MAKE BELIEVE BRIDE

"So what do we do now?" Flame asked, her tone anxious.

"Well, the way I see it," Stone answered thoughtfully, "we can go on like we've been doing and in the meantime I'll go back to that house where I found you . . . see who lives there, ask some questions."

"I guess that's a good idea." Flame agreed, although her tone said that she wasn't quite sure. She had a feeling she didn't want to know the people who lived in that house.

There was a long silence, then she asked, "What if you don't learn anything about me? What then?"

"Don't fret about it." Stone grinned. "You're a married woman, remember. You'll stay right here with your husband," he teased with a laugh.

Flame was silent for a moment; then she asked in a serious tone, "Don't you have a woman in your life?"

"No. No other woman." Stone stared out into the darkness.

"You understand, don't you, Stone, that it's all pretend?"

Pretend? A hot wave rushed through Stone. There was no pretense in the way he felt about her, the way he wanted her, dreamed of having her every night. How long could he feign mere friendship? This constant ache he felt all the time would have to be soothed before long. . . .

SNOW FIRE

NORAH HESS

LEISURE BOOKS NEW YORK CITY

To my favorite son, Bob

A LEISURE BOOK®

March 2000

Published by

Dorchester Publishing Co., Inc.
276 Fifth Avenue
New York, NY 10001

ISBN 0-8439-4691-1

Printed in the United States of America.

Chapter One

It was just before dawn, as the sky was beginning to turn silver, when a tall man stepped out of a large frame house standing proudly beneath a wide cottonwood tree almost a hundred years old. It had been only a sapling when his grandfather had planted it.

His shirt and pants were faded, his boots dusty and run down at the heels. The hat he held in his left hand—he always kept his right hand free in case he had to draw his Colt—had seen many seasons of rain and snow. A stranger seeing Stone Falcon for the first time would never guess that he owned one of the largest cattle ranches in all of Colorado.

He was a ruggedly handsome man with

strong features and black unruly hair that hung to his shoulders. His steel gray eyes, however, detracted a little from his good looks. They were as cold as ice on a river in January. He was thirty-five years old, born of a wild breed high in the Rockies. Friends and enemies alike said that he was part puma and part rattler. What they didn't know was that his grandfather, old Stonewall Falcon, had taught him that if he was in the right, it didn't matter how dirty he fought.

He breathed deep of the clean, pure air. He had borne the long lonely days of winter holed up on his ranch during blizzards and snow that fell at least once a week for four months. There were spots where the snow had drifted seven feet deep.

Spring had finally arrived now, sending melt water down the mountain and thawing out the passes that had kept him isolated from the rest of the world. He was tired of having no one but his cowhands to talk to.

Stone stretched his long, lean body, then looked up at the towering overhead mountain. Most folks believed there was only one way up the mountain. He knew differently, however. He and his Indian friend, Shilo, had found half a dozen ways to come in and out. They had practically lived on the mountain as boys.

He turned his head and peered down the path that led to the Ute village a couple miles away. He hoped that his friend would get back from his hunting trip in time to bid him goodbye.

There was no sign of the tall Indian. Picking up the gear and bedroll he had brought outside with him, Stone walked down the muddy path to the stables where his Palamino was housed.

The stallion was a handsome devil with pale gold hide and ivory colored mane and tail. He was a mean-eyed mountain horse that only Stone could ride. Stone was very proud of Rebel. He claimed that the stallion was better than a watch dog when it came to watching over a camp site. The big animal had raised many a ruckus that had probably saved his life.

He had just finished saddling the big horse and was leading him outside when, from the corner of his eye, he spotted his friend loping down a much worn path that had mostly been put there by the two of them.

Stone smiled. His boyhood friend was an arresting looking male. He was dressed in fringed buckskin, including his knee-length leggings. He wore a red cloth sash around his lean waist with a gun and a wicked-looking knife stuck in its folds. He was an expert in handling both weapons. His hair was raven black and hung halfway down his back.

"So you're going to try to find her," Shilo said when they met, faint derision in his tone.

"You know that I am."

The Indian shook his head as if in disbelief. "You see this maiden one time, and at a distance, and you want her."

"Yes, I want her and I intend to have her."

"You stupid fellow, did it ever cross your

mind that she may not want you?" Shilo asked, serious now.

Stone looked blank for a moment. Of course she would want him. His feelings for her were so strong, she'd have to return his sentiments. He looked at his friend and said with confidence, "She'll want me."

"I hope you're right, Stone," Shilo said quietly, then asked, "How long do you think you'll be gone?"

"It's hard to say," Stone said, then grinned and added, "I've never courted a woman before."

Shilo's black eyes glittered with humor. "You're not noted for having a silver tongue, so I'll look for you when the geese fly south in the fall."

Stone's eyes crinkled at the corners. Shilo was right. He had no trouble talking with light-skirts, but when it came to polite conversation with decent women, he was like a mumbling idiot. "Very funny, friend," he growled. "However long it takes, will you check on things around here once in a while? See if the house has been broken into. The cowhands will take care of the barn and outbuildings, but I can't trust them to remember the house."

Shilo nodded that he would, and with a wave of his hand he turned and walked toward his village. He shook his head at his friend's foolishness. This Indian knew more about white women than Stone Falcon did. About decent women, that was. He had scouted for wagon trains a few times and the white women traveling across the country were a far cry from the whores and loose women that Stone was used to. He wouldn't have the slightest idea how to go about courting a lady. She'd have his tongue tied in knots within five minutes.

The poor dunderhead, Shilo thought, feeling sorry for his friend. Stone was going to be mighty disappointed.

The air grew warm as Stone let the stallion choose his own pace. It had been a fickle spring. There had been thaws that two days later would freeze over again. But by every indication winter's back was finally broken now. The aspens showed green leaves budding out, as did the willows along the many creeks and streams.

Stone nudged the stallion to a faster pace. He wasn't sure how far he would have to ride in his search. This was a trip that he looked forward to with mixed emotions. The question of whether the young woman would want him niggled uneasily at his brain despite his earlier assurance that she would.

As the stallion loped along, Stone fell to thinking of the girl who had been on his mind all winter long.

It had been in late November when he saw her. He was on his way to the nearby town of Dogwood to get in a last few days of carousing in the saloons and several visits to Miss Opal's fancy girls at the Red Lantern. Once the blizzards began to roar across the range, blocking all passes, there would be no more riding to town until spring, when most of the snow had melted.

He had been thinking about Opal as Rebel topped a hill just outside town. He'd quickly reined him in and out sat staring at a feminine figure riding toward him at an easy canter. He didn't know what had made him back Rebel into a clump of pines that hid him from the girl's view.

As she rode nearer, the first thing that struck him about her was the color of her hair. It was a rich, burnished mahogany. Then the sun slid from behind a cloud and flames seemed to shoot off the long tresses that hung down her back.

As she came opposite him, Stone had leaned forward so that he could study her face. He had stared and stared. Never had he seen a woman so beautiful, or so graceful, he added mentally, watching the way her willowly body moved with the little black mare.

There had grown inside him the sure knowledge that this woman was meant to be his lifetime mate. Next spring, as soon as the snow melted, he would come back here and discover where she lived; then he would court her. He had not wanted her to see him then. He'd looked like a saddle bum. He hadn't shaved in four days and his hair was in need of a trim.

When the girl rode out of sight, he had ridden on into town, picked up his mail, then ate lunch at the Sage Hen cafe. He'd returned home before dark. The desire to spend time with Miss Opal's girls had left him.

As Stone rode along, the unwelcome thought his friend, Shilo, had brought up continued to nag at his brain. What if the young woman wouldn't have him? It had never entered his mind that she wouldn't, but now, thanks to Shilo, he had to consider that possibility.

"Damn you, Shilo," he muttered. "Why did you have to put that thought in my head?"

A few minutes later Stone drew rein at the South Platte, the river that flowed from northern Colorado. He sat in the saddle, studying it. It was a treacherous stream, he knew. It was given to unexpected floods and had beds of quicksand. A very dangerous water to cross. The only good thing about it was that it never ran dry.

After watching the current a minute or so, Stone lifted the reins and urged Rebel into the water. He was confident that the stallion would avoid the pockets of sucking sand.

When Rebel reached the opposite shore, Stone guided him up the hill where he had first seen his mystery girl. He paused there, debating the best way to go about finding her. Should he make inquiries in Dogwood, or search the outlying ranches first? Deciding to begin in town, he turned Rebel's head in that direction.

After a day spent questioning everyone he came across, Stone was beginning to feel like a fool. No one knew anything of a girl with hair like flame who rode a little black mare. His last hope was the trading post ten miles down river.

It was growing dark as the stallion approached the long log building only a few feet away from the river's edge. He reined Rebel in and sat for a minute, scrutinizing the six horses tied to the hitching post. He recognized a couple of the horses as belonging to mountain men. They mostly minded their own business, only occasionally getting drunk and raising hell.

It was well known that some of the men who frequented the post were barely on the right side of the law. Actually, he felt pretty sure that a couple had stepped over that line a few times. With the exception of the mountain-bred horses, all wore brands and looked well cared for. Their owners were not the type that would be running from the law.

Stone decided that he wouldn't have to watch his back if he entered the saloon. He dismounted and tied Rebel to a tree, well away from the other mounts. The big devil was always ready for a fight. To be on the safe side, he checked his Colt to make sure both cylinders were loaded. They were, and shoving the gun back in its holster, he stepped up on the narrow porch and pushed open the trading post door.

The big room was crudely constructed and

was poorly lighted by a few hanging lanterns. His gaze skimmed over the room. He was surprised at the number of men lined up at the bar of rough planks supported by three barrels. He realized then that probably half the men had arrived by boat. There were several trappers mingling with the men he knew.

Stone's attention was drawn to a group of four tables in the back of the room. One was unoccupied. The other three were peopled by a group of men, each of whom dandled a scantily dressed saloon woman on his knee.

As maudlin laughter rang out from the drunken women, Stone strode through the dirt and sawdust-covered floor and found himself a place at the bar. Big Cal Broden, the owner of the place, greeted him with a wide smile and a loud, "Stone Falcon, you old wolf. What brings you so far away from your ranch?"

The men at the bar came to attention at the name, Stone Falcon. Each man there either knew, or had heard of the big rancher. They all knew he was not a man to cross. Some spoke to him, others gave him a friendly nod.

"I've got some business to take care of in the area," Stone said in answer to Broden's question. But when he went on to describe the girl he was looking for, no one could recall seeing her.

Knowing better than to ask Stone what he wanted with the girl, the bartender didn't press him, and poured him a glass of whiskey. When he put the cork back in the bottle, he asked a

17

safe question instead. "What kind of winter did you have? Did you lose any cattle?"

"It was pretty bad." Stone picked up the glass. "We were snowed in tight for three months. Couldn't get through the passes. Lost a couple dozen head of cattle. Some to the weather and some to the wolves," he added before tossing the fiery liquid down his throat.

"It was bad here, too," Broden began, then stopped. The outside door had banged open and he and the other men at the bar stared at the four men who noisily entered the post. They pushed two Indian women ahead of them.

"Hell," the bartender muttered, "I wish them Jackson brothers would stay the hell out of my place. I've told them a dozen times not to bring Indian women in here. It riles up my girls. They don't want any competition."

"The young one doesn't look more than thirteen years old," Stone said, studying the thin girl. "And she's scared to death," he added as one of the twins sat down at the empty table and jerked her onto his lap.

Stone frowned when the man began to roughly fondle her, running his hand over her small breast and sliding his other hand up her doeskin shift.

The older woman being pawed by two of the other men watched anxiously as the young girl fought to push away the rough hand that squeezed her tender breasts while the other one tried to pry her legs apart.

Anger began to grow inside Stone as the girl struggled against the man, who only laughed at her small fists beating against his chest. Stone gritted his teeth but kept his mouth shut. He told himself that the maid hadn't been struck, that maybe the bully was just having sport with her.

Suddenly then everything changed at the table. One of the girl's hard little fists connected with her tormentor's eye. The laughter died on his face, replaced by black anger. He jumped to his feet, dragging the girl up beside him. With an arm around her waist holding her fast, he called out to Broden, "I'll be using one of your rooms for a while, bartender. The little squaw here is gonna let me have a poke."

As the terrified girl hung on to the table, tears running down her cheeks, her companion cried out, "Please, she has never been with a man before."

"Now ain't this my lucky day," the irritated man crowed to his brothers. "I'm gonna have me a virgin. And she's gonna pay dearly for striking a white man." He broke the girl's grip on the table, snarling, "Come on, bitch, give me a good time."

Stone's anger turned to rage. The one soft spot in his nature was for the weak and the helpless. Barely aware of his action, he slammed his glass down, its contents splashing all over the bar.

The sudden loud thud on the bar caused a deathly silence to descend on the room. The only sound was the ticking of the clock on the wall behind the bar and the girl's soft sobbing. Everyone's attention was focused on Stone, whose eyes were glittering like shards of ice, sending a clear message to the abuser.

Young Jackson grew visibly pale as he recognized the big rancher. He shuffled his feet and looked at his brothers for support. When they looked away from him, he knew he was on his own.

He grew more uneasy. He had seen Stone Falcon almost cripple a man once in a barroom brawl. He wasn't about to let that happen to him. A nervous smile twitched his lips, and giving the girl a push that sent her stumbling toward Stone, he said, "Take her. I didn't much want her anyway."

Stone caught her by her thin arms as she reeled into him. When he steadied her slight body, he looked across the room to see if he would have a fight on his hands from the Jackson clan. The brothers were headed for the door, pulling the older woman along with them.

"Please, won't you help her, too?" the girl begged, gripping his arm hard.

Stone understood why she wanted to save her companion, but he didn't want to press his luck. There were four brothers and he didn't know how many men in the post would help him out. He had saved the girl with just a threatening look, but when the older brothers saw that they might lose the chance of having a woman to pass among themselves, he would probably have a fight on his hands—one he might not be able to win.

"I'm sorry," he said gently, "but I don't think they will give her up without a fight. Anyway," he added bracingly, "she looks tough enough to hold her own with them." He pretended not to hear her soft sobs as he turned back to the bar.

The other patrons went back to their drinks also, but they listened closely to Stone's ensuing conversation with Big Cal.

"What are you gonna do with her?" the bartender asked as he refilled Stone's glass.

"Dammed if I know. I hadn't planned on her being handed over to me." He looked down at the small, shivering female. "Where are your people?" he asked. "Where is your village?"

She gripped her hands together to stop their trembling, but her voice was wavery as she answered, "My aunt and I are Utes from northern Colorado. Our chief is moving our village to a new summer location. Up in the mountains, I think."

"How did those men get hold of you and your aunt without your menfolk seeing them?" Stone asked.

"We were the last ones in a long line, and no one was paying any attention to us. The men had no trouble grabbing us and dragging us into the forest."

"Why weren't you and your aunt with the other women?" Cal asked with a frown. "It always appears to me that when a tribe is on

21

the move the women and children walk in the middle of the men for protection."

A solemn look came over her small, dusky features. "We are not welcome in our village anymore." When Stone gave her a questioning look, she haltingly explained.

"My aunt's husband, my uncle, died last year of a white man's sickness. We were left with no man to provide for us. We are resented now for the food we eat."

Stone and Cal nodded their understanding. It was the Indian way. "I don't expect they will come looking for you then," Stone thought out loud.

"No, they will not," the girl agreed, her narrow shoulders slumping.

Pity for the girl's plight welled up inside Stone. "What is your name?" he asked quietly.

"I am called Little Bird."

An apt name, Stone thought. She looked like a hungry little sparrow.

Cal bent a somber look on Stone. "Well, friend, again I ask—what are you going to do with her?"

Stone shook his head. "And, again, I answer: Damned if I know. I know that I can't leave her here. The Jacksons will be coming back through here in a couple days and some of the characters that hang around are no more trust worthy that the Jackson brothers."

He poured himself another drink, and after tossing it down his throat, he said thoughtfully "I'll take her to my camp for now. Maybe I'll come up with some kind of solution by tomorrow morning."

Big Cal propped his elbow on the bar, and after studying Little Bird a minute said, "You know, if she was scrubbed up, she'd look pretty fetching. Since you haven't found that gal you're looking for, why don't you keep this one for yourself?"

Stone smiled as he thought of the woman he had been dreaming of all winter and shook his head. "I've already chosen the woman who will share my home from now on."

The bartender waited to hear more about the mystery woman. When Stone didn't add to his remark, Cal shrugged. He'd find out in time. He doubted that Stone was planning to get married soon. The Falcon men remained bachelors until they were almost forty.

Stone slapped some money on the bar and said, "Let's get going, Little Bird."

"See you next time, Falcon," Big Cal said as he scooped up the coins.

"Is he keeping her for himself?" a half dozen voices asked Cal as the door closed behind Stone.

"Naw, she's too young for him."

It was dark when Stone and the weary girl stepped outside and Stone closed the door behind them. As though anxious to get the night over and done with, an early full moon was shining its silvery light on the river. Stone boosted Little Bird onto Rebel's back, then climbed up behind her.

The girl was in no shape to ride back to the ranch tonight, Stone thought. Within a few minutes he had chosen a campsite beside the river. Before he could help her to dismount, Little Bird slipped from the saddle and sat down on a large boulder that had at some time been dropped at the river's edge when the Platte was in flood.

She looks worn out, Stone thought as he stripped the saddle off the stallion, then let him roll in the sand for a few minutes. When Rebel lunged to his feet, sand and gravel clinging to his beautiful hide, Stone staked him out to graze in a patch of grass. Then, walking over to Little Bird, he asked, "Are you hungry?"

Little Bird didn't pretend that she wasn't starving. She nodded eagerly. "I haven't eaten since early this morning. My aunt and I were given a strip of pemmican to share."

Stone wasn't surprised at the girl's answer. Actually, he was surprised that the two lone females were allowed to remain with the tribe at all. Most clans would have driven them away when they had no male to support them.

When Stone had a cookfire burning, he doubled the number of bacon strips he usually fried in the battered skillet. He also opened two cans of beans, thinking to himself that the girl looked like she could eat one can by herself.

The pot of coffee he had set to brewing earlier was ready by the time the meat was cooked and the beans heated. He divided the meal into two equal parts and added a piece of hardtack to each plate. He handed one to Little Bird and said, "Eat up, girl." He started to sit down beside her, then noted that though she eyed the food hungrily, she made no effort to begin eating.

It took but a moment for Stone to understand her hesitation. He knew the girl wanted to attack her food like a hungry little animal but would hold back if he sat beside her. Without an audience, she could gulp down her food as fast as she could chew it. He took his supper and walked the few feet to the river bank. He sat down on a large rock, and with his back to her, he dug in.

When Stone had finished his meal and rolled a smoke. He looked out over the river as aromatic smoke drifted from his nostrils. What was he going to do about the girl? he wondered. He couldn't take her with him. It just wouldn't do to go courting a white woman with a skinny little Indian maid tagging along behind him. And despite today's frustrations, he meant to continue his search.

With a sudden flash, his friend Shilo came to mind. If he could get the girl to the Ute village, he wouldn't have to worry about her. Shilo wouldn't want to take on the responsibility of the girl, but he would do it. Of course he would complain about it every time they saw each other. Which was almost daily. But then, the big Indian grumbled about everything. He had done so as long as Stone could remember, and that was back to the time they were youngsters.

The sudden crunch of gravel brought Stone to his feet, his right hand dropping to the handle of the Colt strapped around his waist. Had the Jacksons followed him, intent on getting the girl?

"Don't shoot, young feller," an age-cracked voice called out from down the river.

Stone peered into the shadows of the willows and made out the shape of a mule plodding toward him. A wide smile lit up his face when he recognized the old mountain man astride the gray-faced pack animal. Caleb Greenwood. He had lived in the mountains over forty years. Nobody knew, not even himself, how old he was.

"Caleb, it's been a long time." Stone stepped forward, his hand outstretched.

"Nigh on to four years, as I recollect."

"Every bit of that," Stone agreed, shaking the gnarled that had reached for his. "You were taking your winter's catch to the trading post the last time I saw you. Where are you heading now?"

"Back up the mountains. Had to come down to Dogwood for some supplies. Ran out of flour and coffee a couple weeks back. Been waitin' for the dang-blasted passes to open up."

"I don't have any cooked grub to offer you, but I have half a pot of hot coffee and some hard tack. Help yourself if you've a mind to."

"That's the best offer I've had since I can't remember." Caleb squatted beside the campfire and reached for the coffee pot. Using

Stone's cup, he filled it with the steaming, dark brew. When he raised it to his mouth and took a long swallow, he smacked his lips and looked heavenward. "There's nothin' so tasty as good, strong coffee." He lifted the cup to his mouth again.

When Caleb had emptied the cup and refilled it he asked, "Where are you off to, Stone?"

"The same place you're coming from," Stone answered cautiously, tired of explaining his foolish search for a girl who had disappeared into thin air.

A wide smile exposed Caleb's toothless gums. "I see you got yourself a young squaw. She looks kinda scrawny. Did she keep your bed warm this past winter?" He gave a cackle of laughter. "I bet she didn't. I bet that's why you're takin' her back to her father."

"It's not what you're thinking, you old reprobate," Stone snapped, "so wipe that smirk off your face."

"If it's not what I'm thinkin', then what is it?"

With as few words as possible, Stone explained how he had come to have an Indian maid in his camp.

Caleb was silent as he sipped his second cup of coffee. When he set the empty cup down beside him he said, as though to himself, "I bet I passed where them men are camped a few miles back. I could hear by the way they wuz talkin' and laughin' they wuz drinkin' so I stayed out of their sight. I went close enough, though, to see there wuz four men and a middle-aged Indian woman with them. They wuz takin' turns with her."

Stone took a hurried look at Little Bird. He hoped that she hadn't heard everything Caleb had said. She was upset enough about her relative.

As Caleb went into a long tirade about the evil that lived in some men, an idea struck Stone. Maybe the old man could help him get rid of Little Bird. When Caleb finally stopped talking, Stone looked at him and said, "You say you're on your way back up the mountain?"

"Yep, and I can't wait to get back there. Civilization ain't for me."

A piece of wood burned through and Stone pushed it back on the coals with the toe of his boot. Then, avoiding Caleb's eyes, he said, "I'm wondering if you would do me a favor. A big one." He looked at the old man then.

Caleb looked into the dancing flames and glowing coals a moment, then gazed at Stone. "Something tells me to say no right off. It's somethin' to do with the little squaw, ain't it?"

Stone picked up a brittle stick and snapped it between his fingers. He could not help the amusement that flickered in his eyes, and he lowered his lids to hide it. It was typical of Greenwood to come straight to the point. He could do no less.

"Yes, it is," Stone answered. "I would appreciate it if you would take her to my friend, Shilo. His village is close to my ranch. He will take her in."

Caleb looked a little alarmed. "I don't want to have much truck with that big Injun. Sometimes he speaks to a man, then a week later looks straight through him as though he'd never laid eyes on him before. He makes me nervous."

Stone's lips twisted in a grin. "He makes a lot of people nervous. But if he's left alone, he won't bother anybody. He's a bad one, though, if he's picked on."

Stone picked up a small, flat rock, and drawing his arm back skipped it across the water. "I never thought I'd see the day that Caleb Greenwood would be afraid of an Indian."

"Hold on there now!" Caleb bristled. "I didn't say I was afraid of the Ute. I just said that he makes me nervous."

Caleb scratched his white beard as he studied Little Bird perched on her boulder. "She looks mighty puny," he said after a while. "She won't get sick on me or anything like that, will she?"

"She's not ailing with anything, if that's what you're thinking. She's half starved, that's all. A few good meals and she'll be fine."

After another close scrutiny of Little Bird, Caleb muttered, "Alright, but I'll be leavin' at first dawn. See that she's ready to travel." He glanced at the stallion staked out in the grass. "I don't see any extra horses anywhere, so that means she'll have to walk."

"Do Indian women ever get to ride?" Stone asked with a sardonic twist of his lips.

"Not very often," Caleb agreed, "but I saw it

29

once," he added as he walked over to his old mule. "She was an Indian princess. She sure was a beauty. She sat her horse real proud-like."

Caleb turned to the mule, and talking to it as though it was human, he unsaddled the old animal. He picked up his bedroll then and spread it under a tree. When he rolled up in the blankets, Stone asked, "Aren't you going to stake him? Won't he stray away?"

"Naw. He never goes far away from me," Caleb said with a yawn. He was snoring when Stone hunkered down beside Little Bird. She looks dead tired and half asleep, Stone thought. He wondered how she would take to the idea of riding with a crusty looking old mountain man tomorrow morning. When she looked up at him, he said with a jerk of his thumb at Caleb, "He's an old friend of mine."

"Yes, I could see that," Little Bird said, wariness coming into her eyes.

She knows, Stone thought and there was a slight hesitation before he said, "I have made arrangements with him to take you to my friend, Shilo. Shilo is the Ute chief in the village near my ranch. He will take you in and see to your needs."

Little Bird looked at him, her eyes wide with dismay. Stone realized that she had been thinking he would be the one who would look after her. As she continued to look at him with big solemn eyes, he explained, "That's the best I can do, Little Bird, since I can't take you with me."

As Stone waited for her to say something, a

night bird flew out of the willows. The moment was poignant as the bird swooped out over the river, its soft song fading behind it. He waited another few seconds, then said softly, "I'm sorry, girl, but it's impossible to take you with me."

"Do not apologize, Stone Falcon. I am grateful for what you have done for me already. It was enough that you saved me from those awful brothers." She gazed out over the river. "I worry about what is happening to my aunt."

Moonlight glittered on the tears that slipped down her cheeks. Stone spoke gruffly to hide the compassion he was feeling. "They'll turn her loose in the morning," he said, not believing a word he said. The only hope the woman had was to slip away in the night.

Stone stood up and walked over to where he had stashed his bedroll. "I'll divide my blankets with you." He dropped one down beside Little Bird. "Roll up beside the fire and try to get some sleep. The old man wants to get an early start in the morning."

Chapter Two

The soft gray of dawn had arrived when Flame awoke. She lay a moment watching her familar room take shape. There was the rickety table beside her narrow bed, and the battered-looking dresser with its cracked mirror. A straight-backed chair completed the room's furnishings. It was placed with its back propped against the doorknob. It provided the only privacy available to her.

She stretched her slender body and yawned widely. She hadn't slept well last night. She had been awakened numerous times by moans and grunts and squeaking bed springs next door.

I should be used to it by now, she thought

grimly. That racket had been going on every night for two weeks. Her mother, Bertha, shared her bed with a new man these days.

She recalled the day Deke Cobbs rode up to the ranch. She had pegged him at once as a down-at-the-heels saddle tramp. He was riding the grub-line, looking for a hand out. She had stood at the kitchen window watching him dismount, praying that her mother wasn't around to see him. He wasn't bad looking, in a hard sort of way, and her mother was man-crazy. If the stranger were willing, Bertha would move him right into their home.

She remembered sighing as her mother walked into the kitchen and spotted the man. She almost knocked over the table in her hurry to get through the door and greet him. She gave the stranger a coy smile and ran her fingers up his arm. He in return grabbed her hand and kissed her knuckles. Everything was happening as she had feared it would. The saddle bum had taken one look at the big woman, and understood the invitation in her eyes. Flame had seen the smirk on his face that said he had found himself a home.

"I know all there is to know about cows," he'd announced.

As Bertha tittered, Flame slipped through the back door. She had spent the day riding fence. When she came home that evening, Deke Cobbs was firmly ensconced in their home. And plump, slovenly Bertha, who had never before had the attention of a younger, attractive man was crazy about her new lover. Flame firmly believed that the woman would kill for him.

A shiver passed through her. Pray God her mother never noticed that her new man also had eyes for her daughter. Bertha was stronger than most men and could easily break Flame's back if she suspected that Deke was interested in her.

Flame laid her arm across her eyes as she thought back over the years. She was nineteen and had been fighting off her mother's many men since she was thirteen. She had had no help repelling their advances. She didn't dare tell Bertha how the string of men who came and went in their lives tried to coax her into their beds. They would only stop when she threatened to tell Bertha.

Her lips twisted wryly. The men didn't know it, but that was an empty threat. She had complained to to her mother the first time she had been cornered by one of the men in the barn. She fought him off with a pitchfork, then ran crying to the house. Frightened, her dress torn and tears running down her cheeks, she sobbed out what had happened.

Her mother called her a liar and gave her a beating. Ever since then she had been watched with suspicion every time one of the men came around.

Flame sighed as she turned over on her side and gazed out the window. There had never been a loving relationship between her mother and her and she doubted there ever would be. They only seemed to grow farther apart. She realized that Big Bertha was jealous of her youth and freshness. Hatred was in her eyes every time she looked at Flame. Her slitted eyes said that Flame was no longer welcome in her home.

But Big Bertha wasn't ready to get rid of her only child yet.

And Flame knew why. It was her hard work that brought in money so they could continue to live in the four-room house that was so dilapidated there was danger of the roof blowing off every time the wind roared across the range. It was she who ran the hundred head of cattle, herding them, branding them, preparing them for spring and fall market. She had scant help from the men who shared Bertha's bed. Certainly Deke Cobb spent more time in her mother's bed than out on the range.

At least, she thought thankfully, her mother had enough sense to stretch the money between the seasons so that they could buy food to put on the table. The taxes, however, hadn't been paid in years. She was surprised they hadn't been forced off the property a long time ago.

She stared through the grimy window, where objects were beginning to take shape in the arriving dawn. She made out the tool shed with the leaking roof, the run-down chicken house whose wire fence had been broken down years ago; the hens laid their eggs in the weeds somewhere. Then there was the barn, the double doors sagging inward, and only a half roof to keep their three horses protected from the wind, rain and snow.

Wouldn't I be better off if we were forced off the land? Flame wondered. If that happened she would strike out on her own. Hadn't she yearned to be free of the long hours of hard labor that began at first light and ended well past sundown? She longed to throw away her faded, worn pants, the shirts with the elbows out of the sleeves. She didn't own a dress or the fancy undergarments that went with one. To her recollection she had never worn female clothing. Her only feminine garments were rough muslin pantaloons with matching camisoles. She yearned to wear pretty dresses and soft slippers. Maybe own a bonnet trimmed with lace and ribbons.

Flame remembered her school years. They hadn't been many. She'd had to stop going after fifth grade. Her mother claimed they couldn't afford a cowhand and that she would have to see to the handling of the cattle. She was ten years old and thin as a whip.

She had so envied her classmates as she compared their clean, starched dresses, full of ruffles and bows, to her ragged trousers. She had pretended not to see their contemptuous sidelong looks or to hear their giggling laughter at the dusty, worn boots that she had worn. She had lifted her chin when they snickered and pointed at her elbows sticking out of her shirt, her bare knees showing through her pants.

A humorless smile twisted Flame's lips. When she complained to her mother that she needed new clothes, Bertha always answered that she should be glad that she had food to put in her stomach. It was only when the clothing was so thin and couldn't stand up under another washing that Bertha reluctantly bought her a pair of pants and a shirt.

As if the teasing and snickering and being shunned wasn't enough, as she grew older she had something else to contend with. Her body had matured at an early age. She dreaded having to go to town where she must bear the men's insolent eyes roaming over her slender, budding body. About the same time she stopped going to school, she also began avoiding trips into Dogwood. Year in, year out, she saw no one but her mother and the men who occupied Bertha's bed.

Flame had borne the loneliness and the abuse from her mother simply because she was afraid to strike out on her own. According to Bertha the only way she could make a living was to sell her body. She had cringed at the thought. She would starve to death first.

"What else could you do?" Bertha would sneer. "You can't cook. You can't keep a house clean. You're too skinny and plain looking to serve drinks in a saloon. You're too standoffish to sit on a man's lap and let him fondle you a little.

"Face it, girl," she'd always finish her tirade, "you should be thankful that I let you continue to live with me."

Flame only half believed her mother. It was true she didn't know how to cook much, or to keep house. She'd always had to do work outside doing things that men usually took care of. But she had worked like a slave, getting no recognition or thanks for it.

As usual when Flame remembered the past, she thought of her father. The father who had left them when she was four years old. She had been too young to understand why he had been so angry with her mother, why he had taken his fists to the man who had been working for him. Nor could she understand why the father she loved so dearly had given her a fierce hug, then walked out of the house, never to return.

It was from him she had received affection, and she had cried for days for him to return. She stopped crying out loud the day her mother slapped her across the face and threatened her with a beating if she ever heard her blubbering for that man again. She had continued to cry, though, but only in secret.

Where had Rudy Martin gone? Flame asked herself the years-old question. Was he still alive? If so, did he ever think of his daughter? She understood now what the fight with the hired hand had been about all those years ago. Her father had caught her mother in bed with another man. Even back then Bertha was man-crazy.

Flame gave a tired sigh, and sitting up she swung her feet to the floor. The hay mattress rustled as she bent over to pick up her worn pants and pull them up over her long legs. She stood up to draw them over her small rear and narrow hips. When she had buttoned up the fly, she sat back down on the edge of the bed and picked up her dusty boots. Before tugging them on she held them a moment, studying them. Besides being badly scuffed and run-down at the heels, the soles had holes in them the size of a silver dollar. She wondered what her chances were of getting a new pair before winter set in. Slim, she imagined.

When she had strapped on her heavy Colt, she removed the chair from the door knob and eased the door opened. When no noise came from the room next door, she quietly slipped down the hall to the kitchen. She wanted to eat and get out of the house before Bertha and Deke got up. She would have to make breakfast for them then and she had a hard day's work ahead of her. She wanted to get started on it.

Flame made a fire in the rusty stove, then put a pot of coffee on to brew. After she washed her face in the chipped basin of water and slicked back her hair and tied it with a string of rawhide, she went to the larder. She would fry some bacon and eggs for her breakfast.

She stood in the open door and stared. The shelf where those two items were always kept was bare. "That can't be," she exclaimed, and started sorting through the other shelves that held air-tights and other staples.

After several minutes of searching she found, hidden behind a bag of flour, half a slab of bacon and two eggs. Anger and hurt gripped her. Her mother had secreted them there for Deke's breakfast. She didn't care a whit that her daughter wouldn't have a hot breakfast, her only meal until supper, before riding out to work the cattle all day.

Flame had noted as she rummaged through the larder that they were low on supplies. Why hadn't Bertha gone to town to purchase more?

A thought crossed Flame's mind. A thought she didn't want to believe. Were they out of money already? Had Bertha given it all to Deke to buy whiskey?

The more she thought about it, the more convinced she became that this was exactly what had happened. Her mother was that besotted with the saddle bum. She knew the only way to hold him was to feed him, keep him in whiskey and please him in bed.

She shook her head, wanting to reject the idea that her mother would do practically anything to keep the man with her. Even kill. She shivered when that thought crossed her mind. She wasn't exempt if Bertha went into a rage that concerned Deke Cobbs.

Her soft lips tightened in a firm line. Let them hide the food. She would get by. She would live off the land. She would shoot prairie chickens and other small game and catch fish out of the Platte. She would cook them over a campfire and eat her supper before returning home every evening. Bertha wasn't allowed to run up a bill at the mercantile so it wouldn't be long before her new man got on his horse and vamoosed.

A mischievous look twinkled in her blue eyes. She was going to have a hot breakfast this morning. Let ole Deke whistle up a tree for his bacon and eggs.

She sliced the bacon and laid the strips in the black cast iron skillet that had been around as long as she could remember. When the meat began to fry she closed the kitchen door. She crossed her fingers that the aroma of frying bacon wouldn't creep into her mother's bedroom. If that happened she wouldn't put it past Bertha to come stomping into the kitchen and maybe attack her.

Minutes later, although the bacon wasn't as crisp as she would have liked, she ate the meat and eggs. She hurriedly gulped down two cups of coffee and left the house just as the sun was coming up.

The slap of a beaver's tail on water awakened Caleb Greenwood, the mountain man. He knew it was time to get up without looking at the eastern sky. He rolled out of his blankets, climbed to his feet and stretched the stiffness out of his old joints and muscles.

He sniffed the air. It smelled of woodsmoke and fresh-brewed coffee. He looked to his left and was surprised to see Stone hunkered down beside a small fire turning strips of salt pork in a blackened frying pan.

"I didn't expect to see you up this mornin'," he said on his way to the river to wash his face and hands.

"I wanted to make sure Little Bird had something in her stomach before she started out. I remembered that you're not one to stop along the way to fix something to eat."

"That may be," Caleb said, kneeling on the river bank and scooping water into his hands, "but I wouldn't do that to a girl who looks half starved already."

He stood up, dried his face and beard on a handkerchief he pulled from his back pocket. He ran his fingers through his long, gray hair, then slapped an old, floppy hat on his head. He walked over to where Little Bird still slept in her blanket. He nudged her hip with his bare toe. When she jerked awake, he said gruffly, "Get up, girl. We'll be hitting the trail pretty soon."

Little Bird brushed the hair off her face, stared sleepily up at Caleb, then scrambled out of the blanket. She stood a moment, getting her bearings, then moved down to the river to wash up. After she stood up and wiped her face dry with her hands, she moved deeper into the willows for privacy.

When she returned to the campfire, Stone handed her a tin plate of fried salt pork and a piece of hardtack. "Don't look so worried," he said, smiling at her. "I know the people who live in the village near me. They will treat you kindly. You will be expected to work, though," he added.

Little Bird gave him a surprised look. "Did you think that I would not?"

Stone looked uncomfortable a moment. "No, I didn't think that at all, Little Bird," he said. "Please forget I even said it."

"It is forgotten." She smiled at him, then asked, "Your friend, Shilo, will he take kindly to me?"

A wry grin twisted Stone's lips. "That big Indian doesn't take kindly to anyone. But don't pay any attention to his gruffness. That's just his way."

"Will I ever see you again?" Little Bird asked shyly.

"Of course you will." Stone looked at her and smiled. "The village is only a couple miles from my place. Shilo and I see each other most every day."

"That is good." Little Bird smiled back at him.

"It's time we get goin', girl," Caleb broke in on their conversation. He stood up and handed her his empty plate. "Wash mine, too, will you? And don't lollygag."

A couple minutes later Stone watched the pair take off down the river trail. Caleb on his old gray mule and Little Bird walking behind him. He shook his head. Indian women didn't have an easy life. No woman in the West did.

* * *

When Flame entered the barn her little mare Lady stuck her head out of the stall and whinnied a soft greeting. She scratched the mare's long, pointed ears a minute, then tossed a saddle on her pet's back. When she had tightened the cinches and tested the stirrups she swung onto the mare's back.

She set Lady to an easy canter and let her gaze travel over the range. She loved this time of year. Scattered about were patches of red and purple wildflowers that had changed the dull winter landscape to a thing of beauty. The grass was tall and green, and the hardwood trees were leafed out.

Lady topped a hill and Flame forgot the beauty of her surroundings as she looked down at the holding pen where a dozen yearlings milled around, stirring up clouds of dust. Sighing, she put everything else out of her mind while she concentrated on branding the cattle.

By high noon Flame had bull-dogged and branded half the yearlings. Six more to go, she thought as the sun beat down on her head. Sweat formed on her forehead, and trickled down her face and between her breasts. She took off her hat, dusty and floppy from much use, and hung it on the saddle horn. She next removed the bandana from around her neck and tied it Indian fashion across her brow. It would catch the perspiration before it could get into her eyes.

Flame stretched her aching back, then

looked at her mare. Lady looked as weary as she felt. "Come on, girl," she said softly, taking hold of the reins. "Let's go down to the river and cool off for a while."

Reaching the Platte, she slid off the mare and went to kneel upstream from her. She dipped her hands into the silent, cold current. When her wrists felt cool she scooped up palms full of water and brought them to her mouth. The water still had the taste of snow.

When she had quenched her thrist, she bathed her hot face. Then, with a cool breeze fanning her face, and the dank smell of the river in her nostrils, she sat down at the base of a willow and leaned back against its trunk.

This was one of her favorite places on the ranch. She could remember her father bringing her here, playing with her by the cool water. His initials were carved into the broad trunk at her back. R M. Another set of initials was carved below. R C. She'd always wondered what those letters stood for. Not her mother's name, certainly.

She allowed herself to rest ten minutes and was preparing to go back to work when she heard the anxious bawling of cattle. She jumped to her feet and listened. The clamor was coming from where part of the herd was grazing. Her face grew tight. Had a pack of hungry wolves come upon them?

She sprang into the saddle and sent Lady tearing up the knoll that hid the cattle from sight. When she reached the summit of the steep hill, she pulled the mare to an abrupt halt. She sat there staring in disbelief. At least a dozen of her longhorns had been cut from the herd and were being driven away. And if that wasn't shock enough, Deke Cobbs and a stranger were doing the rustling.

She must ride to the ranch and alert her mother, she was thinking when suddenly Deke whirled his horse and rode toward her, leaving the other man to drive off the cattle.

"What do you think you're doing, rustling our cattle?" she demanded hotly when he brought his horse to a plunging halt in front of her. "Wait until I tell Bertha what you're up to. She'll kick you out faster than you can blink."

"You foolish girl, you really believe that, don't you?" Deke sneered. "Bertha knows just what I'm doing. You might as well know that we're planning to sell the herd as soon as you've finished branding the yearlings."

As she stared at him in disbelief, Deke moved his horse up alongside her mare. "If you'd be a little nicer to me, I'd get Bertha to take you along with us. She plans on leaving you behind."

He gave her a look whose meaning was crystal clear. "What say we take a dip in the river? Get to know each other better."

Contempt flared in Flame's eyes. "I know you as well as I want to, you grub-liner. I wouldn't go anywhere with you if it would save my life." She kicked the mare and sent her galloping back to the river.

Frustrated tears glimmered in Flame's eyes. What kind of promises had the saddle bum made to her foolish mother?

As the cattle and the drivers disappeared out of sight, Flame slumped in the saddle, the reins lying loosely in her hands. It appeared she would be going out on her own sooner than she'd expected. With the cattle gone, and no money to buy more, she could no longer make a go of the ranch.

What would she do? Flame stared unseeingly out over the range. The tears she had held back now brimmed over.

She had to come up with a plan of her own, she thought, tying Lady to a willow branch. But what it might be, she had no idea.

The day wore on, the air becoming heavy as Flame sat in the shade of the willows. She skimmed flat stones across the Platte as she tried to come up with a solution to her dilemma. The only idea that came to mind that she didn't dismiss immediately was finding work on a ranch. She knew every aspect of ranching.

The more she thought about it, the more the idea appealed to her. She would pose as a teenage boy. She would cut her hair short and bind her breasts. Her five foot, seven inches would help her to look like a gangly teenager. She didn't plan any further than that before sleep overcame her and she nodded off.

It was nearly sunset when Flame's stomach gave an empty growl that awakened her.

Almost at the same time she heard the clucking of prairie chickens. She rose quietly to her feet and went in search of them. Fifteen minutes later she returned to the river, a fat hen dangling from her hand. She had shot its head off. She laid it on the ground, then built a small fire among the trees. When she had rigged up a tripod of green wood and dressed out the hen, she hung it over the fire. A short time later her supper was ready.

The meat was crispy and tender as Flame sank her white, even teeth into it. Although the absence of salt was noticeable, nevertheless the meat filled her empty stomach. She now had the courage to ride back to the ranch.

Chapter Three

The sun was sinking low in the West. Dusk would be settling in soon, Shilo realized. Standing on a little knoll, he looked down in over a serene and slumberous valley. He loved this time of day when the elders gathered around the big fire in the middle of the compound and talked of olden days while the women cooked their families' evening meals.

Shilo had been hunting deer up in the high country. He had only seen does with their fawns. He hadn't, of course, shot the mothers. Without nourishment from them, the youngsters would starve to death within a couple days, or be brought down by a pack of hungry wolves before then.

49

So, he thought dejectedly, he was returning to the village empty-handed. He hoped that the other braves were having more luck than he'd had the last couple days.

The handsome Indian gave a long sigh as he continued to stand on the grassy knoll. The responsibility of leading his people lay heavy on his shoulders. He had not thought the obligation of looking after them would be his so soon, had never given much thought to how it would be when he was chief.

Six months ago his carefree days had ended when his father's horse had gone down in a buffalo hunt and their chief was trampled to death. Now at age thirty-three, he was responsible for those who lived in the village. Was he capable of it? He had never taken life seriously before. As a teenager he had led a wild, carefree existence, hunting and fishing with his friend, Stone Falcon. Later, when they were adults, they drank the white man's whiskey, lay with the white whores Stone snuck into his barn. And he musn't forget the Indian women they'd had as well. Those included widows and the ones who cheated on their husbands.

As Shilo started walking down the hill toward the Platte he reflected that those lazy, idle days were a thing of the past. What worried him most was the question of whether he could give wise counsel to his people. Would they listen to him? He hadn't shown much wisdom in the past. Another long sigh feathered through his lips. It was also expected that he would now choose a wife, settle down and have children.

As Shilo came to the Platte and took off down the river trail, he pictured in his mind the young maids in the village. None appealed to him. He always had privately thought that his village had the most unattractive females of all the Indian settlements up and down the Platte.

"I'll think about that later," he muttered as he stopped at a low spot in the river. He waded into the shallow water and began to move through the tall reeds that reached as high as his waist. He looked for the canoe he had hidden there before setting out on his hunt. He hoped some young brave hadn't found it and paddled away. If it was gone, he would have a long walk home.

He found the birch canoe where he had left it. Giving a sigh of relief, he pushed the canoe into the mist-shrouded water. The current was swift and soon took him to where the river forked. He guided the birch into the slower-moving water on his right. In a short time he came to the sandy bank where he wanted to go ashore.

Stepping into the water, he dragged the light vessel onto the shore and hid it among another patch of tall reeds. When he had anchored it with a large rock, he started climbing the path to the village.

Something drew his eyes to the top of the path and he paused for a moment. Silhouetted against the gray twilight was the figure of a mule with a man sitting astride it. The small shape of a girl stood at the mule's head. His hand went to the gun tucked into the sash wound around his lean waist and he resumed climbing.

"Are you lost, old man?" Shilo demanded when he reached level ground and looked into the bearded face of the old mountain man. "On this side of the river you are on Ute land."

"I know where I am." The old man bristled. "I walked this land before you was born. I probably smoked the peace pipe with your grandpappy."

Shilo firmed his lips to hide the amusement that twitched at their corners. He had no doubt that the crusty old fellow was telling the truth. He had often heard the elders of the village talk with respect of the mountain men. They told of the many times mountain men spent entire winters in their villages, helping to hunt game so they could survive.

"Have you come to smoke the peace pipe again?" Shilo asked. "Or do you plan to steal one of our maids while we sleep?"

"Neither." The old man's answer was sharp and swift. "I'm here on an errand for a young feller named Stone Falcon."

All levity left Shilo. His tone was also sharp as he took a step forward, demanding, "Is everything alright with my friend?"

"I'll tell that to the man I'm supposed to talk to."

"Well, who is that man?" Shilo barked impatiently.

Caleb squinted at the angry-looking Indian. How far could he push him? he wondered. When Shilo glared back, Caleb decided that the Ute could be mean if he wanted to.

Nevertheless, his answer was a little testy. "I don't know if its any of your business, but the brave's name is Shilo."

An oath ripped out of Shilo's lips. "You old fool, why didn't you say so right off? I'm Shilo. Is Stone alright?"

"Don't go gettin' huffy with me, red man." Caleb's gnarled hand swept to the handle of a wicked looking knife tucked in his belt. "This old white man can still whittle you down to size."

Shilo's features softened. In his worry for his friend, he had unintentionally insulted the old man. His age demanded more respect. "Forgive me. I did not mean to speak so harshly. I'm concerned about Stone."

"That's more like it," Caleb said, mollified by Shilo's apology. "Stone looked alright the last time I saw him." He gave Little Bird a shove in the back with the toe of his moccasined foot. "He said to ask you if you'd make a place for her in your village. She's a Ute from up north a piece. Her name is Little Bird. She don't talk much."

As Little Bird stumbled forward, Shilo gave her a sharp look and thought to himself that the old man must be lying. Stone would never

Norah Hess

be attracted to a creature like this one. He ran his gaze over her dirty face and feet, her snarled hair, the ragged shift that hung from her narrow shoulders.

He looked back at Caleb. "When Stone asked you to bring this . . . this girl to me, had he been drinking?"

"No. He was sober as a judge. They had just finished eatin' supper."

When Shilo made no response, only stared out into the gathering darkness, Caleb demanded, "Are you gonna take her or not? I'm not gonna drag her along with me. I got no use for her."

"Neither have I." Shilo swore fluently in his native tongue. "But if Stone has taken a fancy to her, I'll find a place for her in the village."

"Good," Caleb said with relief, and while Shilo looked Little Bird over again with curled lips, the mountain man and his mule silently faded from sight in the shadows of some boulders.

"You sneaking old varmint," Shilo muttered angrily when he looked away from Little Bird and found that Caleb had left. He wanted to ask him if he knew when Stone would be returning to his ranch. He wanted to get the girl off his hands as soon as possible.

Without sparing her a glance, Shilo growled, "Come on, girl, let's go." He started walking so fast, she had to half run to keep up with him.

His fast pace continued. After a while Little Bird's breath was coming in labored bursts.

Resentment stirred inside her. The arrogant man was doing this on purpose. She had seen the contempt in his eyes when he looked at her. She knew he didn't approve of her and was only letting her come to his village because of his friend.

Would she ever see the rancher again? she wondered. She hoped so. He had been kind to her in a casual, off-handed way and she felt that she could count him as a friend. She thought of her aunt, hoping that thinking of her would dull the ache that was developing in her side.

It only worked for a few minutes. Leaning against a tree, her hand pressed against her side, she panted, "I can't go on. I've got to rest awhile."

Shilo, a half dozen paces ahead of her, stopped and turned around. Frowning, said coldly, "Stop sniveling. You can rest when you're dead."

Little Bird wished that she had the strength and the nerve to spring at him, fasten her fingers in his long hair and pull him to the ground where she would pummel him with her fists.

She knew it was a foolish thought and eased herself to the ground. Leaning her back against a tree trunk she said, "I can't walk another step."

His fists planted on his hips, his long legs apart, Shilo growled, "Sit there then. When you've a mind to walk again, follow this path to the village." Without a backward glance at her he struck off, walking at the same fast pace.

Little Bird called after him, "How much farther is it to your village?" He didn't let on that he heard her. She muttered an Indian insult at his back and wished again that she was strong enough to tackle him.

She waited until her breathing returned to normal and her side stopped hurting, then stood up and plodded on up the path.

Several minutes later she heard the laughter of playing children and barking dogs. At last, she thought thankfully. She rounded a pile of boulders that looked like a giant hand had dropped them there and was met by half a dozen dogs barking and snarling. She stepped back, her hand going to her throat, her heart thumping.

The children ceased playing, and after staring curiously at her for a moment, they yelled for the dogs to be quiet. They gathered around her and one of the boys asked, "Are you lost?"

"I don't think so. Not if a brave called Shilo lives here."

"You know Shilo?" a little girl around eight asked doubtfully, her eyes ranging over Little Bird's dirty face and feet and ragged doeskin shift.

Little Bird started to answer when Shilo came walking through the door of a large lodge. As he strode toward them, his face was as forbidding-looking as it had been after the old mountain man shoved her at him.

Ignoring her, he glared at the children and ordered them to go away. Aren't any of these people friendly? she was wondering when she saw an attractive middle-aged woman walking behind Shilo. She wore a very pleasant expression on her face.

"You will stay with my mother until I figure out what to do with you," Shilo said, his voice harsh and cold.

"But will I not be staying here in your village?" Little Bird asked anxiously as he started walking toward a teepee in a stand of aspens.

When he gave her no answer, his mother said gently, "Do not worry, young maid. You will be taken care of. Do not pay any attention to my son's rudeness. That is his way." She took Little Bird's arm and said, "Come, I will give you something to eat. Then you will bathe and get dressed in clean clothes."

Little Bird smiled shyly at the woman, wondering why she looked so sad. "You are very kind," she said. "My name is Little Bird."

"I am happy to meet you, Little Bird," she said. "I am called Moonlight. You remind me much of the daughter I lost to small pox when she was around your age."

"I am sorry to hear that. It is hard to lose loved ones."

"Let's not talk of sad things now. We will go to my lodge where I will feed you."

Shilo was waiting impatiently outside his mother's lodge when they arrived. Looking only at his mother he asked gruffly, "Do you have everything you need to clean the maid up?"

Moonlight gave him a chastising look before

saying, "Her name is Little Bird. And, yes, I have everything I'll need. Although," she added, "I would like for you to ask one of the maids to heat some bath water and bring it to us."

Shilo stalked away, making no answer.

"Your son does not want me here," Little Bird sighed. "He will tolerate my presence only because his friend Stone Falcon wants him to."

"Maybe he's afraid that you will come between him and Stone. They have been very close since they were children," Moonlight said as she stirred a long wooden spoon in a bubbling pot hung over a small fire in the center of her lodge.

"He need not worry about that," Little Bird said. "The rancher has no interest in me. He is a good man. He saved me from white men who wanted to take me to their camp and use me. I will always be grateful to him."

"Yes, and so you should be. They would have ruined you for life. No decent man would have wanted you after they tired of you. You are too young for that to happen to you."

"I am older than I look," Little Bird said shyly.

After giving the young maid's face a close scrutiny, the older woman said, "I would say you are no more than twelve years."

"I am sixteen," Little Bird answered in amusement.

"You certainly don't look your age." Moonlight reached for a wooden bowl sitting on a flat rock next to the fire. As she ladled thick, rich stew into it, she said, "It is time for you to find a young brave and get married, have a wigwam of your own to care for."

"To have my own home has been my dearest wish for a long time. I lost my parents when I was twelve and lived with my aunt and her husband until a year ago. Then my aunt's man fell sick and died." Little Bird's small face turned sad and solemn. "We had no male relative to care for us then and my aunt and I became pratically slaves in our own village. We had to obey every order given to us by the women. If we dared to refuse, we didn't eat that day."

Moonlight sympathized with the orphan girl but didn't speak her feelings. It was the Indian way that if a female had no man to take care of her, she must either marry again or work hard for a blanket and a few scraps of food. Sometimes these unfortunate women were driven away from their village to fare the best they could. Sadly, many of them became whores. Stone had saved the little one from that shame.

While the hungry girl ate, Moonlight went to a far wall of the teepee and knelt in front of a large chest constructed of buffalo hide. From it she selected three articles of clothing. A cotton camisole, a soft deerskin shift with a fringed hem and a pair of beaded moccasins.

Little Bird finished eating just as a girl around her own age entered the dwelling, carrying a bucket of warm water in each hand.

She slid Little Bird a curious look as she set the pails on the floor. She next took a large earthenware basin from the wall and placed it near the fire. She looked at Moonlight then and Shilo's mother dismissed her with a smile.

"I think I will wash your hair first." Moonlight lifted one of the pails, dumped half its water into the basin, and motioned to Little Bird. "Come, bend your head over the water, little one."

It took three scrubbings to fully cleanse the hair and scalp. The first two washings sent rivulets of dirty water running down Little Bird's neck and face. But the third washing left the black hair that reached to her waist shiny as a raven's wing.

Moonlight wrung the water from the long tresses, then fastened them on top of Little Bird's small head with two long thorns cut from a locust tree. "Now," she said, "step out of that dirty shift and throw it in the fire."

Little Bird got rid of the stained, dirty clothing while Moonlight tossed the dirty water out of the teepee, then emptied the second pail of water into the basin. Kneeling, she picked up a pink bar of soap that lay on top of the clean clothing. She held it up to Little Bird's face and said, "Smell its fragrance. Shilo bought it for me from a white woman. It will make you smell like wildflowers. It will draw the young braves to you."

Outside the teepee two teenage boys looked at each other, their hands clamped over their mouths to keep from laughing out loud. They knew that the white woman hadn't sold the soap to their new chief. She had given it to him, like many other things she gifted him with. Most everyone in the village knew that Opal would give tall Shilo most anything he wanted if he would sleep with her regularly.

"It does smell sweet," Little Bird said of the soap, but I doubt that it will draw any young braves to me. My face is too ugly."

"Who told you that?" Moonlight asked sharply.

"Every one in my village. I am called the Ugly One by them."

Shilo's mother cupped Little Bird's face in her hands. She slowly scanned the fine features and soft brown eyes, then said, "They said that because they have never taken the time to look beyond the dirt. When I have cleaned you up, you will be quite beautiful. We will start with your bath."

As Moonlight lathered a piece of cloth with the pink bar of soap and started moving it over Little Bird's face, she said, "Tell me how you and your aunt came to be with the white men."

Little Bird squeezed her eyes shut against the soap suds running down her face and told the tale.

"And then all four of those bad men left the saloon, taking my aunt with them," she concluded. "I am so afraid for her."

And well you should be, Moonlight thought sadly. The woman probably wouldn't live long.

It was terrible the way some white men treated Indian women. But then, there were many Indian men who treated their wives badly, too.

She sighed at the cruelty of man, then asked, "What happened after that, Little Bird?"

"Stone Falcon didn't want me, didn't know what to do with me. He took me to his camp and fed me. When an old mountaineer came along, he talked him into taking me to your son. He said that Shilo would find a place for me."

As Moonlight toweled her slim body, Little Bird said solemnly, "Shilo was not happy to have me pushed off on him."

Moonlight made no answer, but smiled to herself. My son will get over that, she thought as she slipped the soft deerskin shift over Little Bird's head. His whole attitude toward the maid would change after he saw her later tonight.

It was eight o'clock by the time Flame returned home, stabled Lady and approached the house. Her nerves tightened as she stepped up on the rotting porch. Bertha and Deke sat there in the dark, arguing about a wagonload of settlers who were camping on the ranch. A fast glance at Bertha's bleary eyes and slack mouth told her that the big woman had made much use of the bottle sitting on the floor between the two of them.

"I tell you, I want them off my property tomorrow morning," Bertha slurred. As usual she ignored her daughter. The only time Flame got any attention from her was when she was angry about something.

Deke, however, gave her one of his appraising looks, his gaze drifting from her breasts to the spot between her hips. His eyes said plainly what he was thinking. He sent a sidelong look at Bertha, and when he saw that she had slumped over, he ran his palm down the length of his fly in a suggestive manner.

"You look tired, honey," he said in a low, soft voice that Bertha wouldn't hear. Rubbing himself he said, "Why don't you meet me in the barn later? I can take the tiredness out of you. I'll make you feel real good."

Flame gave him a scorching look. "The only way you could make me feel better is if you fell dead at my feet."

"You don't mean that." Deke leaned toward her. "Let me show you what I've got for you." His hands went to the buttons of his pants.

For a moment Flame couldn't believe that he was going to expose himself to her with her mother sitting right next to him. But he was as drunk as Bertha and was capable of doing anything. He might even attack her.

She reached her hand down into her right boot and pulled a knife from it. When she pressed a button on the handle, the six-inch-long blade that whipped out was lethal looking. She moved to stand over Deke. "Let me help you there," she whispered harshly, her eyes glinting dangerously.

"Hey!" Deke whispered hoarsely, pressing

back in his chair. "I was only joshin' you. Put that thing away."

"I will in just a minute," Flame said very softly, then fast as lightning, her hand shot out, the long blade slicing quickly down the length of his crotch. Buttons spilled all over the floor.

"You crazy bitch," Deke gasped, grabbing himself. "You better not have cut me."

"You low-life—" Flame's eyes shot hatred at him—"the next time I'll geld you."

When she wheeled and walked into the house Deke snarled after her, "I'll get you alone someday when you don't have that pig sticker on you. We'll see how brave you are then."

Flame ignored his threat. Holding her breath against the stench of stale alcohol, unwashed bodies and spent sex, she walked down the short hall. She released it when she opened the door to her bedroom and stepped inside.

Bone weary, and trembling with anger, she kicked off her boots, shed her clothing and turned back the blanket on her narrow bed. She reached under the pillow and pulled from it her thin nightgown. As she pulled it over her head, a flash of lightning lit up the room. We're going to have a storm, she thought, remembering how humid it had become that afternoon.

Flame had barely lain down and stretched out when the air crackled with lightning and thunder rolled. She lay in bed as a gusty wind blew rain against the window pane.

At the first slash of rain Flame heard Deke and her mother stumble into the house. She smothered a snort of laughter as she wondered how Deke was going to explain the missing buttons on his pants.

When all was quiet in her mother's room she thought with a curl of her lips that probably both had passed out. "Damn," she muttered as she turned over on her side, "I forgot to put the chair under the door knob." She debated getting up and barring the door.

In the end she decided she would be safe enough tonight. Deke was dead to the world. She could hear him snoring. He would sleep all night in his drunken state. Besides, she was tired to the bone.

Flame was drifting off to sleep, wondering what tomorrow would bring, when suddenly the creaking of the door brought her wide awake. She smothered a gasp when the door eased open and a dark shape filled the opening. She sat up in bed just as a flash of lightning lit up the room.

Her heart began to pound. Deke was carefully coming toward her. "What do you want?" she whispered as she scooted across the bed until she came up against the wall.

"You know what I want." Deke leered down at her. "I want to get between them long legs of yours. That's all I've been thinkin' about ever since the first time I saw you."

Flame clutched the blanket up to her chin, silently cursing herself for not barring her door, for forgetting to put the Colt under her pillow. She knew there was no use calling out to her mother. Bertha was dead drunk; she would never hear her. And even if she weren't, she might blame her daughter for luring her lover to her room.

"What about my mother?" she said, trying to reason with Deke. "She cares deeply for you. It would hurt her very much to learn that you wanted to sleep with me."

"I don't give a damn how that fat cow feels," Deke sneered. "I've just been killin' time with her until we could get together. Since she's drunk herself into a stupor, now's our chance to do some lovin'."

"Never," Flame ground out, clutching the cover to her chin and gathering herself to spring out of bed. But before she could lunge out of bed, Deke jerked the blanket out of her hands and flung it on the floor. In a flash he had her on her back, his hands clawing at the hem of her gown, shoving it up past her hips.

With a determination born of desperation she silently fought the rough hands that were trying to force her legs apart. Deke only laughed when she attacked his face. But when she ripped her nails across his flesh, an oath erupted from him. And though he slapped her hard, she fought on until she was exhausted. In defeat then she lay quietly, giving in to what was going to happen to her.

She lay helpless as Deke pulled her weakened legs apart. He was crawling between them when roar of fury exploded in the room. Holding a lamp shoulder high, Bertha glared down at them. "What in the hell is goin' on here?" she yelled, her face twisted in rage.

Even though Flame's mind had shut down momentarily she was still aware of how swiftly Deke removed himself from her. She listened in disbelief as he began to blame her for what Bertha had seen.

"Bertha, honey," he whined, "you know how she always flaunts herself at me, always hangin' round me, rubbin' herself against me. Well, when you passed out tonight, she came to our room and crawled in bed beside me. She began strokin' me, whisperin' all the things she could do to me. I'm sorry, honey, but I grew weak. After all, I'm a man. Will you please forgive me for following her in here?"

Bertha didn't answer Deke's plea, but before Flame could call him a liar, her mother was upon her. With a screech of rage her big hand slapped her daughter's delicate face. "Bitch!" she shouted. "I knew all along that you wanted Deke."

"You're wrong," Flame protested, her hand going to her stinging cheek. "I never—"

She didn't get to finish her denial. Bertha had fastened both hands in her long hair and jerked her to the floor. As she lay there, stunned, the breath knocked out of her, Bertha's hard, man-sized fist began to pummel her face and breasts. Every time she tried to crawl away from the punishing blows, she was dragged back for more.

Just when she was sure the beating would

never end, Deke pulled the enraged woman off her. "Bertha, that's enough. You're gonna kill her," he warned.

Bertha lowered her raised fist and stared down at Flame with hate-filled eyes. When her daughter moaned and grabbed her rib cage, Bertha heaved herself to her feet. She stood panting a moment, then reached down and grabbed her daughter by the hair again.

"Open the door, Deke," she ordered and followed him down the hall to the kitchen. "This piece of baggage is going out where she belongs."

Chapter Four

The storm had hit with a fury, catching Stone unprepared. There was blinding lightning, crashing thunder, and rain coming down in sheets. Stone peered through the deluge of water striking him in the face. Would he find any shelter around here?

He had ridden all day in search of his mystery girl, stopping at isolated ranches and exploring hidden valleys. His travels had brought him in a rough circle, until now he judged he was within ten mile of his own spread.

In the next flash of lightning he saw an up-thrusting of rocks about a quarter of a mile away. He felt a little better. He would find some kind of protection there. Maybe even a cave.

He kneed Rebel down the hill and was about to urge him into a gallop when he drew back on the reins. He saw, in the distance, a dim light shining from a dark bulk of trees. He pulled the stallion in and studied the pale yellow orb. The steady flame told him it was lamp light. Flames from a campfire would be dancing and uneven and it was unlikely a fire could burn in the wind and rain. He turned Rebel's head in the direction of the beckoning light.

He was still some distance away from the hope of shelter when over the racket of the storm he heard shrieks of anger and cries of pain. He slowed Rebel to a walk. Did he want to get involved in whatever was going on there? he asked himself. It was usually a good idea not to interfere in family disputes. But the one voice was crying as though in mortal pain.

Suddenly then, as though a door had been flung open, a narrow swath of light struck through the darkness. "What the hell?" Stone muttered when a flash of lightning revealed a large woman tossing the limp body of a slender girl out into the storm. As he swiped at the rain striking him in the face, the door slammed shut. His gaze swerved back to the crumpled body. The girl lay on her back, the rain beating on her pale face. Was she to be left there to drown? Stone was appalled that such a thing might be possible.

When several seconds passed and no one came out to check on her, Stone knew that he could not ride off and leave the girl at the mercy of the storm. He swung out of the saddle, then stood there, staring in disbelief. The girl had managed to get up on all fours and was crawling toward a small building that might be a barn. When she disappeared inside it, he told himself that at least she was out of the weather.

Still, he lingered. Something told him that the girl needed more than warm quarters. After all, she hadn't been able to walk. But should he interfere? he asked himself again.

As he dithered, trying to make up his mind, there emerged from inside the building a horse and rider. He stared at the slender body lying full length on the animal's back, her arms clutched around its neck.

He swore under his breath, his mind made up. If she was trying to get away from the woman who had tossed her into the storm, the girl feared for her life. And if she fell off the horse, she could be trampled to death.

Stone swung back into the saddle, and with a jab of his heels sent Rebel after the smaller horse. He caught up with the animal in a matter of seconds. He drew alongside and reached out, grabbing a handful of mane so could he guide it toward the large out-cropping of rocks.

He thought he would never reach the promise of possible shelter. He had to keep the horse at a walk so that the girl wouldn't lose her grip and fall off its back.

Then, after what seemed an eternity, they reached the jagged formation. He loosened the reins and let Rebel pick his own way among the debris of rocks and boulders while he kept his attention on discovering a suitable spot where they could find cover from the drenching rain.

Stone had just about given up hope of ever finding such a place when a streak of lightning lit up the entire area. He uttered words of thanks when he saw, only a few feet away, the dark opening of a cave. He pulled Rebel in, then reached behind himself to unfasten the bedroll tied behind the cantle. He slid to the ground, waiting for the sky to light up again. A moment later it did, and six running steps took him into the cave.

It was dry but musty-smelling and not very large. He thought maybe around four feet wide and eight feet long. And tall enough that he didn't have to bend his head to stand up in it.

In the inky darkness he hurriedly unfolded the bedroll on the gravelly floor. He rushed back outside just in time to catch the girl as she started slipping from the mare's back. When he carried her inside he had to stand and hold her while he waited for the next flash on lightning to show him where he could lay her down.

The cave was soon lit up again and he lowered her onto the bedroll he had unfolded. He took her wrist then and felt for a pulse. She was so pale and quiet, he feared she was dead. His heart jumped in thanksgiving when he felt a steady throb against his fingers.

"I must get her warmed up," he thought out

loud, "and the first thing to do is get her out of this soaking wet night gown."

Without hesitation he pulled the thin garment over her head and tossed it to the floor. By feel alone in the darkness he wrapped the blankets around her shivering body. That done, he sat back on his heels and in the darkness began to smooth the wet hair off her face.

The next time nature lit up the sky, Stone noticed the stub of a candle near the wall about four feet from the bedroll. And if he wasn't mistaken, he had glimpsed a pile of dead tree limbs in a corner.

"Please let them be dry," he prayed of the matches he pulled from his vest pocket. With fingers that shook, he scraped the sulphur end against the stone wall.

The breath he had held hissed through his lips when a yellow flame leapt into the air. Its flickering light guided him to the candle. In its illumination he carried enough wood to make a fire a few feet from where the girl lay. She still shivered. But within five minutes he had a roaring fire going.

In the fire's dancing light Stone made a closer inspection of their quarters. His lips twitched in amusement when he saw a broken rifle leaning against a wall, and a pocket knife with one blade missing. Lying beside it was a handful of marbles in a round circle scratched out on the floor, and several dry apple cores. Evidently some boy had come here to play.

Stone turned back to the girl when she rolled over on her back and moaned. He hurried to the bedroll and knelt down. It was then that he got his first full look at her face. He stared at her in total disbelief. There before him, lay the little beauty to whom he had lost his heart. He reached his hand out and gently touched a large bruise on her chin, then another on her jaw, and yet another one on her delicate cheek bone. From her moaning and shallow breathing, he was afraid she had some broken ribs also. And how many bruises were hidden under the blankets? he wondered.

He continued to kneel beside the girl, his forehead furrowed in a frown. He wanted to learn how badly she had been battered, but he couldn't bring himself to uncover her. He had thought nothing of stripping away the wet gown when he didn't know who she was. But now that he knew, he couldn't help feeling that it wouldn't be right to look at her nakedness in her helpless condition.

There was only one thing to do, he realized. He must keep her warm until daylight. He would go looking for help then. He remembered there was a small cow town not too far away.

Stone was laying a piece of wood on the fire when from outside he heard the strident voice of a woman calling, "Cletie, are you in that cave again? I'm gonna take a switch to you. I've been worried sick."

Stone stood up and walked to the entrance of

the cave. Maybe this woman could help the girl. As he stood peering out he became aware that the storm had moved off and that the rain had gone with it. He started to step outside, then paused.

A tall, rail-thin woman with a lantern in her hand came out of the darkness, worry written all over her face. Her features were sharp, thrown into relief by the thin hair pulled away from her face and fastened in an untidy bun at her nape. Her beady black eyes stared at him suspiciously.

"Who are you, stranger, and what are you doin' here?" she demanded, her eyes sweeping over the cave.

How much should he tell this sharp-tongued woman? Stone wondered.

"My name is Stone Falcon, ma'am," he answered finally. "I haven't seen your son."

"What's happened to your woman?" The thin woman walked over to the bedroll and placed her hand near the girl's head.

"How did she get in this shape?" The woman looked at him accusingly. "She looks half drowned and as if someone tried to beat her to death." She pinned him with narrowed eyes.

"Not me!" Stone groped for an explanation that would not prompt questions. "We got separated in the storm. When I finally found her someone had gotten hold of her and did all that to her. She's been unconscious ever since I found her so I haven't been able to question her."

He heard the horses stamping outside and had an idea. "Whoever attacked her was trying to steal her mare, I think. The saddle is gone.

"From the way she's breathing I'm afraid she may have some broken ribs. Would you help her, please? I'd gladly pay you for your trouble."

Stone didn't miss the interest that shot into the sharp eyes at the mention of money. He wasn't surprised when she knelt on the bedroll and said, "Let me take a look at her."

The woman's feet were shod in a pair of men's worn boots, and her dress was so faded it was hard to tell what its original color had been. But her work-hardened hands were as gentle as a child's when she pulled the blankets apart, then slowly moved her fingers over the battered body.

"Poor little thing," she said softly as she pulled the blankets back into place after the examination. "Whoever done this to you hates you real bad."

She looked up at Stone, who had turned his back the moment she laid hands on the bedding. "She has two broken ribs, maybe three. Her body is bruised all over."

"Can you help her?" Stone's question was a plea.

"I can bind up her ribs and treat her bruises." She paused a moment. "But if one of the broken ribs has punctured her lungs, we'll have pneumonia to deal with. You never know how things will come out with lung fever."

"She doesn't have any clothes," Stone said,

his face pale from the mention of pneumonia. "And we don't have any food either. We were on our way home when the storm hit."

"Where is home?"

"I have a ranch east of here."

The woman nodded. "I figured you to be a rancher from the looks of them horses out there." After a pause she said, "I guess some of my duds will fit her. Ain't got no shoes though. The grub won't be fancy, but it will stick to your ribs."

She stood up. "My name is Pearl Harding. Our wagon is on the other side of these rocks. As soon as I can find my boy, Cletie, I'll be back. One of our mules spooked in the storm, and he's out lookin' for it."

Stone walked outside with her. "I'd like to borrow your lantern for just a minute, Pearl," he said. "I want to look my animals over, see if they have any cuts on them."

Pearl handed over the light and Stone carefully went over Rebel. The stallion had a few scratches on his legs but otherwise he was in good shape. He was running his palm over the little mare's rump when his hand encountered what seemed to be a line of letters. He raised the lantern up to shine on the small ridges.

The word Flame sprang up at him. It had been neatly branded on the hip. A wide smile curved Stone's lips. The must be the girl's name. The mare belonged to her and she wanted it to be known in case her pet was ever stolen.

"Thanks, Pearl," he said and handed over the lantern. "The animals seem to be fine."

Pearl nodded, then walked away into the darkness. Stone grinned at her abrupt departure, then returned to the cave. He crossed over to the bedroll and knelt down, gazing at the still-unconscious girl a moment, then stroked his rough palm over the curls that were nearly dry now.

Would she learn to love him? he wondered. And really, who was she? She wasn't just Flame. She had a last name. Who was the woman who had treated her so harshly? And what about the man he had glimpsed in the shadows when Flame was flung outside? Why hadn't he stopped the woman? Were the man and woman relatives of the girl? Mother and father? Surely not.

As Stone continued to stroke her hair and murmur soft words of comfort, his eyes went often to the opening of the cave. He was anxious for Pearl Harding to return. There was a capability about the skinny woman that made him think everything was going to be alright.

According to the position of the moon that was visible through the clouds, Stone judged it to be near midnight when Pearl returned. A tow-headed youngster of around nine came with her. He carried a lantern in one hand and in the other a cloth bag whose contents rattled around inside it. Pearl carried a flat bundle under her arm.

"This is my youngun', Cletie," Pearl said as

she knelt beside Flame and untied the paper-wrapped package. Stone stood over her, watching as she unfolded the wrappings. On top of some folded clothing lay a bottle of clear liquid and a small, flat tin can. Pearl took up the bottle and gently patted its contents on the bruises, explaining, "This will take away the swelling."

When she had tended to the discolored spots on Flame's throat, arms and shoulders, Pearl corked the bottle and laid it aside. She picked up the tin then and explained as she smoothed the gray-colored salve on the discolorations, "This will help heal them."

Snapping the lid shut, she said, "Now let me doctor her body." She looked at at Cletie and ordered, "Go sit over there in the corner, son. Give the lady some privacy."

When the boy jumped up to obey his mother, Stone followed close behind him. He had no business watching, either.

It took Pearl close to an hour to probe Flame's ribs, then tightly bind the two she found broken. When she had treated the many bruises on her slender body she turned her hand to getting Flame dressed in rough muslin underwear. Next she got her into a much worn dress and a pair of heavy woolen socks that would take the place of shoes. All the articles were clean, smelling of soap and the out-of-doors.

"Well," Pearl said as she stood up and brushed off her skirt, "she has two broken ribs, but neither one punctured a lung so we don't have to worry about lung fever. The bruises will clear up in a few days and she'll be good as new. She appears to be in good health, and a hard worker according to the callouses on her palms."

She gazed down at Flame, who now slept peacefully. She looked up at Stone then and said, "You sure have a pretty wife. Ain't never seen her likes around here before."

"Thank you, Pearl. She's the prettiest woman I've ever seen."

"Well—" Pearl began rolling down her sleeves—"me and Cletie had better be gettin' back to our wagon. My old man will wake up and wonder where we've gotten off to." She pointed to the bag the boy had carried. "There's some grub in there. Some bacon and sourdough, and a jar of vegetable soup I made this morning. There's a pot to heat it in and a skillet to fry the meat in. You're probably ready for supper by now." She pushed Cletie toward the cave's opening. "I'll stop by tomorrow morning to see how your wife is doin'."

"I can't thank you enough for what you've done," Stone said, without correcting her assumption that they were man and wife.

She waved his words away and said gruffly, "Just be ready to cross my palm with money in the mornin'."

Stone shook his head in amusement as mother and son disappeared into the darkness. The skinny woman wasn't afraid to speak frankly. Anyway, he didn't care how much she charged him. The sharp-tongued woman had been very gentle with Flame and she seemed to know how to doctor her.

When Stone went back inside the cave, his gaze lit on the jar of soup. His mouth watered and his stomach rumbled. Pearl was right. He was more than ready for his supper. He dumped the soup into the pot and placed it near the fire to heat. When a delicious aroma began to drift through the cave, he sniffed appreciatively. He imagined that Flame was smelling the soup, too, for suddenly he felt her gaze upon him.

There was bewilderment and alarm in her eyes when he knelt down beside her. When she shrank from his touch, he said gently, "Don't be frightened. I'll not harm you."

She tried to sit up, then lay back with a moan. "Who are you?" she gasped. "Where am I? Why do I hurt so? I feel sore all over."

A frown creased Stone's forehead. Was it possible she didn't remember the beating the large woman had given her? He said finally, "My name is Stone Falcon and you're in a cave."

"In a cave?" The girl looked more bewildered than ever. "What am I doing in a cave?"

Stone looked at her with growing concern. "Don't you know what happened to you?" He watched her face as he waited for her answer.

She frowned and chewed her bottom lip, then shook her head. "I vaguely remember being hurt and thinking that some crazy woman was trying to kill me. I can't remember anything else."

"Can't you remember why she was beating you? Had you made her angry about something?"

There was a brief flash in her eyes as she tried to recall the events of the evening. It looked for a moment as if she had succeeded; then her eyes were damp with tears. "I'm sorry. Nothing comes to mind."

"Don't cry now. You remember your name, don't you? Where you come from?"

Her lower lip quivered and the tears slipped down her bruised face. "I can't remember anything," she whispered.

It took Stone a moment of realize that Flame had amnesia. She must have hit her head on something when she was flung from the house. Neither he nor Pearl had thought to examine her head.

"Do you know my name? Where I come from?" Flame asked as Stone walked over to the mouth of the cave.

Staring up at the sky where blackness was turning to gray, Stone wondered if he dared do what he was thinking. It was a dastardly thing he was contemplating, but he was desperately afraid of losing her. He firmed his lips. God help him, he couldn't take that chance.

Stone walked back to the bedroll and lowered himself to the gravelly floor. When she looked at him with wistful eyes, he swallowed a few times before saying, "Your name is Flame Falcon."

He watched her mull this information over in her mind and wasn't too surprised when she looked up at him and said, "My last name is the same as yours. Are we related?"

After a slight hesitation during which he expected to be struck dead from his lie, Stone said, "We are husband and wife."

Stone wondered how much wider Flame's eyes could grow. She looked down at her ring finger, then back at him. "I don't feel married and I don't wear a wedding band. Do we have children?"

Stone squirmed uneasily. This was becoming more complicated than he had imagined. She was asking questions, demanding more answers than he had. He turned his profile to her and answered, "We don't have any children. We haven't been married long enough."

"How long have we been married?"

It's not getting any easier, Stone thought and lied again, "Only a couple days." It was quiet for a moment and Stone held his breath for the next question.

When Flame said, "I'd like to see the marriage certificate, please," it was no easier to answer that demand than it had been the questions.

He took a deep breath and told another lie. "I don't have it yet. The preacher said he had to get it registered before he could give it to me."

She startled him by switching to another

subject. "Where were you when I was being handled so roughly?"

To give himself time to think up yet one more lie, Stone laid an unnecessary piece of wood on the fire. To kill more time he moved it around as though trying to position it just right. Finally he knew he had to answer her.

He sat back on his heels, and stared into the glowing coals. "We were on our way to my ranch when we got caught in the storm. It was the worst I've ever been in. The rain came down in sheets, blinding us. Somehow we got separated. When I finally found you, someone had beaten you almost unconscious. I managed to get you on the mare, then started looking for shelter. I finally found this cave and got a fire going."

Flame ran her fingertips over her face, then slipped her hand under the blanket and felt the bandage around her rib cage. Looking up at Stone, she asked, "Where did you get the salve I feel on my face?"

Stone had felt all along that she was suspicious of his answers. He relaxed a bit. She had finally asked him something that he could answer truthfully.

"We really had a streak of luck there," he said and proceeded to tell her about Pearl. "She was out in the storm, too, looking for her young son. She came to the cave because the boy plays here. I asked her to help you and she did after she found her son. She'll be stopping by later this morning to see how you're feeling."

He pointed to the pot. "She brought us this soup. Would you like some?"

"I sure would." Flame eased herself up on an elbow, her lips curving in a crooked smile. "I can't remember when I ate last. And I mean that literally," she added, amusement glittering in her blue eyes.

Stone smiled at her witticism, at the same time hoping that she wouldn't ask him when they had eaten last. He was getting tired of lying.

"We'll eat as soon as I check the horses." Flame nodded and he walked outside, thankful to be finished with answering questions for a while. He felt sure, however, that there would be plenty more of them as time went by. This woman that he was determined to have was full of inquiries.

Stone led Rebel up close to the mouth of the cave, and the little mare followed them. He unsaddled the stallion and tied the horses to a tree only a few feet from the cave. If a bear or a pack of wolves came nosing around, he would hear the horses' neighing and could quickly come to their rescue.

He picked up Rebel's saddle, and carrying it into the cave, he dropped it at Flame's shoulder. He knelt beside it and asked, "If I prop it behind you, do you think you could sit up and eat?"

Flame nodded. "I think so. My ribs are bound tight."

"Let me ease you up." Stone placed a hand

on either side of her waist and carefully raised her to an upright position. "Are you alright?" he asked, looking for a pained expression on her face.

There was no grimace on her delicate features. She sat a moment, looking at him; then she smiled. "I think I feel better sitting up than I do laying down. I can breathe easier."

"Good." Stone smiled, too, and propped the saddle behind her back. "I'll see to our supper now."

He rummaged through the sack a minute then grumbled, "There are no bowls in here. Just a couple of spoons. I guess we'll have to eat out of the pot."

"That's fine with me, if it's alright with you." Flame reached for one of the spoons.

Stone nodded that he was agreeable and they both dove in.

The soup disappeared quickly as they silently appeased their appetites. When the pot had been scraped clean, Stone fed more wood to the fire and Flame scooted down in the bedroll and rested her head on the saddle.

"Tell me about your ranch," she said after a small yawn. This was a subject Stone loved to talk about. He could talk for hours about the ranch his grandfather had started when he was a young man.

"It's a big place; four bedrooms. When my grandfather, Stonewall Falcon, came West and built it, he planned that he and my grandmother would have a passel of children. They only had one child. A son, my father, Riley.

Stone shook his head with a wry smile. "My mother presented my father with only one child also. So, for all these past years there are two bedrooms that have never been used." He didn't add that he hoped that he and Flame would fill those rooms with little Falcons.

"The place isn't run down," Stone continued, "but I guess it needs a little fixing up inside. Paint and such. Everything in it is older than me," he chuckled. "Sometimes I have a woman come in and clean it up some."

He didn't tell her that a young widowed Indian woman came to the ranch during the winter months to take care of all his needs. Sometimes he got snowed in at the ranch for months on end and it was impossible to get to Denver and Miss Opal's Red Lantern. The young widow wasn't bad once he got used to the stench of the bear grease she used in her hair.

Stone didn't think that Flame would approve of his arrangement with Gray Dove so he said, "I had a very happy childhood growing up. I played mostly with the Indian children from the nearby Ute village. My closest friend is an Indian named Shilo. We are like brothers. He taught me how to fish, trap and shoot a bow and arrow. He also taught me to love and respect nature. I, in turn, taught him how to herd cattle, how to rope and brand them.

"I tell you, Flame, there's no finer place in the world than a ranch to raise a family."

Flame blushed slightly, realizing what starting that family entailed. In her case it meant going to bed with a stranger, making love with him. Something told her she wouldn't like that part of marriage. Something told her it would be a vulgar act. She smothered another yawn and drifted off to sleep.

Flame hadn't voiced any thoughts, good or bad, as Stone gave her a short version of his childhood and thirty-five years of life. He looked at her face, her closed eyes, the slight rising and falling of her chest and shook his head in amusement. At what point in his story had she fallen asleep? he wondered. He had the feeling that he would have to go over the whole thing again later.

He wondered if he would ever get her story. Would she ever regain her memory? What if she never recalled her past; what would he do then? He had already had told her that they were married, so it was too late to stand in church and recite their marriage vows.

"Damn," he muttered as he pulled off his boots and stretched out on the cave's floor. "I wish I'd kept my dumb mouth shut."

Stone's last disturbing thought as he fell asleep was that he couldn't in all conscience make love to her until they were legally married. He would be taking advantage of her in the worst possible way. And there would be hell to pay if later he weakened in his determination and a baby arrived as the result of his desire for her. And what would happen if her memory returned and she realized she had been living in sin?

And that was only the beginning of things for him to worry about. What was she going to think when he didn't take her into his arms when they went to bed at night? She was bound to think that mighty strange.

Chapter Five

Stone awakened to a woman's sharp, chastising voice. When he opened his eyes, he found himself staring at a rough granite ceiling. Where was he? He tried to recall the events that had brought him to this cave. He became aware of something sharp poking him in the back. He supressed a moan as he shifted to his side. When he caught sight of the girl sleeping beside him it all came surging back.

He had rescued her from a mad woman and brought her here. The woman outside who was yelling at her son had come along and patched her up. But Flame still had a very serious ailment. She had lost her memory. Would she remember who she was this morning, remember her name and where she come from? he wondered, a worried frown etching his forehead. If her memory returned, would she recall all that he had said to her, all his lies? If she did, what would she say or do to him?

Bright sunlight flooded the cave suddenly and Stone had his first clear view of her in the daylight. She lay sleeping, a slender, workworn hand curled under her chin. Long dark lashes laid shadows on her delicate cheek bones. He wondered what color her eyes were. He could see that even with the bruises on her face her skin was clear and unblemished. A stray curl of burnished mahogany hair had fallen across one corner of her slightly parted lips. He gazed longingly at their softness, thinking how he would love to feel them beneath the firmness of his own.

Would he ever be able to do that, though? he asked himself. He thought of the words he had recklessly spoken last night, claiming that they were husband and wife. That lie might have jeopardized for all time any chance of his courting her, of her ever returning his love. His friend Shilo had said that he was loco, thinking he had fallen in love with a woman he had seen only once, and that at a distance. But crazy as it might seem, he had done exactly that.

Stone sat up when Pearl Harding's thin body darkened the cave's entrance.

"You still asleep?" she scolded as she advanced inside. "The sun has been up a couple hours." Cletie entered behind her, a cloth bag slung over his shoulder. When he started to lay it down, Pearl cautioned him to be careful. As she rolled up her sleeves, she said, "I brought you some more soup and a different kind of lotion I want you to rub on your wife's bruises."

She looked over at the bedroll. "How is she this mornin'?"

Before Stone could answer, Flame carefully sat up. "I'm feeling ever so much better this morning," she said cheerfully. "Whatever you used on my face and body has certainly helped."

Stone saw the pleased light that flickered in Pearl's eyes and knew she was touched by Flame's praise.

Her tone was sharp as ever, though, when she knelt down beside Flame and asked, "How are your ribs?"

"They're still sore, but not like they were last night. But the back of my head still hurts."

Pearl gave her a startled look, then turned to Stone. "You didn't mention that she'd hurt her head."

"I didn't know about it while you were here," he said, defending himself against her accusing eyes.

"Turn your back to me, honey, and let me feel your head," Pearl said softly. She helped Flame shift to her other side and started gently moving her fingers over Flame's scalp.

"Aha," she said, her fingers lingering on a spot just above Flame's left ear. "You've got quite a goose egg here. Something sharp has cut your scalp, for you have bled some."

Stone was trying to decide whether to tell Pearl about Flame's memory loss. Maybe she knew something about amnesia. Before he could make up his mind, Pearl was turning Flame over onto her back.

"The bump on your head will be sore for a while, but it's nothing to worry about. I'll take a look at your face now." A smile of satisfaction twitched the corners of Pearl's lips as she began to carefully scrutinize Flame's face.

She sat back on her heels. "All the bruises on your skin will be gone by the end of the week. If you kept your horse at a walk, do you think you could ride?"

"Yes, I'm sure I could. Do you mean today?"

Pearl pushed herself up. "Stayin' in this damp cave ain't gonna help your ribs to heal. You need hot sun in the day and a warm, comfortable bed at night." She turned to Stone. "How far away is your place?"

"Just ten miles away. Do you think that's too long a trip for her?"

"Not if you go slow. It's important not to put too much strain on the ribs."

"I'll see to it that she gets plenty of rest," Stone assured Pearl.

"Well then—" Pearl picked up the bag Cletie had placed next to the fire—"while I fry some salt pork and heat some more soup, you go saddle your horses. I want you to get on the trail as soon as possible."

Stone was both nervous and excited at the same time as he prepared the mare and stallion for traveling. He couldn't wait to get Flame to his home, but at the same time, he worried that she would not like the solitude there. It wasn't right that she hadn't been given the chance to decide if she would like ranch life. Maybe a person had to be born and raised on a ranch to appreciate it and love it as he did.

He would know soon enough, he thought as he led the animals to a tree and turned back to the cave. In the meantime he could only hope for the best.

Flame had left the bedroll and was sitting in front of the fire eating Pearl's crisp salt pork and vegetable soup. Her hair was a mass of curls and her eyes were still sleep-filled. He gazed at her beauty, her soft pink lips and shook his head. What a fool he was to think that such a woman would ever consent to be his wife. She was going to hate his ranch and would sooner or later leave him.

Pearl broke in on his gloomy thoughts when she handed him a bowl of soup and some salt pork on a tin plate. "Eat up," she said gruffly.

Flame looked up and gave him a bright smile. "This is the best breakfast I've ever eaten."

Pearl looked at her and wondered with a raised eyebrow why she should be so pleased with such a plain meal. "Do you like to cook?" she asked.

Stone saw the confusion that swept over

Flame's face and felt sympathy for her. She didn't even know if she could prepare a meal. He hurried to answer for her. "She's a real good cook. She's never cooked over an open fire though."

Lord, he thought, will I never stop lying?

"Food cooked over a campfire does have a better taste," Pearl agreed as she scattered the fire and stamped out the live coals that remained. "I've been cooking that way while we're traveling west. Rudy always talks about how much better everything tastes cooked over an open fire.

"Still, I'll be happy to be in a real house again," Pearl continued as she began shoving cooking utensils back into the cloth bag. "We're hoping to homestead nearby, but the lady who owns this place wants us off her ranch, so we'll be moving on today."

Stone and Flame had wiped clean the bowls and plates Pearl had brought and when Pearl had added them to the bag, she stood awkwardly before them. After a moment she cleared her voice and said, "I guess it's time you settled your bill so me and Cletie can get back to the wagon."

"Of course." Stone stood up. "How much do I owe you, Pearl?" he asked as he stuck his fingers in his vest pocket and pulled out some bills.

The way she shifted her feet back and forth, Stone imagined that she had never before charged anyone for her help. Dire times were making her do it now. His guess was confirmed when she mentioned a sum so small it was hardly worth asking for.

He counted out triple the amount she had hesitantly asked for. "Here you are, Pearl." He handed her the greenbacks. "And thank you very much for everything."

Pearl looked down at the money pressed in her hand, her eyes staring almost in awe. "You've given me too much, Falcon," she protested. "I only asked—"

"I know what you asked, and it was too little. You probably saved my wife's life last night. There's not enough money in all of Colorado to pay for that."

Pearl's harsh features softened. "I'm surely obliged to you, Falcon." Her eyes were moist as she folded the money and shoved it into the pocket of her faded apron. Me and my man will put it to good use. Maybe buy a hog and a few chickens once we get settled. Pork sausage and eggs tastes real good on a cold winter mornin' when the snow is up to your rump."

She gave the bag to Cletie, then stuck out her hand at Stone. "Good luck, Falcon." She turned to Flame and offered her hand. "You be careful of your ribs for a month or so. Let them knit properly before you do any hard work."

"I will," Flame answered, wondering what kind of hard work would be expected of her. "Thank you for everything." She smiled up at the woman who wasn't so tough after all.

Pearl nodded and nudged her son toward the

cave opening. "Let's get goin', son. We've got to hitch up the team."

The pair was gone then, Cletie looking over his shoulder at Flame, a love-struck look in his eyes.

Flame and Stone looked at each other in amusement. "It looks like I have an admirer," Flame said with a grin.

Stone wondered jealously how many other admirers she'd had. There had to have been many. Any single man who saw her must have wanted to court her. He refused to think about that. Reaching his hand to her, he said, "We'd better get going."

"I'm ready," Flame said, and grasping his wrist she carefully pulled herself up to stand beside him.

She looked so pale and frail in Pearl's ugly dress that Stone asked anxiuosly, "Are you alright?"

"I'm fine. I just felt a little wobbly for a minute. I'll need some help to get onto this pretty little mare."

"Don't you recognize her?" Stone asked as he carefully grasped her waist and sat her astride the mare.

"Is she mine?" Flame looked down at Stone, her eyes sparkling.

"Yes, she is," Stone said firmly. He didn't know if the mare belonged to her or not but he'd challenge anyone who tried to take it away from her.

"Why doesn't she have a saddle?" Flame

automatically clamped her legs around Lady's belly.

"It got lost in the storm." Lying was coming easyily to Stone now.

"Maybe we should go look for it."

"Like Pearl said, we ought to get you back home. But I promise I'll come back to this area someday and have a look around." Which he intended to do, but not neccessarily to look for a saddle. He wanted to find out all he could about the people who lived in the vicinity of that shack. He would learn whether Flame was related to them in any way.

Flame watched the graceful sway of her husband's back as he rode ahead of her. She had no memory of this man. Her blue eyes darkened in thought. How could she have no recollection of a man she must have loved deeply? Especially one so virile and handsome?

Had they made love on their wedding night? she wondered. Would he expect to make love tonight? She hoped not. Right now he was a stranger to her and she was not yet ready to surrender her body to him.

Would he force her? The thought was alarming. She dismissed the idea of that immediately. It was true she knew very little about this man she was married to, but she had an innate feeling that he would never use his power to get from a woman what she didn't want to give.

Had there been many women in Stone Falcon's life? she wondered. He looked old enough to have had many. The lines at the corners of his eyes and the ones that slashed down his lean cheeks suggested that he had lived hard, had sown his wild oats many times.

It was close to ten o'clock when Stone decided it was time for a rest. When they came to a spot where some falls splashed down a jumble of rocks, then flowed on into the Platte, Stone reined Rebel in.

"I want you to rest awhile, Flame," he said as he slid out of the saddle and removed his bedroll from behind the cantle.

"I was getting a little tired," she admitted when he had unrolled the blankets and reached his arms up to help her dismount.

She sighed in relief as she stretched out. When she smiled at Stone and closed her eyes, he sat down and relaxed against a tree. The only sound was the soft tumbling of the waterfall. Stone thought Flame had fallen asleep until she began asking him a string of questions he was totally unprepared for. "Do I come from around here? Had we known each other long before we married? How did we meet? Do my parents like you? Do I have any sisters and brothers?"

Stone stared up at the quaking aspen leaves. Why hadn't it entered his mind that sooner or later she would ask him such questions. It was only natural. Now that she was feeling better, all kinds of questions would pop into her mind.

He silently cursed himself for a fool. He was getting deeper and deeper into his lies. Now he had to make up whole families, their names, and where they lived.

He couldn't do it. He didn't have any more lies left in him. But was she ready to hear the truth?

He stood up and reached a hand down to her. "If you're rested, I guess we ought to get going. When we arrive at the ranch I'll answer all your questions. It's a long story."

Chapter Six

Deke awoke with a grumbled curse. Water was dripping from the ceiling, hitting him in the middle of the forehead. He sat up and swiped at his wet face with the corner of the sheet that was wadded up between him and Bertha.

"Damn it to hell," he swore when he realized that the whole bed was wet. He shook his snoring bed partner by the shoulder. "Bertha, wake up. The damn roof is leakin' again. The bed is soakin' wet."

Bertha's big feet hit the floor. "We'll go get in Flame's bed," she muttered, heaving her large body off the sagging mattress.

"She may be in it," Deke grunted. "You beat her up pretty bad last night.

"She knows she'd better be up by now. It's almost nine o'clock and she still has some yearlings to brand."

"And it's important that they get branded." Deke followed her down the hall. "The sooner she finishes that bunch in the branding pen, the sooner me and you get out of here."

Deke bumped into Bertha when she came to a sudden stop in front of Flame's bedroom door. "What in the world!" she exclaimed. "Who made this mess? Even the bed is broken down."

Deke looked over her shoulder at the bedside table, which had been knocked over. The lamp chimney had been smashed and oil had spilled all over the floor. A chair lay on its side with one leg missing. Bed clothing was scattered all over the floor.

"You made the mess and broke the bed last night, Bertha," he said. "Don't you remember? You thought me and Flame was carryin' on. When I explained to you how she had coaxed me into her bed, you went crazy. I had to pull you off of her before you killed her."

Bertha's little pig-like eyes glared at him as a vague remembrance of the previous night came to her. "Yes, I remember that," she muttered, "and I'm not sure that I believe everything you said. Now that I think it over, it looked more like she was fightin' you off."

"Now, honey babe, you know I wouldn't look at her if she hadn't flirted with me. You know you're the only woman I care for."

A worried frown formed between Bertha's eyes. She was beginning to remember other things. She recalled how she had beaten her daughter, thrown her out into the storm wearing only a thin gown. After a while she looked at Deke and asked in a small voice, "Where do you suppose she slept last night? It's plain she didn't use the bed."

"You threw her out in the rain. Maybe she slept in the barn."

Bertha was worried. There was a hint of fear in her eyes. Had she beaten her daughter too severely? Had she gone too far this time? What if she had killed the girl?

Her voice was brisk when she ordered, "Get dressed. We'll go check the barn."

In less than two minutes Deke had pulled on his pants and boots. Bertha had pulled on a wrinkled robe and a pair of boots. They stepped out the kitchen door and stared at the barn in astonishment.

The side of the building that housed the horses had blown away in the storm. It lay in pieces, scattered all over the ground. The three horses were gone.

"Do you think she's in this rubble?" Deke asked, his face pale.

"How in the hell do I know?" Bertha snapped impatiently. "Come on, let's go look."

They searched through what was left of the barn. There was no sign of Flame, not even a footprint.

"Let's go back among the trees." Bertha

started walking toward the growth of pine and aspen. "She might have gone there."

"I hope so," Deke said. "And I hope she's still alive. If we find her dead, you're gonna hang for it, Bertha."

"What do you mean, I'll hang for it?" Bertha swung on Deke. "You was there too, so you're just as guilty."

"You're crazy. I didn't lay a hand on her."

"But you was ready to," Bertha sneered. "You'd have done a lot more to her if I hadn't come on the two of you when I did."

"Let's stop arguin' 'bout it and see if we can find her." Deke struck out through the trees behind the ruined barn.

They splashed through mud and puddles of water for over an hour and found no trace of Flame. All they found were horse prints going in all directions.

"It's gonna take half the day to find them," Deke griped. "The storm spooked the hell out of them."

"Maybe she's at the branding pen," Bertha said, her uneasiness building. "Let's go look there,"

"That's a long walk, Bertha," Deke complained.

"Oh, for heaven's sake, stop your whinin' and come on." Bertha started walking in the direction of the branding pen. "We've got to find her."

"Why are you suddenly so concerned about your daughter?" Deke asked, reluctantly following Bertha's waddling body. "You never gave a damn about her before when you was beatin' hell out of her. I can't believe that you've suddenly found motherly love in that hard heart of yours."

A malevolent grin stirred Deke's lips and he thought, she's afraid that she's killed her, the fat bitch. He gave Bertha a sidelong look and asked in sly tones, "What are you gonna do if we find her and she's dead?"

Bertha stopped and spun around, her eyes so hard and threatening, Deke caught his breath. "You mean what are *we* gonna do, don't you?" She took a step toward him, her big hands clenched into fists. "You continue to forget that we're in this together."

"I'm sorry, Bertha." Deke backed away. "I'm just gettin' awful nervous."

"Well, stop being nervous. If we find her dead, we'll tie a rock around her neck and drop her in the deepest part of the Platte."

"What will we tell anyone who asks about her? Sooner or later she'll be missed."

"If she's dead, we won't be around here long enough for anyone to ask questions. If she's not at the branding pen, we'll drive what cattle you've gathered into Kansas like we planned. We'll just have to leave the rest behind. Can you get hold of your friend?"

"Yeah, he's in town waitin' to hear from me."

Bertha and Deke were almost in sight of the branding pen when they spotted the two horses. Deke's gray and Bertha's roan. Moving slowly and speaking in soothing tones, they had no problem approaching the two frightened animals. They each grabbed a handful of mane and walked the animals where the yearlings were penned.

There was no sign of Flame ever having been there. There was only mud churned up by cloven hooves. Bertha leaned on the pole corral, staring thoughtfully at the bawling cattle. After a moment she looked at Deke and said, "Boost me up on my horse. We might as well start getting out of here before somebody else finds her."

Deke almost threw his back out heaving Bertha onto the roan. His face was red and sweat popped out on his forehead before the deed was done. When they arrived back at the house they rode the horses to the part of the barn that was still standing. They found three saddles, untouched by the storm, still hanging on a partial wall. Deke saddle the two horses and tied them to a tree. He followed Bertha into the house then, looking over his shoulder every few steps. It was strange they had found no trace of Flame.

"Here's some left over coffee I heated." Bertha handed Deke a mug of dark liquid.

"Ain't we got nothin' to eat?" Deke complained. "We didn't have much of a supper last night, you know."

"We've got less this morning," Bertha snapped. "I was gonna send Flame to town today to pick up some supplies," Bertha added, shoving the empty coffee pot into a haversack. As tin cups and plates and flatware were added, she ordered, "Get your clothes and bedroll together. I'll have mine ready by the time you bring the horses around." In a separate bag she put a skillet, a cook pot and some sugar, salt and coffee.

Only a few minutes passed by the time they met where Deke had tied the horses. This time Bertha managed to climb into the saddle by herself.

"When we get to where I've got the cattle penned up," Deke said, leading out, "you can wait there while I ride into town and find my friend, Hoss." He gave Bertha a big smile. "Then we'll be on our way just like we planned."

"What about the yearlings in the pen? Ain't you gonna take them too?" There was a hint of scorn in Bertha's voice.

Deke caught the barely hidden contempt and his face flushed a deep red. "Of course I'm gonna take them," he growled.

Bertha realized she had never noticed before that he wasn't too smart. She decided that she had better take over when it came time to sell the cattle.

Deke had herded about 60 head of cattle into a short dead-end canyon only a couple miles away. A drift fence kept them penned in. When they arrived he helped Bertha to dismount, then swung back into the saddle, ready to ride into town and meet his friend.

Close to an hour passed before Deke returned to where he had left Bertha. His friend was with him. Bertha thought that she had never seen a bigger, uglier man in her life. Yet she had never been more drawn to a man. Deke introduced him as Hoss Jenkins.

Her eyes were drawn instantly to the great bulge in his crotch. He's like a bull, she told herself with a rushing tightening in her body. She blushed lightly when she lifted her gaze to his face and saw by his knowing grin that he had read her mind.

When Deke was busy tying his horse to a tree, Hoss rubbed his palm down the front of his fly and winked at Bertha. She gave a lascivious swipe of her tongue across her lips and bucked her wide hips at him. Excitement grew in her eyes as she watched the bulge in his pants grow to an enormous size. Her brain started working on ways to get rid of Deke. He wasn't too bright and he might lead them into trouble with the cattle. But right now he was needed to help drive the longhorns to Kansas. She'd see what happened after that.

"Well, let's get started," Deke said. "I'd like to get out of this area as soon as possible."

"That's fine with me," Hoss said and put his left foot into the stirrup. He started to swing his right leg over the stallion's back, then gave a loud curse. The saddle had loosened and shifted. "The damn belly strap has broken," Hoss exclaimed angrily. "We can't go anywhere until I get a new one."

"Maybe we can mend it," Deke suggested and started to dismount.

"Naw, it can't be fixed," Hoss said impatiently. "It's been put back together three times already. You're gonna have to ride back to town and buy me a new one."

Deke's frown said plainly that he didn't like the idea of leaving Hoss alone with Bertha. It wasn't that he cared what they might do in his absence; his only concern was that if Bertha found big Hoss a better lover than he, she wouldn't hesitate to kick Deke out of her bed. He didn't want that to happen until the cattle were sold.

Deke was afraid of Hoss, however, and all he said was, "You'll have to give me the money to pay for it. I'm stone broke."

"Ain't you always?" Hoss half sneered as he handed him some bills.

As soon as Deke and his horse were out of sight, Bertha and Hoss lunged at each other. Bertha hitched up her skirt and Hoss tore open his fly as they they fell to the ground. The cattle grew uneasy and milled about at the sound the pair made as they came together.

Half an hour later Hoss rolled off Bertha. They lay still a moment, panting like a pair of buffalo. Hoss sat up after his breath was under control and said, "I expect we'd better straighten up our clothes. Ole Deke will be comin' back pretty soon. You don't want him gettin' suspicious of us, do you?"

"I don't care how suspicious he gets," Bertha

said with a curl of her lips. "Did that belly strap really break?" she asked as she brushed grass and pine needles out of her hair and the back of her skirt.

"Naw," Hoss laughed. "I just wanted to get rid of him." He walked over to his big stallion, and removing the belly strap from the saddle, flung it into a nearby ravine.

He and Bertha were each sitting on a large rock when Deke rode up ten minutes later.

Chapter Seven

Little Bird snuggled deeper into the furs as she slowly woke up. She tried to hang on to the dream that was quickly slipping away.

Glancing around the lodge, she compared it to the pitiful dwelling where she and her aunt had been living. In rain it leaked, and in the winter the wind and snow crept inside. There had been no soft fur to sleep on, only a couple raggedy blankets to share. They were little protection from the cold dirt floor; a floor that had no fur or mats covering it.

Little Bird remembered the soft furs her bare feet had sunk into last night when she walked about. She wondered how long she would be allowed to stay with Shilo's kind mother. Not long, she imagined. Her arrogant son would see to that.

She had never before had anyone take such an instant dislike to her. Even when she and her aunt were veritable slaves in the village, no one had looked at them with such scorn. Shilo didn't even look at her if he could help it.

He had been part of her dream. They had been walking together along side the river. They were laughing and talking and holding hands. Just before she awoke, Shilo had looked at her and said softly that he wanted her for his bride. The dream had vanished before she could answer him.

It was only a dream, and don't you forget it, Little Bird chastised herself. Tall, handsome braves were not for the likes of her. She would be lucky to marry a short, squat, ugly man with crossed eyes. One who would probably beat her.

Little Bird's thoughts turned to Stone Falcon. He was so kind and handsome. She wondered if she would ever see him again. Since he was a friend of Shilo's it was likely, she thought. She wanted to thank him again for saving her from those awful brothers. Also, she wanted to ask him to do another favor for her. She wanted him to keep an eye open for her aunt. She had prayed hard and long last night that her aunt was alive and well.

When Little Bird heard the laughing voices of children, she sat up and reached for the shift folded neatly on the floor. She was very proud of the soft deerskin garment. It was the nicest she'd ever owned, and the first one that hadn't been worn by someone else before.

She smoothed her hands over the leather fringe that hung from her knees to mid-calf. After she had stroked her palms over the butter smoothness of the dress, she pulled it over her head. She'd heard Moonlight talking to a man who sounded like Shilo.

Little Bird was slipping a pair of beaded moccasins on her slender feet when the lodge flap was lifted and Moonlight stepped inside. When she had fastened the flap to a pole that would keep it open she looked at Little Bird and smiled.

"You must be rested and hungry by now," she said, a twinkle in her eyes. "You have slept ten straight hours."

"Oh, dear, I should have been out working with the women. They will think that I am lazy." Little Bird scrambled to her feet, running her fingers through her hair, smoothing out the tangles.

"No, little one, tomorrow will be soon enough for you to have duties assigned to you. I want you to rest today. You are much too thin and run-down."

As Moonlight talked she knelt on the bed of furs behind Little Bird. "I intend to put some meat on those fragile little bones," she continued as she drew a bone comb through the long,

113

black, shiny tresses. "When I have braided your hair we will go outside to our campfire and have our morning meal."

Little Bird wished to herself that Shilo wouldn't be eating with them. But she wished in vain. When Moonlight finished dressing her hair and they stepped outside, the proud chief sat scowling into the fire. When she said good morning to him, he only glared at her.

"I hope that you don't plan on making us wait for breakfast every morning," he griped, his voice harsh and cold. "You're in for a big disappointment if you are. There are no lazy people in this village. Those who do not work do not eat."

Little Bird was too near tears to respond to his unpleasantness. She could only sit and stare at her fingers clasped tightly in her lap. Moonlight didn't say anything either. But the look she gave her son kept him quiet for the rest of the meal. When he had finished eating the flat cornmeal cakes his mother served him, he stood up and stalked away without a word.

Moonlight gazed after Shilo, bafflement in her eyes. It was not like her son to be so rude. Especially to a young maid Stone had asked him to befriend.

A sudden thought came to her. Was it possible that her son was attracted to the frail little orphan? She was a pretty little thing. She was quiet and modest, her voice soft. She was just the sort of young woman Shilo should marry.

Sadness clouded Moonlight's eyes. Her son

had finally fallen in love, but with a maid his closest friend wanted. Shilo would never try to come between them. And because of this he was angry at his helplessness. To hide his true feelings, he treated Little Bird badly.

Moonlight's serene countenance hardened a bit. She would not give up the hope that some day Little Bird would be her daughter-in-law. In the meantime she would see to it that Little Bird was kept in view of her son as much as possible. If he grew to care enough for her, he would pursue her despite his long friendship with Stone.

At least she hoped that would happen. Her son was much like his dead father. He would love but once. It would sadden her to see her only living child go through life without the comfort of wife or children.

Moonlight drew in a deep sigh. There was another reason she wanted Shilo to marry. At his father's death he had become chief of the tribe. The people expected him to take a bride and have fine, healthy children. Many of the young maidens already were casting longing looks at him. He hadn't shown interest in any of them yet.

Little Bird looked at Moonlight with a wan little smile. "As you know, your son is not happy about having me thrust upon him."

"Don't worry about my son's behavior." Moonlight patted Little Bird's hand. "We will see how things are a couple moons from now."

A toddler, around three years old, came to

Moonlight, clutching a small bow and arrow in his chubby hand. With a gamin grin he pretended to shoot an arrow at his aunt. She chuckled and pulled his little bare body into her lap.

"Bad boy, Little Turtle. You would shoot your aunt?" She set him giggling when she tickled his fat little belly. When he reached for a flat cake, Moonlight looked at Little Bird and asked. "Do you like children?"

"Oh yes. Little ones are so innocent. You always get the truth from them. In my village it was my job to look after them. I especially liked tending the babies. I will miss the children."

Little Turtle scooted off his relative's lap, gleefully shooting imaginary enemies as he ran away. "Little Bird," Moonlight said when the child disappeared from sight among some trees, "I think I have just the job for you."

"You do? What is it?"

"Tending the children here in our village. We need someone to look after them when their mothers are fishing or gathering grains and roots for our meals. What do you think? Is it a good idea?"

"I think it's a fine idea." Little Bird's eyes shone with pleasure. "When do you want me to start?"

"Tomorrow morning. We have many children in the village and you will need help in caring for them. I must decide which of our maids will make you good helpmates. Some of them are only interested in our young braves right now. We don't need their sort looking after our children, don't you agree?"

"Indeed, I do," Little Bird agreed. "Children are precious gifts from the Great Father and we must see to it that they grow up safe, and healthy and honorable."

Moonlight smiled in pleased agreement. "I will take you to meet the elders now," she said.

As they walked toward the long council house, Moonlight noticed that the young men eyed Little Bird with much interest. It surprised her that the girl seemed unaware of their appreciative gazing. She was pleased with Little Bird's demeanor when she was introduced to the wise men and the medicine man. She even knelt in front of Shilo, giving him the respect a chief deserved. She wanted to laugh out loud at how uncomfortable that action made her aloof son. He had to acknowledge her as he would any member of the tribe. She knew that he would have rather chewed rocks.

A long breath of relief feathered through Little Bird's lips when she and Moonlight left the council house. Ever since she could remember, the elders of her tribe had frightened her. They looked so stern and forbidding. She used to dream that they were chasing her, their faces painted red and black.

"I imagine you're glad that's over." Moonlight linked her arm with Little Bird's. "The old men are so solemn and fierce-looking. To this day I'm a little frightened of them."

Little Bird started to admit that she felt the

same way; then she became aware of the females gathered around Moonlight's lodge. "They have come to meet you, to look you over," Moonlight whispered. "Do not be nervous."

The majority of the females who stood staring at her were teenagers. The adults sent her friendly smiles, as did a few of the young women. But most of the younger ones gave her cool looks and turned away before Moonlight could introduce them. The mothers frowned at their daughters' rudeness, but did not rebuke them. They knew that jealousy of the new maid's looks made them act so. She was a threat to them. Each girl was looking for a husband, and they didn't want any added competition. The mothers knew that when Little Bird found one of the braves to her liking, she would be welcomed into the group.

It helped Little Bird's hurt feelings when the girls who had smiled at her remained to welcome her and invited her to go swimming in the river with them later in the day.

When she and Moonlight entered the lodge, Little Bird said, "The girls who just left are very nice. I wonder why the others were so rude to me."

"Actually, they are nice, too. They are simply jealous of your looks and fear you will take their young men away from them."

"But I'm not interested in their young men," Little Bird protested earnestly. "I don't think I would like being married."

"Why is that, child?" Moonlight looked surprised. All maids wanted a husband.

"In the village where I lived, husbands often beat their wives. My aunt's husband did not do this, and she tells me that my father never laid a hand on my mother in anger. Nevertheless I do not want to chance it."

"What you say is true sometimes," Moonlight said sadly. "It happens often when our men drink the white man's whiskey. Some of them go a little crazy and abuse their women.

"But you must realize, Little Bird, that you will have to take a husband sooner or later. You will need a man to provide for you."

Little Bird had already admitted that to herself. She was aware that a woman without the protection of a man had little security.

"I hope that the husband who is chosen for me won't be too old and will not beat me," she said quietly.

"Little Bird!" Shilo's mother exclaimed, shocked. "You will choose your own husband when the time comes. No one will tell you whom you should marry. Our young braves show much interest in you. Soon they will come to Shilo requesting permission to come calling on you."

And Shilo will waste no time in allowing the first brave who asks to come courting, Little Bird thought, recalling the courtships between the young people in her old village. She remembered the weddings, the gifts of horses

119

and furs and other items of value that were exchanged.

She had never dreamed as she watched the merry-making that some day a young brave might want her in his teepee. And now that it was a possibility, she wasn't sure she was happy about it.

But hadn't Moonlight said that she could choose her own husband? She could claim that none of them suited her, couldn't she?

That was wishful thinking, she knew. Shilo would press her into choosing someone right away. It was plain that he wanted to be rid of her as soon as possible.

Chapter Eight

"We'll be home pretty soon," Stone said. "The ranch house is just over this ridge."

A couple of minutes later he was pointing toward a stand of aspen and saying with pride, "There it is. The place where I was born and raised. It's almost a hundred years old. My grandfather, the first Stonewall Falcon, had it built."

When they drew rein Flame could only sit and stare at the big, sturdy building. It was set in the juncture of two streams that flowed down from the mountain. What a picture it makes, she thought, gazing at the white painted walls shining softly in the golden glow of the setting sun.

Its wide porch and window trim blended with the color of the grass growing around it. A heavy vine climbed up the fieldstone chimney and spread halfway across the porch roof. She counted four tall windows in the front of the house. They had heavy shutters that would keep out the cold in the winter and the heat in the summer.

It looks so cozy and inviting, Flame thought. Then she glanced over the grassy area surrounding the house. Some care was needed here. She could make out that at one time there had been flower beds alongside the house in front. She could see that even now young plants were struggling to push through a mat of weeds and leaves. In each chimney corner was a large old rose bush, filled with buds. She wondered what color the blossoms would be.

Stone was becoming nervous as Flame sat and gazed at the house he loved so much. Had she hoped to see a fancier place? But why should she do that? She had no memory of her past, what kind of home she came from.

He was about to suggest that they go inside when she turned glowing eyes on him.

"I love it, Stone. It seems to be saying, 'Welcome, Flame.'"

"And I second that." Stone smiled at her, and taking her by the waist, he lifted her out of the saddle and stood her on the ground. "Are you tired? Would you like to rest out here on the porch awhile before going through the house?"

"I'd like to see it now, if you don't mind."

"Fine. You'll be able to have a good look before the sun goes down. I've got to warn you though, I'm not much of a housekeeper."

Stone opened the large front door and stepped aside so that Flame could enter. He followed her inside and said as he waved his hand around, "This is the main room, as you can see."

The first thing that caught her attention was the enormous fireplace in the center of a wall that was made entirely from fieldstone. The fireplace itself could hold two big backlogs at the same time. Its hearth was a foot and a half off the floor and the same width. It would give off a lot of heat, Flame thought, not like . . . not like what? she wondered, frowning. She strained to recall, to remember that fleeting thought that had swept through her brain. When nothing came to mind, she gave her attention to the furnishings.

She thought the furniture was old, but she could tell it was in good condition. The settee and large chairs were of soft leather that looked like they would be very comfortable to sit on. There were three end tables in the room, with a pretty kerosene lamp on each one. There was a long, low table in front of the settee, with books scattered on its top. The table sat on a beautiful Mexican woven rug. She noticed that dust lay heavily on everything.

Stone next led Flame down a long hall. There were four doors opening on to the bedrooms. She only gave the rooms a peek as they walked past them. She did notice, though, that two of the rooms had the appearance of having never been used. She saw also that in one room the bed was made up and everything was neat. The fourth one was a total mess. The bed was unmade, dirty clothes were strewn about the floor, a shirt and pants hung on the bed posts, and boots and dirty socks were scattered everywhere.

She thought he wouldn't hear her whispered, "Phew," but he did.

"I guess it's pretty bad, huh?" He gave her a sheepish grin.

"I really don't know." She grinned back at him.

"That's right, isn't it?" Stone laughed and hugged her. He was relieved at her smile, but he knew he had to stop living like a pig.

He led her into the dining room next. This room was large also, and faced the front of the house. Its table was long enough to seat ten people. It, too, had a fireplace, though not as large as the one in the main room.

The kitchen came next, another large room with many cupboards. Pots and pans and other cooking utensils hung on the wall behind the big, black stove. Clearly, they had not been used in a long time. Everything, including the stove, a long table and two benches, was covered with dust. Stone was relieved when Flame didn't remark that she could write her name in the dust. Actually, she hadn't even seemed to see it. Strange, he thought. But maybe she didn't want to embarrass him by mentioning it. She only asked, "Don't you ever cook?"

"No. I eat with the cowhands at the cookhouse. I look forward to the meals you'll cook for me."

"I hope I can remember how." Flame looked a little worried.

"You will." Stone laughed. "It will come naturally to you."

Flame hoped so, but she somehow doubted it.

"You're looking tired." Stone searched her face. "Why don't you lie down and rest until supper is ready? Charlie, the cook, has it on the table around six o'clock. He'll yell when it's ready. You'll hear the men coming in from the range around five-thirty."

"I am a little tired," Flame admitted, and Stone led the way to the first door on the right side of the hall.

Flame wasn't surprised to find that the room, like all the others, was large. The bed was big, as was the dresser, the wardrobe and the bedside table. Flame shook her head in amusement. The house, and everything in it, had been built and bought with big men in mind. She tugged off the socks Stone had bought from Pearl and when he turned back the covers, she lost no time lying down. The sheets smelled dusty from disuse, but she was asleep before she really smelled them.

Stone stood a long time gazing down at Flame's sleeping face. He had changed his mind a half dozen times about telling her the truth about their relationship. He still didn't know what he was going to tell her when she woke up and began to demand answers to her questions. He didn't want to admit that he had lied to her about their being married. She would leave him then and he would lose his chance to make her care for him. It was important that they spend time together, that she get to know him.

His gaze fell on her bare feet and he remembered that she had no shoes. And that ugly dress of Pearl's had to be replaced. He would take her into Dogwood to buy new clothes as soon as her ribs were healed, but what would she wear until then?

He walked over to the window and gazed outside. A look of pity and amusement twisted his lips when he saw his young horse wrangler moping about the corral. Charlie's niece had visited him for a couple weeks and the young man had been smitten with her immediately. It had been a hot and heavy romance for two weeks, but then the girl had to return home. Young Jamey had been heart-sick ever since. He felt for the lad.

Then his sympathy for Jamey was forgotten. Charlie's niece had gone off and left one of her valises. Maybe there were some dresses and women's clothing in the bag. The two girls were of the same size. Charlie had been threatening to throw the valise out, saying he didn't have room for it in his one-room living quarters.

The impatient stamping of the stallion and

the mare at the hitching rack brought Stone outside. When he had taken care of Rebel and the mare, he joined his cook in the long cookhouse.

"You weren't gone long," Charlie greeted him as he mixed up a bowl of sourdough. "I see you've come back with a pretty lady, though."

"I sure did." Stone poured himself a cup of coffee from the pot that was kept hot all day.

Charlie looked at him and raised a questioning eyebrow. "She gonna be stayin' here long?"

"I hope so. She's my wife."

"What!" Charlie dropped a bread pan holding a loaf of raw dough. "You mean you went and got married?"

"I sure did. Her name is Flame."

"Well, I'll be hornswaggled. Do you think you're ready to settle down to one woman? That ain't your style, you know."

"I'm sure, Charlie. I've been thinking about her all winter. Funny thing is, she's been living on a ranch not ten miles away, and I never knew it. We got married a couple days back."

"Then you're on your honeymoon, ain't you?" Charlie gave him a sly grin.

Stone took his time stirring sugar into his coffee before answering slowly, "We're not on our honeymoon, exactly. The night of our wedding we were caught in a real bad storm. Flame's horse threw her and when she fell, she hit her head on a rock. She's got some broken ribs and a lot of bruises. But the worst thing is, she's got amnesia."

When Charlie gave him an uncertain look and asked if it was catching, Stone explained, "She can't remember anything of her past. Not me, not her home, or her parents. She can't even remember that we're married."

"You mean she lost her memory." Flame's ailment was clear to Charlie now. He drew a breath of relief. "That's too bad, Stone. I knowed a couple fellers that happened to. One got over it in a few months, but the other poor feller went to his grave not knowin' who he was. He died all by his self. He had a wife, but when he couldn't remember her, she up and left him. She said it was like sleepin' with a stranger—made her feel like a whore. Is there anything I can do for your wife?"

"Just treat her normal. She's not crazy or anything like that. She just can't remember her past. But if you still have those duds that belong to your niece, maybe Flame can borrow some of them. We lost her clothes in the storm."

"Sure. She can have them all. I was about ready to throw them out. There's no tellin' when she'll be back for another visit. I don't know what all is in the bag. I know it's mighty heavy."

Stone drained his coffee cup and stood up. "Thanks, Charlie. I'll take the clothes over to the house right now."

"The bag is in my room, in a corner. We'll be eatin' in about a half an hour."

Charlie was right, Stone thought as he carried the bag across the yard and into the house. It was mighty heavy.

With the setting of the sun, Flame's bedroom was in shadow. Stone placed the bag on the floor at the foot of the bed. He lit the lamp on the bedside table, then looked down at Flame. She still slept soundly, a hand curled under her chin. He stood, just looking at her for a moment, then gently shook her shoulder. She stirred, slowly opened her eyes, then turned over on her back. Her eyes widened in fear and she shrank from Stone.

"It's alright, Flame," he soothed softly. "It's me, Stone."

"Oh, Stone." She gave a deep sigh of relief. "I was having an awful dream. I was fighting off a man who had sneaked into my room and was trying to get in bed with me."

"Do you remember what he looked like?" Stone hoped that the dream was a sign of her memory returning.

"I do, and I don't. For an instant his face was very clear, but then it faded away before I could recognize him. But I feel strongly that he is a part of my past. The dream was so real."

"Was there anyone else in your dream? A woman, maybe?"

Flame frowned in thought. "I remember vaguely that an angry woman was shouting at me." She leaned on her elbows. "I don't want to think about it any more, Stone. I'm getting a headache."

"I understand, Flame. Don't think about it

now. When your brain is ready, you'll remember everything. Now, I've brought you some clothes that belonged to Charlie's niece. I don't know what all is in here." He lifted the valise onto the bed. "Why don't you sit up and we'll take a look."

Flame watched eagerly as Stone unstrapped the carrier and laid aside the lid. "Oh my!" she exclaimed at the sight that met her eyes.

When she only continued to stare at the stack of clothing Stone urged, "Go through it. See if you think anything will fit you." As Flame lifted each carefully folded garment onto the bed, she found that the bag held everything a female might want or need. There was fine lawn underclothing, dresses, some the likes of which she had never seen before. Some were very fancy, made of silk, velvet and thin muslin. There were also everyday dresses of homespun cotton and linen. In the bottom of the bag were several pairs of shoes and a pair of boots.

Flame looked up at Stone, her eyes glowing. "Everything looks like it will fit me, and everything is so grand. I'm sure I've never owned anything like this before." She smoothed a hand over a pink lawn nightgown.

Stone repressed a groan. How lovely she would look in the flimsy garment, lying in bed, her arms lifted to receive him. He imagined how it would feel when he stretched out on top of her soft, slim body, then slid himself inside her.

When Flame spoke, bringing him back to reality, he found himself hard and hurting. "I can't wait to put on one of the dresses ... I think this one." She held up a small flowered calico. "What do you think?"

"Yes, that one will be fine," he managed to say. "Charlie will be calling out that supper is ready pretty soon. I can't wait for him and the men to meet you."

Flame lifted her hands to her face, covering the bruises there. "Could I meet them tomorrow? I need a bath and I have a bit of a headache."

Stone knew the real reason she was hesitant to meet his men. She didn't want them to see her battered face. He fully understood and went along with her wishes. "Sure you can." He grinned as he added, "It's no big deal meeting those yahoos anyway. I'll go to the cookhouse and fix us a couple plates. We can eat here in the house."

"If it's not too much trouble, Stone, I'd appreciate it."

"No trouble at all. I'll go see what Charlie has cooked up."

Flame went to the window and watched Stone walk across the yard to the cookhouse. She wished that she could remember him. What she did know of him she liked very much. He was polite and caring of her welfare. He hadn't yet made any sign that he wanted to be her husband in all ways. He understood and respected how she would feel about making love to a man she didn't know.

Flame's lips curved in a slight smile. She had

a feeling it wouldn't be too long before she got to know him again in the biblical sense. She sighed. He was so handsome. She couldn't believe that she couldn't remember him.

The cowhands were at the table when Stone walked into the long building. He was immediately bombarded with congratulations and insults. "Who is the woman that was foolish enough to marry a roughneck like you?" one man asked, while another wondered if she was blind. Someone asked him if she was from the area.

Stone laughed and shrugged off their razzing. All he said was that she wasn't a local girl and that they would meet her tomorrow. "She's tired now and needs rest."

As soon as the last words left his mouth, he knew he shouldn't have uttered them. When he saw in his peripheral vision that some of the men wore knowing grins, he knew there were going to be some suggestive remarks made as to why his wife was tired.

He pinned them all with a frosty look and said, "There will be no more discussion about my wife."

The men looked sheepish and gave their attention to the food on their plates. It was plain that they were to respect Mrs. Stonewall Falcon or get a thrashing they would never forget.

"That fried chicken sure looks good, Charlie." Stone walked over to the stove and gazed down at the contents of a big black skillet. "Flame will sure like it." He took two plates from the back of the stove and began to fill them with chicken, mashed potatoes and gravy, string beans and biscuits. Charlie brought a big tray from under the sink. When Stone loaded the plates on it, the cook held the door open so that he could pass through.

When he was out of hearing distance, Charlie spoke. "The boss is a bit touchy about his bride right now. A couple days back when they were on their way home, they got caught in a storm. His wife got thrown from her horse and hit her head on a rock. She can't remember her past. She can't even remember him. She can't remember that they are married."

Amusement was wiped from the men's faces. This was serious. A hell of a thing to happen to a man, a new husband at that.

"Poor ole Stone." One of the men shook his head. "He waits all this time to get married and now his wife don't even know him."

"Wonder if she lets him poke her?" Jamie, the teenage horse wrangler, said.

"Damn it, Jamey, don't you think of anything else?"

"Hah!" Jamey snorted, "as if the rest of you aren't thinking the same thing."

No one denied his charge.

When Stone entered the house he found Flame in the kitchen. She had filled a basin with water from the small hand-pump installed in a tin sink, and had just finished washing her face and hands.

"Mm, that smells good." She smiled at Stone

133

as she smoothed her hands over the tangles in her hair.

"It's fried chicken." Stone removed the cloth Charlie had spread over the plates as he placed the tray on the table. "If you'll get the plates off the tray I'll get us some silverware to eat with."

It was soon done and they were digging in. "This is the best fried chicken I've ever eaten." Flame took a second bite of the crispy chicken leg.

Stone looked at her and teased, "How do you know it's the best you've ever had if you can't remember your past?"

Flame grinned and took another bite of chicken. "If I'd ever had chicken like this, I'd remember it."

They had eaten every morsel of food on their plates when Charlie appeared at the kitchen door. He held up a pot of coffee. "I thought that right about now you two would like some coffee to finish off your meal," he said, stepping inside.

"You must have read my mind." Stone stood up and went to a cupboard, where he took out a couple cups. "Do you like coffee, Flame?" he asked, placing them on the table.

"I think so." She sniffed the aromatic brew as Charlie filled the cups. "It sure smells good." She took a careful sip of the steaming liquid and smiled widely. "Indeed I do like coffee." She looked up at the slender man with the graying hair. "You are a great cook, Charlie."

"I'm sure you can cook better," Charlie said,

blushing with pleasure. "You can probably cook up fancy dishes like the Frenchies do."

"I have no idea what I can do in the kitchen." Flame sighed and lifted the coffee to her lips again.

"I'd better be getting back to the cookhouse." Charlie turned to the door. "I have to keep an eye on that Toby if I'm to get any work out of him. I'll see you folks in the morning."

When Charlie had left Stone explained, "Toby is the teenager who helps Charlie in the kitchen. The kid is a hard worker, and actually Charlie is very fond of him." Stone gave a short laugh. "My cook is a complainer."

Stone refilled their cups. "What do you say we go out on the porch and drink our coffee? It's a beautiful evening."

Flame agreed it was a beautiful evening as she and Stone sat on the top step of the porch sipping their coffee. They watched the men leave the cookhouse, some going to the bunkhouse, the others going to the stables to saddle up and ride into town. They smiled at the men's horseplay, their colorful language which they used because they were unaware that Stone and Flame were within hearing distance.

As darkness closed around them and a full moon began to rise, Flame turned her head and looked at Stone. "What can you tell me about my past?"

The time had come. The words he would utter in the next few minutes could sign the death warrant on any future they might have together. He turned his head away from her and looked out into the moonlit darkness. He couldn't go on with his lies anymore. Now that he was thinking clearly, he realized how stupidly he had acted. But he wouldn't tell her how he had seen her last fall, riding her mare or how he had fallen in love with her. How he waited for spring to arrive so that he could go looking for her. She would think him an idiot, a callow youth.

With an inward sigh, Stone placed his cup on the floor beside him and said, "I don't know much more of your past than you can remember."

He told her then about the storm, how he had been looking for shelter of some sort. He told how he came upon the old house and found a big woman beating her.

"Before I could stop her, she threw you out of the house into the rain and lightning. You crawled to a barn and managed somehow to mount the little mare you've been riding."

He skimmed over their wild ride to where he'd found the cave. "And then Pearl Harding came along. She just assumed you were my wife and I never corrected her. You see, all you were wearing was a wet night gown that clung to your bare body." He paused a moment, then added, "Charlie and the men think we are married, too."

Stone got up the nerve to look at Flame, to see how she was taking his news. "I'm sorry, Flame," he said. "I thought it was the best thing to do. I won't be surprised if you cuss me out proper."

Flame's body had stiffened at first. But as Stone continued to explain everything, she relaxed and listened quietly to him. Sadly, the story he told did not stir her memory. However, he spoke so sincerely, she believed what he said.

After a moment or two she said, "I think you did the best thing, considering the circumstances."

Stone wanted to shout his relief at her reaction. Maybe he still had a chance.

"So what do we do now?" Flame asked, her tone anxious.

"Well, the way I see it," Stone answered thoughtfully, "we can go on like we've been doing and in the meantime I'll go back to that house where I found you . . . see who lives there, ask some questions."

"I guess that's a good idea," Flame agreed, although her tone said that she wasn't quite sure. She had a feeling she didn't want to know the people who lived in that house.

There was a long silence, then she asked, "What if you don't learn anything about me? What then?"

"Don't fret about it." Stone grinned. "You're a married woman, remember. You'll stay right here with your *husband*," he teased with a laugh.

Flame was silent for a moment; then she asked in serious tones, "Don't you have a woman in your life?"

"No. No other woman." Stone stared out into the darkness.

"You understand, don't you, Stone, that it's all pretend?"

Pretend? A hot wave rushed through Stone. There was no pretense in the way he felt about her, the way he wanted her, dreamed of having her every night. How long could he feign mere friendship? This constant ache he felt all the time would have to be soothed before long.

"Of course," he answered after a moment, then drawled, "My bedroom is at the other end of the hall . . . with a lock on the door." He gave her a wicked grin.

"Hmm," Flame teased back, "I wonder if there's a lock on my door?"

"Will you be worried if there's not?" Stone arched an eyebrow at her.

"Should I be if there's not?"

"I don't know. I can't promise. You're awfully fetching. Would you shoot me if I came visiting in the middle of the night?"

"I don't know. I can't promise either. Maybe one of us should sleep in the barn," Flame teased.

"Or maybe you could bunk in with Charlie," Stone suggested.

"Or maybe we both should shut up." Flame braced her hands behind her, throwing her firm breasts in sharp profile. Stone zeroed in on them and thought to himself he'd better stop the bantering before he lost control.

"Yeah, you're right. I'll go get you some

warm water from the cookhouse so you can take your bath before you go to bed."

"Thank you, Stone," Flame said softly, "and goodnight." She knew that if there was a lock on her door she would never use it against him.

Chapter Nine

Shilo stood under the hot sky, looking down at the silent current of the river. His gaze followed it as it swung southward between green borders of willows and cottonwood.

He'd been there close to an hour, trying to come to a decision. What was he to do about Little Bird? In the week she'd been living in the village she had become a different maid from the scrawny-looking creature the old mountain man had dumped on him. With regular meals she had put on weight; her eyes were bright now and her hair was soft and silky looking. And her joyous laughter rang often through the village.

She was wonderful with the little ones, too,

kind and gentle. He sometimes hid himself among the trees just to listen to the musical sound of her voice as she told stories to her little charges.

He wasn't the only man in the village who was attracted to the newcomer. The young braves watched her, too. He knew that they would soon start coming to him, asking his permission to walk with her in the evenings. In the white man's language, to court her.

Shilo frowned down into the water. What would he answer them? And what was he going to answer the elders when they hinted that it was time he took a wife? Even his mother thought the same.

His lips twisted wryly. If he didn't know better, he'd think that his mother wanted Little Bird for a daughter-in-law. She made it plain in countless ways that she cared for the little orphan. But although Little Bird was a Ute, she was from a different tribe. His mother and the villagers would expect him to marry a maid from their own tribe.

Then there was Stone. What were his feelings for the girl? He had returned with his bride almost a week ago and had brought her to the village this morning to meet Moonlight and the elders. Her name was Flame and she was a great beauty despite her unfortunate loss of memory. Stone had said they had no idea when or if she would ever remember what her life had been like before her accident.

Shilo remembered how the beauty had

frowned at the warm greeting between Stone and Little Bird. The look had told him that the wife was jealous of the little Indian maid. And well she should be, he thought. He hadn't liked the way Stone and Little Bird smiled at each other, either. Had they known each other sexually? Did they intend to remain lovers? Little Bird didn't pay any attention to the interest the young braves showed her. Was it because of Stone? Maybe he should tell the braves to speak to Stone Falcon about courting Little Bird.

Shilo's moccasined foot kicked out at a rock. What was Stone thinking? he asked himself angrily. Did he think he could have both women? Did he think that he could be married to one and make the other his personal whore? It wasn't like him to do something so underhanded, but both women were very beautiful. Still, Little Bird didn't deserve that kind of life. She shouldn't live alone in a teepee with everyone talking about her, being shunned if she had little half-breed children. Was Stone so taken with her, he would do that to her?

He gave a start and looked down the river when feminine voices reached him. He saw several village women with baskets of soiled clothing in their arms. They were going down to the river to sand-scrub their weekly wash. His eyes searched through them, looking for Little Bird. When he didn't see her he remembered that she was busy tending the children.

Most likely his mother would wash her clothes. She was quite taken with the maid.

Shilo didn't want to be waylaid by a group of giggling, coy young females, so he quickly turned and walked toward his lodge. When he was almost there, his face darkened. Little Bird and Stone sat in the shade of the trees with several small children gathered around them. They were laughing gleefully at a story Little Bird was telling them.

What was Stone doing here today? Shilo grumbled to himself. He was here yesterday with his wife. He looked around for Flame and did not see her. Why had Stone come by himself? Was it because he wanted to spend time time alone with Little Bird?

His face wore a scowl when he approached the laughing group. Stone looked at him and his lips curved in a grin. "Friend," he called, "you look angrier than a bear with his tail caught in a trap. What's wrong in your world today?"

"Where is your wife?" Shilo asked gruffly, ignoring Stone's question and Little Bird's presence.

Stone gave his friend a searching looking. He seemed grumpier than usual. "You are in a bad frame of mind today. Did you have a bad vision, or are you just being your usual sour self?"

When Shilo only grunted, Stone looked at Little Bird with a wide grin and said, "Have you ever seen Shilo smile?"

Little Bird's eyes twinkled with mischief. "No, I haven't. I heard that his lips can't turn upwards." She looked at Stone and asked in serious tones, "Do you think that is true?"

"Let me think on that a minute," Stone answered, then pretended to give her question serious thought. After a moment he shook his head sadly. "Now that you bring it to my attention, I believe that could be true. Poor fellow. That's why he always looks so grim."

"You have no trouble with your lips curving up this morning." Shilo gave Stone a narrow look. "You look like a foolish, grinning opossum. I guess marriage agrees with you, even though you go off and leave your wife alone."

"I invited her to come with me, but when she learned I was going to ask you to come hunting with me she refused. Said she didn't want to go traipsing in the woods all day looking for some poor animal to shoot. Anyway, she's still pretty weak and her ribs are real sore."

"She needs to drink a lot of deer and beef broth. She'll get her strength back then."

"What do you think I've been giving her? She's drunk so much of the stuff, she can hardly look at it anymore. Do you want to go hunting with me? I saw a small herd of young antelope down in Quail Valley yesterday."

"Might as well." Shilo shrugged a shoulder indifferently. "My people could use some fresh game. My mother has been hinting that she would like some roast turkey."

"Can I go with you?" Little Bird asked

eagerly, her eyes shining at the thought of spending the day in the forest.

"Sure, come along," Stone said, "We'll—"

"You will not come with us." Shilo gave her a dark look that bored into her. "You forget that you are to tend the children."

"Oh, I did forget that." Little Bird blushed in embarrassment. "I am sorry, Shilo."

Shilo's only answer was a grunt.

Stone wondered why Shilo was so short spoken and cold to Little Bird. She was quiet and well-mannered. He couldn't begrudge her the small amount of food she ate. Besides, she was earning her keep by looking after the children.

It came to him then. Shilo had fallen for the little maid and was angry at himself, and her, because of it. He was too stubborn to admit that he loved an orphan maid who would bring no wealth to their marriage.

On second thought, that was not like his friend. Shilo cared very little what people thought about his actions. If he wanted to marry Little Bird he'd do so. There had to be something else that made him act so badly toward the girl.

Shilo went inside his lodge and picked up the rifle leaning against the buffalo-hide wall. "How are you fixed for shells? I'm just about out."

"I've got plenty for both of us." Stone patted the cartridge belt wrapped around his lean waist. "I picked some up in town yesterday."

"Come on then, let's get going," Shilo grunted impatiently.

"I'll see you later, Little Bird." Stone stood up and brushed off the seat of his pants. "I'll see if I can shoot you a couple squirrels."

"Thank you, Stone. I like roasted squirrel." Little Bird smiled up at Stone. It was a warm smile that Shilo didn't miss.

As soon as he and Stone were out of hearing distance of Little Bird and the children, Shilo demanded sharply, "Why should you shoot game for her?"

"It's no more than right that I shoot some meat for her once in a while since I asked you to make a place for her."

A tight silence grew between the two men; then Shilo asked a question that was so sharp, Stone stopped and stared at him. "Is Little Bird your woman, too?" His tone was angry. "Isn't one woman enough for you?"

"What's wrong with you, man?" Stone grabbed Shilo's arm and swung him around so that he could look his friend in the face. "I don't want any other woman but Flame."

"Then don't concern yourself whether or not Little Bird gets enough to eat."

"Hey, you long-legged Ute, have you made her *your* woman?" Stone demanded.

"I have not!" Shilo snorted scornfully. "I like my women to have some meat on their bones. I don't want to be obliged to shake the furs on my bed to find her. Besides, I'd split her in half if I ever lay with that skinny one."

"I doubt that," Stone laughed. "I grant you that Little Bird is small and frail looking, but the life she's had to lead recently has put a lot of steel in her spine. It's my opinion she could outlast you in the bedroom."

"Bah! You'd better stop smoking so much loco weed," Shilo advised gruffly. "You know my stamina in the furs."

Stone grinned and the subject was dropped. It was time to stop talking anyway if they were to slip up on some game.

Although he wasn't speaking as he walked carefully and silently behind Shilo, Stone was thinking a lot. Had his friend fallen in love with the scrawny little orphan? She had turned out to be a pretty little thing. He was very glad that he had saved her from the Jackson brothers. If he hadn't she might be dead by now, or wishing that she was. He hoped that the proud Indian had fallen in love with her and would marry her some day.

Stone wished more strongly that he could marry Flame some day.

Deke Cobbs lounged back in the saddle and gazed down at a string of holding pens at the edge of town. He and Bertha and Hoss Jenkins had been on the trail for two weeks.

They had arrived here just after dawn, and watered the cattle at a stream about a mile from town. The sun was well up now and it was time to drive the longhorns down to the holding pens. There would be buyers arriving soon to inspect the cattle that would be there. Some would be small-time ranchers looking to add a dozen or so to their herds. The majority would be government men, looking to buy beef for Indian reservations. Thanks to Flame, their beef was all prime stuff. To make sure they arrived in Hays in good condition, they hadn't pushed the cattle.

A dark frown formed on Deke's brow. "I'll have to take the bitch with me," he muttered in a voice that dripped venom. "They know her in town, know her brand."

But that was alright. He had his plans. Hoss was going to be in for a big surprise. He knew that his supposed friend and Bertha were lying together every chance they got. He knew that they had been since day one. They were beginning to get very careless about it, too. Sometimes they hardly bothered to hide their fornication. They had awakened him many times with their loud panting and the sound of their fat bare stomachs slapping together.

Deke's lips lifted contemptuously. The bitch hadn't felt the weight of his body these past two weeks. His lips twisted in a coarse grin. She had given him satisfaction, nevertheless.

He stretched his stiff muscles. He'd be glad to sleep in a bed again. He looked forward to tonight. He would sleep in a clean bed, and with a young whore who would smell of flowers. But right now he had to get the two sluggards up and get the cattle started down the hill.

When Deke got back to where they had unrolled their blankets four hours before, Bertha and Hoss were snoring away. He gave them each a hard jab in the rear end with the toe of his boot. "It's time we get the cattle down to the holding pens," he explained when he received black, threatening looks. When Bertha reached for her shirt and trousers, distaste clouded Deke's eyes. "Bertha," he said, "why don't you wade out in the creek and wash the whore smell off you. And put on some clean duds, for Pete's sake. None of the buyers will come around our cattle if they get a whiff of you first."

Bertha jumped to her feet, her face beet red with fury. As she came waddling toward Deke she screeched, "I'm gonna knock you on your ass, talkin' to me that way."

Deke waited until she was a couple feet from him, then shot out his clenched fist, straight from his shoulder. It landed on the point of her chin. As she went down, flat on her back, the ground seemed to tremble. As she lay there in pained shock, Deke and Hoss threw back their heads and bellowed with laughter.

Bertha ranted and raved, calling the men every insulting name she could think of. They only continued to laugh all the harder.

When she finally wore herself out and was panting for breath, Deke and Hoss each took a wrist and pulled her to her feet. "Behave yourself and get washed up." Deke gave her a smart slap across her fat rear end. "And get into some clean clothes."

When they reached the holding pens, Deke

went to find the man who assigned the pens. He found John Rodgers almost immediately.

"Not a bad-looking bunch of cattle," the man said, pointing out a pen Deke could use. "You'll get a fair price for them."

"What are they going for this year? My missus has her heart set on a fancy ring to celebrate our weddin'." Deke turned his horse's head in the direction of the aspen tree where he had left Bertha and Hoss.

"It goes up and down, but all around the price is good. You should be able to get her a big diamond."

As Deke stood up in the stirrups and waved Bertha and Hoss in, he had to bite his tongue to keep his elation from showing. When he parted company with his companions, he would have a good amount of money in his pocket. More than he had ever seen at one time.

When the cattle had been driven into the pens assigned to them, Deke wiped the sweat off his face and said, "I don't know about you two, but if I don't get some decent food in my stomach pretty soon, I'm gonna keel over. What do you say that while Rodgers is weighing the cattle, we ride into town and find a cafe."

Bertha and Hoss were quick to agree, and half an hour later they were sitting at a table ordering steak and eggs and hot biscuits.

Deke wolfed his breakfast down before Bertha and Hoss had hardly gotten started. He asked the waitress for a second cup of coffee, then said, "I'm going to the outhouse for a minute. We'll leave as soon as I get back and finish my coffee."

He stepped outside and hurried to where the horses were tied, drawing a knife from his pocket. He had purposely tied his horse next to Bertha's mare. He walked behind the animal and looked around to see if he was being watched. When no one seemed interested in him, he lifted the mare's right back foot and pried off its shoe. He dropped the foot then and tossed the shoe into the watering trough. He untied and mounted his gray then. With a jab of his heels in its sides it tore off down the street at a hard gallop.

Luck was still with Deke when he got to the holding pens. He had no problem passing himself off as Bertha's new husband. He was paid a fair price for the cattle, and talked the government man into giving him cash instead of a check.

With the money in his vest pocket, he swung into the saddle and rode off toward Texas as fast as his horse could gallop. How he would like to see Bertha's face when she discovered what he had done. He wished also that he could face her and tell her that he had earned every dollar for all the times he'd forced himself to go to bed with her.

His face split into a grin. She'd find out soon enough that Hoss would ride off and leave her when he learned she had no money.

* * *

When ten minutes had passed and Deke hadn't returned from the privy, Hoss began to grow suspicious. He knew the man well, knew he was capable of pulling all sorts of tricks on a person, even a friend. He looked at Bertha, who was scraping the last crumb of her pie off the plate. "What's keepin' Deke, do you suppose?"

She shrugged her shoulders. "Maybe he fell in the crapper," she laughed.

"And maybe he's gone off and left us." suspicion was bright in the man's fat, slitted eyes. "Let's go outside and wait for him," he said, pushing away from the table. He walked outside, and Bertha followed him.

Hoss swore long and loud when he saw that Deke's horse was no longer hitched with the other two.

"Where do you suppose he's gone to?" Bertha looked up and down the street.

"Where do you think he's gone, you stupid woman." Hoss was so angry, he could hardly speak. "He's gone to sell the cattle."

"He can't do that. They're all wearing my brand."

"Don't you think he'll find a way around that?"

Bertha didn't waste her breath in swearing. "Come on," she gritted out. "We can catch up with the bastard before he can collect the money for them. And when we do I'm gonna put a bullet between his eyes."

They mounted up, but when Bertha's mare

had taken only four limping steps, they knew she had thrown a shoe. They also knew who had caused the loss of the shoe.

"Damn it to hell!" Hoss exploded. "By the time we get a shoe back on the horse, that bastard will be long gone. Do you have any money?" Bertha shook her head. "Not a dime."

"Me neither. I spent my last dollar on breakfast. Hoss's ham-sized fist struck out at the hitching post. "We don't even have the money to get the animal shod."

"What are we gonna do?" Bertha didn't look her usual blustery self. In fact she looked a little frightened.

Hoss sat down on the edge of the narrow porch and stared at the ground. When a few minutes had passed Bertha looked at him an asked crossly, "Are you gonna sit there all day?"

Hoss looked up at her and gave her a slow, knowing look. "Yeah, I think I will. And you, Miss Bertha, are gonna lie on your back all day. Do you get my meanin'?"

Bertha gazed back at him, a puzzled look on her face. A moment later enlightenment came. "You mean—"

"That's right. We're gonna get along just fine. You go down to the livery stable and sneak up in the hayloft. I'll sit here and set you up with customers."

"Start sending them to me," she said eagerly and hurried toward the livery as fast as her great weight would allow.

Chapter Ten

Stone sipped his coffee and let his gaze drift over the valley. Four hundred head of cattle were scattered about, some grazing on the tender green grass, some lined up along the Platte, their noses in the water.

He loved this time of day, when the sun came over the ridge, flooding the valley with a golden light. The mists hanging over the river would begin to rise higher, then gradually disappear.

Stone finished his coffee, set the empty cup on the railing, then leaned against the porch pillar. He had the largest ranch within a hundred miles, ran two thousand head of cattle. He had a fine big house and many friends. He should be the happiest man in all of Colorado.

But he wasn't. He was probably the most miserable fellow in the territory.

The last month had taken a toll on him. He didn't know how much longer he could bear living under the same roof with Flame. Every night he suffered pure hell lying in bed, knowing she was just a short distance away curled up in sleep. He pictured her in a thin transparent gown, her lovely hair spread out on the pillow, her red lips slightly parted as though waiting for his kisses.

She was settling in nicely at the ranch. Everyone liked her, especially Charlie, the cook, and his teenager helper. Her body was completely healed now, but her mind was still empty of her past. It surprised him that she didn't take much interest in cooking or housekeeping. In fact, she was quite lax about dusting and cleaning. He had finally hired a Mexican woman to keep house for them. Maria kept the house spotless, but she only cooked Mexican food, which wasn't to his taste. He and Flame took most of their meals at the cookhouse.

One of the things that pleased him most was how well Flame could ride a horse, and her ability to throw a calf and brand it. She was better and faster than most of his men, yet she had no idea how she'd come to know so much about ranching.

He thought back to the day when he first saw how adept she was at bull-dogging a maverick and branding it.

They had been sitting on their horses watching a cowhand trying to throw an animal onto its side and tie its legs together so that they could apply a hot branding iron to its haunch. Time and time again he failed. The eight-month-old calf was large and strong.

Aggrevated by the man's continued failure, Stone was about to dismount and do the job himself when suddenly Flame was off her horse, a rope whirling around her head. When it landed neatly around the maverick's neck, she commanded her horse to back up, to keep the rope taut between her and the animal. In a flash she was on the prone animal and tying its four feet together. In another second she was slapping a hot branding iron on its hip. As the singed hair sent up a small cloud of smoke, she untied the doggie and it jumped to its feet and ran bawling out onto the range.

"That's how you do it, cowboy." She grinned at the young cowhand. "It's all leverage and speed."

When she climbed back into the saddle Stone asked with admiration, "How did you learn to do that?"

A blank look came into Flame's eyes. "I don't know," she half whispered. She was so confused. Stone felt sorry for her and didn't question her further.

A long breath of air escaped his throat. This woman he loved so desperately was a mystery to him. She wasn't like any other woman he had ever known. He had no idea how she felt about him. She was always pleasant to him. He tried to console himself with that thought, but a moment later admitted that she was pleasant with the help also. And the men, he felt that most of them would lay down their lives for her.

But there was a woman who hated Flame. Had tried to kill her.

A month ago he had spent a day riding to that old house that Flame had fled. In the light of day it looked worse than it had in the rain and dark. It looked ready to fall in on itself. As the stallion approached it, he knew it was deserted. There was a stillness about it that said no one had lived in it for some time.

Dismounting, he stepped up on the sagging floor of the porch and pushed the door open. A stale odor hit him in the face as he stepped inside. After he had walked through the four rooms he knew that whoever had lived here had left in a hurry.

And as hard as it was to believe, Flame had lived here also. The small torn-up bedroom told him that. The few worn clothes scattered about were feminine and her size. Whom had she been living with? Her parents? Surely not. What kind of parents would have beaten her so badly?

He tried to ignore the next possibility that came to him but it persisted. What if she had lived here with a husband? If so, where was he? As for that, where was the woman who had beaten Flame? He had glimpsed a man that night. Was he Flame's husband? And if so, what kind of man would stand by and let someone beat his wife?

He had learned one thing, he thought as he stepped outside and closed the door behind him. Flame had not lived in wealth. The rundown condition of the place said there were no riches here.

But whoever had lived here hadn't needed to live poorly. The ranch was small but it had good grazing land and a year-round creek ran through the property. An ambitious, hardworking man could make a good living here. It was clear that hadn't been the case.

Stone stepped out onto the rickety porch and looked out over the undulating grassland. He gave a start when he caught sight of several head of cattle. They were grazing on a slope that led to the creek. Did they belong to the ranch? Come to that, to whom did the ranch belong?

He hurried to Rebel, swung into the saddle and rode toward the cattle. When he was close enough to read the brand, the Bar X, he reined in and counted. There were thirty-three longhorns, all in good condition.

Someday, when he had more time, he would ride around looking for other ranchers in the area. They would know who owned the brand and what had happened to the people who had lived here.

But first he was going to bring Flame here tomorrow, see what her reaction was when she saw the old house. Maybe it would jolt her mind, bring back her memory.

Flame recognized Stone coming a mile away. Nobody sat a horse quite like he did. What were his feelings for her? she wondered. He was always polite, careful of her welfare. He treated her almost like an ivalid, but she was far from feeling weak and sickly. She had never felt better. Rest and good food had worked wonders on her body.

She sighed as Rebel's galloping pace brought Stone closer to the house. She wished he treated her as he did Little Bird. They joked around, teased each other. Sometimes Stone put an arm around Little Bird's shoulders and hugged her. She hated to admit it, but pure jealously rushed through her at those times.

Shilo didn't like it either. She had seen his face darken with a frown and his hands clench into fists. She didn't understand the tall, handsome Indian. He seldom spoke to the girl when he brought her to visit them, and if he did say something to her, it was always in a gruff voice. Still, the way he watched Stone and the young maid when they fooled around together, he looked as jealous as she felt. If he felt affection for the girl, why didn't he treat her nicer?

Flame wondered suddenly if there was more than friendship between Stone and Little Bird. And if so, did the young chief know it? Did he keep his silence out of loyalty to his and Stone's long friendship?

Where had Stone been for the better part of the day? she wondered bleakly. He was coming from the direction of the Indian village. Had he been visiting Little Bird? Had he wanted to spend some time alone with her? She could understand why he would want to be with the young girl who was always full of laughter and fun, whereas his supposed wife never had anything to laugh about, didn't even know who she was, where she came from.

Stone rode up to the hitching post and swung to the ground. When he had loosened the bit in the stallion's mouth and eased the cinch, he climbed the three steps to the porch. He saw Flame sitting in the wooden rocker and smiled at her.

How pretty she looks, he thought. She had discarded Pearl's old raggedy gray dress and put on one of the dresses belonging to the cook's niece. The color was pink with tiny red roses. The cut was modest, just low enough to give a hint of firm, young breasts.

It was lace-trimmed at the neck and had cap sleeves. A pink ribbon was tied around her tiny waist. Her reddish hair hung to her shoulders in loose curls and waves.

She is a lovely thing, he thought, so lovely, he must somehow make her love him.

I must buy her some pretty clothes of her own, he told himself. Maybe I'll buy her some jewelry. Come to think of it, up in the attic was his mother's jewelry box. He hadn't looked into the velvet-covered box in years, but he remembered vaguely that there were a lot of sparkling gems in it. He'd have to dig it out some day and go through it.

Stone sat down in the chair next to Flame. "How was your day?" he asked, smiling at her. "How did you pass the time?"

My time was not spent as joyfully as yours, Flame thought bitterly. Her voice was pleasant, though, as she answered, "I spent most of the day helping the men with the branding."

Stone's brow furrowed in a frown. "I wish you wouldn't do such strenuous work. You might do damage to your ribs. Couldn't you find something to do in the house? You know, doing embroidery work like ladies do. Or maybe picking wildflowers in the meadows and making bouquets to brighten up rooms. Or maybe you'd like working in the flower beds. I notice they are full of weeds."

Flame flinched at Stone's suggestions. She hated it when he found fault with her. She felt sure that she didn't know how to embroider. She wasn't even sure what the word meant. And though she loved flowers, she couldn't remember ever picking any and bringing them into the house. Maybe the cook would let his young helper, Toby, go with her to pick some flowers.

She looked up at Stone and said quietly, "I plan to pick some flowers tomorrow. The range is full of them."

"Don't do it tomorrow. I thought we'd have Charlie pack us some eats and we'd spend the day riding around. Would you like that?"

"Oh, yes!" Flame's eye sparkled. "I'd love to do that."

"Okay then. We'll leave bright and early tomorrow morning."

It was nearer to noon before Stone and Flame got started on their outing the next day. Two steers had broken down a fenced-in area of quagmire and were sinking into the sucking mud. It was necessary for Stone to help pull the animals free.

When they finally got on their way, the range stretched out of sight, as they put the mare and stallion to an easy canter. Flame hadn't felt so contented in a long time. Stone had been so busy lately with the cattle. They had to be driven to different areas once a week to graze on new grass. Consequently they hadn't spent much time together except at supper time. And that was nothing to speak of. They shared that time with fifteen others in the cookhouse. Most times when the meals were over, the men gathered round Stone asking him questions or just plain talking to him. At first she would go and sit on the porch for a while, hoping that when he finished talking with the men, he would come and sit with her. That seldom happened, though, so she had gradually stopped waiting for him. After all, maybe he didn't want to sit and talk with her. She was probably very boring.

Stone was thinking about how much he was enjoying riding along with Flame. At night, when he saw her sitting alone on the porch, he wanted to join her in the worst way. But he always held back, not sure she would welcome his presence. In the end he would do as his cowhands did, stand back in the night shadows and stare longingly at her from a distance.

He didn't know how much longer he could go on wanting her this way. She was on his mind night and day. Even while he slept she was there beside him, pulled up close to his body, her head on his shoulder.

He was always on tenterhooks that some day a man would come along and Flame would be attracted to him. Would she end this sham they were living? Maybe she would even want to marry the stranger.

Stone drew rein at the end of a long slope that led to the Indian village. Flame's shoulders twitched in irritation. Was Little Bird going to be a part of their one day out together? "Why are we stopping here?" she asked, her annoyance barely concealed.

"I see Little Bird and her charges sitting over there beneath that big cottonwood. I thought it would be nice to stop and say hello." Before Flame could respond, he touched his heel to Rebel's flank and rode off toward the tree.

Little Bird's lips curved in a wide, happy

smile. "What a nice surprise to see you!" she exclaimed. "You haven't come to visit for a while."

What a little liar you are, Flame was thinking. She gripped the reins tightly when she saw that Stone was dismounting. How long did he plan to visit here? He didn't seem to notice her frowning face when he lifted her from the saddle.

"Will you come into my lodge and have some refreshments?" Little Bird invited.

Before Stone could answer, Flame shook her head. "Thank you, but no. We just stopped long enough to say hello."

"And to talk a minute." Stone sat down and reached over to tug at a little girl's braid. That started Little Bird and the children in to laughing and in a matter of seconds Stone and Little Bird were joking and bantering back and forth in their usual manner.

Nearing the end of her patience, Flame glanced away from their tomfoolery and saw Shilo standing in the shadow of a tree, watching the pair stolidly. She became angry with the handsome Indian. Why was he standing over there looking as if he was ready to attack Stone? Why didn't he grab that feather-brained girl and tell her what was on his mind? Why didn't he come right out and tell her that he wanted her for his woman, that she must not carry on with a married man? Everyone, including Shilo, thought she and Stone were married to each other.

Flame gave a silent laugh. Shilo was probably thinking the same thing about her, wondering why she put up with it? Well, she was finished with acting as if the loss of her memory had left her stupid. She stood up, brushed down her skirt and said, brusquely, "Come on, Stone, it's time we got going. Unless, of course, you've changed your mind about our outing and want to stay here with Little Bird."

Stone looked up at her in startled surprise. "Of course I want to go riding with you the way we planned. I was just—"

"Are you sure you don't want to stay here with Little Bird?" Shilo came from the shadow of the trees and stalked toward them. "I've noticed that you enjoy her company very much."

Stone looked at his friend, his eyes questioning. Then a glimmer of amusement sparkled in them. He sounded very serious, however, when he said, "I do like Little Bird's company. She is like the little sister I never had."

Flame and Shilo looked at him, not believing a word he said. Stone only saw his friend's sour expression and it pleased him. He had suspected for some time that Shilo cared for Little Bird and was too stubborn to do anything about it. He needed a little push and Stone Falcon was just the one to give it. By the time he looked at Flame, she had controlled her features and he had no idea of the jealousy burning inside her.

He smiled and helped her to mount. Little Bird returned his goodbye, but Shilo only grunted.

"Most of the day is gone," Flame said peevishly an hour later when they stopped for their picnic lunch.

"Yes. We spent more time with Little Bird than I had planned." Stone was eyeing the dark clouds that were beginning to build in the west.

The air had gone very still and a gray-green darkness had moved in. They had packed up their food and were just mounting as a crackling stab of lightning lit up the sky. It was followed by a loud rumble of thunder. He looked over his shoulder and saw in the distance a sheet of rain coming toward them. He jabbed his heels into Rebel. "Flame," he called over the noise of thundering hooves, "if we don't outrun this storm we're gonna get mighty wet!"

"But where will we go for shelter?" Flame shouted as the mare kept up with the stallion.

"I know of an old run-down house about a mile away. Maybe we can beat the storm there."

At first Flame didn't pay any attention to anything except the ground flashing beneath her mare's thundering hooves. Then as they swept on, she became to feel anxious, unsettled.

They were coming to a fringe of aspen when the rain caught up with them. It fell like a sheer curtain before them but up ahead Flame glimpsed an old house that made a shiver run down her spine. Why? she asked herself. Is it because the trees look gray and ghost-like?

She slowed Lady to a walk and hung back as

Stone continued to race for shelter. He bypassed the house and continued on to a barn that was half fallen down. She was surprised when her mare eagerly followed the stallion. It's as if she knows *where she's* going, Flame thought uneasily. And why do I suddenly feel the same way? She peered through the rain, swayed by unknown and uncontrollable fears.

When her mare entered the barn, Stone had already dismounted. He hurried to help Flame out of the saddle. "Sit down on this bale of hay," he said as he grabbed up a horse blanket and wrapped it around her shoulders. "I'll be right with you as soon as I tie up your mare."

Moving as though in a fog, Flame sat down on the hay, wet and shivering. She picked up a piece of hay and worried it between her fingers as her mind struggled to understand what was happening. She was floating back and forth between two different worlds. One world was hellish, the other safe and sound.

"Let's go to the house," Stone suggested, breaking in on her nightmarish thoughts. "It will be dry there."

"No, it won't," Flame said without thinking.

"Why do you say that?" Stone looked at her, his eyes hopeful.

"I don't know why I said that." She looked at Stone, frightened. "It just popped out."

"Let's go find out," Stone said gently. "I've had things like that happen to me," he lied. He took her by the arm and they ran toward the house, their boots sending mud and water flying.

The porch was leaking like a sieve as they dashed onto it. Stone reached past Flame and pushed open the creaking door, waiting for her to enter. She stopped so suddenly in the doorway, Stone bumped into her with a loud grunt.

"Go on in, honey." He gave her a gentle push. "The wind is blowing the rain into the house."

"I can't," Flame wailed, and turning around, threw herself against his chest.

Stone took her by the arms and held her away. "Why can't you, Flame?" He looked into her face, which was as white as death. "What is it, honey?" He gave her a little shake. "What has frightened you so?"

"I don't know. It's just a feeling I get from this house. It's as if it is evil, that bad things happen here."

Stone saw that she was near tears and said gently, "You've been through a lot today. Do you think you could lie down and rest while I take care of the horses?"

"I guess so, if you're not gone too long."

"No more than ten minutes."

Flame looked in on the two bedrooms and picked the one that looked driest. The bed there, however, had been dragged halfway into the middle of the floor. She pushed it back in place, then changed out of her wet clothes into dry ones hanging on the foot of the bedstead. She didn't wonder that they fit her perfectly, but flung herself onto the bed. Almost immediately she fell asleep.

Chapter Eleven

His boots squelched in pools of water as Stone walked back toward the dark shape of the barn. Inside the building the rain was leaking so badly, it was almost the same as if he was standing outside beneath a tree.

He was peering through the darkness looking for a dry spot when he banged his head against an object hanging from the rafter. Swearing, he reached up and grabbed what turned out to be a lantern. He gave it a shake and heard coal oil splash around inside it. He took a match from his vest pocket, struck it against his thumbnail and held the flame to the wick. The barn was lit up enough then for him to look around.

In a far corner he spotted two stalls that were dry. He led the animals inside them, then stripped off their saddles and other gear. He picked up some gunnysacks he found in a corner and wiped them down. When he went looking for corn or oats, he found neither. But there was a stack of dry, fresh hay and he gave each animal a generous helping of the dry grass.

All this time his mind had been turning over Flame's reaction to the old house. He had hoped that the sight of it would trigger her memory. It had partially done so, but only enough to make her afraid. Maybe it would be best if she never recalled her past. He had a feeling it was so bad, she would fight remembering any of it.

I'm too tired and hungry to think about it any more tonight, he thought as he retrieved his saddlebag and sprinted through the rain to the house. The bag held the remnants of the food Charlie had packed for their outing. He didn't know about Flame, but he was starving. As he stepped up on the rotting porch, he wondered if it were possible that there was some coffee in the shack.

It was dark and quiet in the house. Stone made out the shape of a lamp sitting on the littered table and struck a match to its wick. He picked it up and walked quietly, looking for Flame.

He found her in the first room he looked into. She lay curled on her side, sound asleep.

He smiled softly and shook his head. He wasn't surprised. She was mentally spent. He pulled a blanket up from the foot of the bed and settled it over her shoulders. It was very damp in the room.

He went back into the kitchen and closed the door behind him. As quietly as possible then, he searched the two cupboards for coffee. He nodded and smiled when he found half a tin of coffee beans. He picked up the aged coffee pot and leaned out the door to dump the dried coffee grains out of it. He spent the next five minutes scrubbing it clean and building a fire in the greasy stove. By the time the water was ready to boil, he had ground enough of the aromatic beans to last him and Flame through supper and, if necessary, for tomorrow morning's breakfast.

While the coffee brewed Stone cleared off the table and found two cups in a cupboard. When the coffee smelled as if it was ready, he pulled it to the back of the stove, then spread out what was left of Charlie's lunch on the table. He started to go awaken Flame and found her standing in the kitchen doorway.

She smiled at him and said, "I'm afraid I fell asleep. That delicious aroma in here woke me up."

"Are you hungry?" Stone returned her smile as he poured the coffee. "We've got some cold fried chicken left and a couple beef sandwiches."

"It all sounds good." Flame washed her

hands in the same basin of water Stone had used. "It will make a fine supper."

They sat down at the table and wasted no time beginning to eat. The sandwiches were consumed first, then, having no clean flatware, they used their fingers on the chicken.

Outside there was a steady pelting of rain on the roof and against the windows as they drank their coffee. "From the sound of it, I'd say we're gonna have to spend the night here," Stone said. "I don't have the heart to make the horses go out in this downpour again."

"I agree, the poor things. They must be exhausted."

It grew silent in the kitchen for a couple minutes, then Stone looked at Flame and asked, "Is everything clear in your mind since the time you came to in that cave with me and Pearl?"

"Indeed it is," Flame answered solemnly. "I'll never forget how frightened and confused I was. But you were so kind and gentle, I soon lost my fear and came to trust you."

"So do you still think I did the right thing, telling everyone that we're married?"

"Yes, I do. People would frown on me and talk if they thought I was a single woman living with you."

Stone stood up and poured himself another cup of coffee. When he raised the pot to Flame, she shook her head and he sat back down at the table. "Then we'll continue on as though we are married?"

Flame blushed. "That would be alright with me. How do you feel about it?"

"It sounds fine to me. But there's one thing I'm afraid we haven't given much thought to. How much longer can we go on sleeping in separate bedrooms without causing talk? We've got by with it this long because of your broken bones. But anyone who has watched you bull-dog a maverick and brand him knows there's nothing wrong with your body now."

"Hmm, that is a poser." Flame chewed at her lower lip. "Do you have any ideas?"

"I have one. We start sharing the same room."

"What!" Flame set her cup down so hard, hot coffee splashed over her hand. "I'm not going to live in sin with you, Stone Falcon." Her voice was firm and absolute.

"Am I asking you to live in sin?" Stone's voice was sharp and impatient.

"Not in so many words, but you know darn well we would not sleep together as brother and sister very long."

"So, you don't trust yourself, is that it?"

Flame's face turned pink. She didn't trust herself. If he made one move that hinted he wanted to kiss her, she would melt into his arms. How he would laugh at that. She stuck her chin up in the air and with a haughty, "Hah!" denounced his claim. "It's not me I don't trust."

Stone wanted to grab her and kiss her red lips until she was breathless. Now wasn't the

173

time, though. He was just thankful that he was going to have the time to court her as he had planned.

He raised his head suddenly, listening. "Do you hear anything?"

Flame grew quiet and tilted her head, listening also. "I don't hear a thing," she said finally.

"That's because it has stopped raining." Stone stood up and looked out the window.

Relief was in Flame's voice when she exclaimed, "Good. That solves our sleeping problem. We can go home now."

When they walked into the barn Flame said of the two horses, "They look so comfortable. They're not going to like going out again," she added as she lifted the saddle onto the mare's back.

The horses were rested and wanted to run. "Let them go," Stone laughed and kicked Rebel lightly. The stallion took off at a gallop, Flame's mare hard at his heels. They were home in half the time it took them to get to the small ranch.

The air was fresh and cool from the rain and they were laughing with the exhilaration of children when they pulled up in front of the barn. Stone reached his arms to Flame and she leaned down into them. Slowly, slowly, he let her slide down the length of body. When she stood on the ground she lifted her head to gaze up at him, invitation in her eyes. His arm was clasped tightly around her waist, and he lowered his head, his lips searching hers.

Flame's arms came up and wrapped around

his shoulders. Their lips met, melded. Then a feminine voice called out, "Stone, we have been so worried about you and Flame. We were afraid something might have happened to you in that fierce storm."

Flame and Stone sprang apart like two teenagers caught enjoying their first lover-like kiss. Flame could hardly bring herself to speak to Little Bird when she and Shilo walked up to them. And it was all Stone could do to keep from swearing out loud.

He looked at Shilo and said coolly, "When did you decide that I can't take care of myself in a storm."

"Hell, it wasn't me who worried about your hide." Shilo grunted. "You could have drowned for all I'd care."

Both men knew the other spoke in anger so neither paid much attention to the words that were exchanged.

"I was the worried one, Stone." Little Bird laid her hand on Stone's arm. "I had a dear cousin struck dead by lightning in such a storm when she was only seven. I have been afraid of lightning ever since."

The look Flame shot the Indian girl said that she doubted Little Bird was afraid of anything. Only Shilo saw her disbelieving eyes. He smiled wryly. If the white woman cared for his friend, the little Indian maid would never get him.

"Let's go to the cookhouse and have something to drink . . . coffee or some red-eye," Stone invited.

Little Bird was about to agree but Shilo interrupted. "Another time. Flame looks tired."

"I am, Shilo." Her eyes expressed the thanks she felt. "So, I'll say goodbye and see you another time." She walked toward the house without another word.

Stone stared after her. It was not like Flame to be rude. What had set her off? When he turned his gaze back to his guests, he wondered at the amused twist of Shilo's lips. The Indian was silently laughing at him. Why?

He was about to ask Shilo what he found so funny when the big Indian said, "You'd better go see what ails your woman." Before he could ask what Shilo meant, his friend had turned and walked away. Little Bird hurried after him, leaving Stone standing alone, wondering what had happened.

Flame went straight to her room, closing the door behind her. She was in no mood to talk to that wolf anymore tonight. She undressed, slipped on her gown and sat down on the bed.

What kind of man was Stone Falcon? she asked herself. He had been a split-second from kissing her when Little Bird came running up, interrupting them. But unlike herself, he hadn't seemed to mind Little Bird's sudden appearance. He was all smiles on seeing her.

A long sigh feathered through her lips. Should they continue this sham of a marriage? Stone had said yes, but did he really want to? He was very much a gentleman and would stand by her until her memory came back, or at least until she'd regained her full health and strength. She heard Stone's footsteps and went still. She barely breathed when he stopped outside her door and knocked lightly. After a moment his footsteps continued on down the hall, and she released her breath.

When she finally fell asleep, her cheeks were wet from the tears that slipped from the corners of her eyes.

Chapter Twelve

"Don't walk so fast, Shilo," Little Bird panted, trying to keep up with his long strides. When he made no answer, only walked a little faster, she said, "I think Flame was mad about something when she left us."

She ignored Shilo's grunt of derision and persisted, "Don't you think she sounded kind of stiff when she said goodbye?"

"Don't play stupid, Little Bird," Shilo snapped. "Flame was angry, just as you wanted her to be. That's her husband you've been making up to. You might as well get it in your empty head that you will never take him away from her. He worships the white woman. He might lie with you in the woods, but you'll never be his woman." With that, he struck out at a pace that Little Bird could not keep up with.

Little Bird felt torn between two emotions as Shilo disappeared among the trees. She had discovered tonight that Shilo did care for her, that he was jealous of her laughing and talking to Stone. That made her happy. What she had been striving for had finally happened. But she liked Flame very much and hadn't taken her feelings into consideration when she gave Stone so much attention. She felt ashamed and saddened that she had caused the white woman pain. She looked on Stone as a good friend and nothing more. It was the tall, lean Shilo she had given her heart to.

A mischievous smile curved her lips. From now on she would give him plenty to be jealous about. But never in front of Flame, she thought. She did not want to hurt the poor girl who had lost her memory.

When Little Bird arrived at the village she saw Shilo sitting with the other man around a large campfire where the men gathered at night. There they spoke of the day's events made plans for tomorrow, Everyone except Shilo seemed to be talking, she thought as she stood in the shadow of her wigwam. He sat cross-legged, staring into the flames, his face dark and brooding. She wore a wide, satisfied smile as she opened the door flap and entered her quarters.

She slept like a baby that night, the smile still on her face.

* * *

By night the river was so shadowy, so silent, it seemed unnatural, Shilo thought as he stood on the bank of the Platte staring into its waters. He had left the council fire and walked down to the water when he saw little Bird enter her lodge. She hadn't denied her feelings for Stone. The only reaction to his charge had been startled surprise when he mentioned Flame, It appeared she hadn't given Stone's wife a thought until he had mentioned her. He know the feather-brain wouldn't intentionally hurt the white woman. She liked and admired Flame, it would be interesting to see how she acted toward Stone now.

Why, he thought glumly, did he have to fall in love with a young woman who probably didn't weigh a hundred pounds soaking wet, and who had been abducted by white men? Why was he blinded by her beautiful face, her long, raven-black hair, her soft voice? And how could he respect her when she was trying to steal another woman's husband?

And that husband. He was worse than Little Bird. He had no intention of leaving his wife. Couldn't the feather brain realize that he only wanted to sleep with her.

A wolf howled his loneliness on a distant hill, and Shilo, mad at himself for loving the wrong woman, raised his head and howled back.

Back in the village two women lay on their bed of furs. A knowing smile curved the mouth of the middle-aged woman and the young maids lips curved joyfully in sleep. The tall, handsome Indian was caught. All that had to be done now was to reel him in. Both women knew that wouldn't be easy. Shilo would fight every step of the way.

After a restless night Shilo awakened late the next morning. When he slept it had been in short, fitful spurts. And always his dreams were filled with Little Bird and Stone. Often he argued with his friend, demanding that he stay away from the Indian girl. He pointed out that Stone had a lovely wife and that he should leave other females alone. Stone's answer was, "Sorry, friend, but I want the little Indian beauty."

He heard the children calling Little Bird's name. She would be out soon watching over them. He rolled off his hammock and stretched his long body. He pulled on a pair of leather, fringed trousers, and beaded moccasins, and left his lodge. Those women who were busy at their cookfires smiled and spoke to their young chief.

He nodded gravely and proceeded on to the river. There he climbed out of his trousers and dived head first into the river. When he surfaced the sun glistened on the water that streamed down his lean body and long hair. He sat down on a large rock to let the sun and slight breeze dry him off. As he sat basking in the sun he was unaware that Little Bird had come down to the river to bathe also. He had no idea that she crouched in the willows, her eyes admiring his bare body. She knew it wasn't maidenly to spy on him this way, but she was unable to take her eyes off him. When he stood up to get dressed she turned her head after one swift look at his man-parts.

He is awfully big down there, she thought, a little nervous, as she stepped into the river to have her delayed bath. When she finished her morning ritual and returned to the village, Shilo wondered why she blushed so while they were having breakfast.

Shilo had decided before falling asleep to ask Stone to go fishing or hunting with him. He needed to talk to him about Little Bird. Things could not go on as they were.

"Son," his mother said, "don't forget there is a council meeting this morning. It will start before long. I see that some of the elders have already gathered at the council fire."

Hell and damnation, Shilo thought in words his friend Stone used so often. Those meetings were so long and boring. There would be arguments to be settled, permission to be given to a young couple wanting to be married. Then there would be looks directed at him, asking when was he going to take a wife. If they came right out and asked this morning, it would be very difficult not to slide a covetous look at Little Bird as the people waited for for his answer.

Maybe he could cut the meeting short this morning, he thought. He could try to keep the old men from rambling on and on. In one graceful movement he rose to his feet and stalked away. Little Bird's gaze followed him, longing in her eyes.

It was high-noon when Stone entered the main street of Dogwood and rode to the end of town where Dr. John Williams had his office over the barber shop. He was tired of wondering, guessing and hoping. He should have gone to the doctor a long time ago. He had kept thinking that Flame's memory would return on its own. He was beginning to think it never would.

After he had tred Rebel to the hitching rail he climbed the long flight of stairs to the doctor's office. He sat down in the small waiting room while Williams took care of a patient in a room next door.

The man let out a squeal once that made Stone think the doctor was treating a gun-shot wound. He found out later that the yelling came from having a boil on his neck lanced.

"Come in, Stone," Dr. Williams said as he dismissed his patient. "What brings you here?" he asked as he washed his hands. "You look healthy to me."

"I'm fine, Doc. I'm here about my wife."

"I heard you got married, and to a real beauty. Congratulations. Is your wife expecting?" he asked as he finished drying his hands and hanging the towel up.

"I wish that was the case." Stone sat down in a creaking chair, took off his Stetson and laid it on the floor beside the chair. "A few days after we got married my wife fell in a rain storm and hit her head on a rock. Ever since—it's been a month now— she hasn't been able to remember anything about her past. I'm wondering what you could tell me about memory loss and if you have any idea when everything will come back to her. Is there anything I can do to help her along?"

"Memory loss is a very mysterious ailment. We doctors have not been able to discover much about it. We have learned that it's got to come back on its own."

Williams took off his glasses and as he polished them with a piece of white cloth, he said, "If you tried to force her memory, you might do her permanent damage. All you can do is treat her in a normal fashion. Don't go asking her a bunch of questions that will only confuse her." He put his glasses back on his nose. "I'm pretty sure everything will come back to her in good time."

"Thanks, Doc. That makes me feel better." Stone picked his hat off the floor and settled it on his head. "Send me my bill,"

He was almost out the door when William said with a grin, "Take it easy in the bedroom, too. Remember, you're a stranger to her. Of course, if she hints that she would like a little lovemaking, then it's alright."

Stone felt his face grow warm. "You didn't have to tell me that, Doc," he said shortly. "I can control my urges." He left the office then, his feet coming down heavily on the wooden steps.

Old Caleb had missed the solitude of the mountains and was happy to be going back to them. He had packed a short-barreled peacemaker and a rifle rode in his gun boot. He was ready for anything he might encounter, be it man or animal. Both were known to prowl these upper regions.

The trail was easy to follow and he had made good time. But before he could head for home, he had to make one small detour, to the cabin of his longtime friend, Rudy Martin.

He wished he wasn't bringing him bad news, though. He had been the only link between Rudy and his daughter for fifteen years. During that time he had kept his friend informed of his only child's welfare. No one else knew of the existence of Rudy Martin on top of the mountain.

Caleb was thinking how tired he and the mule were when suddenly a faint light pierced the gathering darkness. "Finally, Bessie, we've made it. And about time, too. I'm so hungry I could eat you if you wasn't so ornery and tough."

Caleb pulled the mule in about a dozen yards from an old but sturdy log cabin situated in stand of aspens. "Hey, Rudy," he called through his cupped hands. "It's Greenwood, here. Tired and hungry."

The cabin door opened, spilling a shaft of light out onto the porch. "Hey you curly ole wolf." A tall, slender man appeared in the doorway. "Come on in. I've got a pot of stew and coffee that's still hot."

"Let me take care of my mule and I'll be right in. She's in the same shape as me, tired and hungry. The climb up the mountain purty much tired her out."

Rudy rolled and smoked a cigarette while Caleb ate a bowl of stew. He knew his old friend was too hungry to talk at the moment. He found it hard though not to pepper Caleb with questions about his daughter. The only news he ever received of her was through the mountain man.

Finally, Caleb pushed away from the table and wiped his moustache with a reasonably clean rag he pulled from his pants pocket. He then began to tamp tobacco into a long-stemmed clay pipe. Rudy managed to conceal his impatience while he lit the pipe from a flaming twig he pulled from the fireplace.

When Caleb had puffed clouds of tobacco around his head, he spoke. "Rudy, I bring you disturbing news this time."

Rudy sat forward in his chair, an anxious Look on his face. "Is my little girl alright?"

"I couldn't say. You see, Bertha ran off with a cowhand, and your daughter has disappeared. I went to check on the ranch like usual, and it's deserted." Caleb looked somberly at Rudy and added, "I think it's time you went home and found out what has happened to your youngun'."

"You're right, old friend, I've hung back long enough. I should have done what I wanted to years ago. Gone and got my little girl and made a home for her."

Rudy and Caleb talked long into the night with Rudy doing most of the talking. He was mostly thinking out loud, figuring out he should do first. There were so many things going through his mind. So many decisions to make.

Chapter Thirteen

Bertha sidled along the back wall of the Painted Lady Saloon. She was looking for Hoss. She hadn't seen him last night or this morning. It was now noon.

She had her suspicions as to where he was and who he was with. An attractive young whore had come to town last week. Hoss had been panting after her ever since. She'd bet anything that he was with her right now in one of the rooms above the saloon.

She would soon find out. All she had to do was step into the saloon's kitchen, and give little Jose, the cook, a knowing smile. While they lay in his room behind the kitchen, he would tell her anything she wanted to know.

Half an hour later Jose had told the jealous woman more than she wanted to know. "I'll kill the bitch," she raged, sliding off the bed. "I'll snap her back in half."

When she started to stamp into the saloon where she could take the stairs to the rooms overhead, Jose ran after her. "No, Bertha, don't go up there. Hoss is with her. He won't take it kindly if you lay rough hands on her."

Even though the hot blood was pounding in her ears, Bertha knew the cook was right. She had received one beating from Hoss already just because she'd complained about the way he was ogling the young whore.

She hadn't mentioned the blond whore again because she felt certain Hoss hadn't been allowed in her bed. After all, what would a young, good-looking woman want with a man who was so ugly, so fat? She now knew, however, that the whore welcomed him in her bed anytime he wanted to be there. And Bertha knew why. Jose had said that Hoss paid her much money to bed her.

"She brags about it," the cook had added. "She claims she made a hundred dollars off him last week."

"That's more than I make in a month," she had screeched. "He's taking the money from our savings to give to her."

"Why are you saving money, Bertha?" Jose had asked in surprise.

"So that we can go to San Franciso. We're gonna open up a big fancy whorehouse."

189

Jose didn't remark on her daydream, but there was pity in his eyes as he watched Bertha leave his kitchen. Poor fat cow, he thought, you'll never get to San Francisco with that one. I'd bet money that before the month is gone he *and* your money will be long gone.

Bertha's angry, heavy tread raised clouds of dust as she headed for the one-room shack where she conducted her business. As she neared the place, she saw four of her regulars sitting on a long bench flanking the shack. For a moment she was tempted to turn around and go to the other shack she and Hoss called home. But she knew better than to take a day off. She had tried it once to spite Hoss. His beating had convinced her the time off was not worth the ensuing pain.

Bertha kept walking. When she approached the men she gave them a salacious smile and asked, "You men ready for some fun?"

The first man to arrive stood up, money in hand. She took the silver and led him into the shack, which held only a sagging bed and a straight-backed chair. There was nothing fancy about the room, but there was nothing fancy about Bertha, either. However, she was cheap and would do anything asked of her as long as it didn't cause pain.

Whipping her dress over her head she lay down on the bed, the man eagerly following her. Her work day had begun.

It was just short of dark when Bertha closed the door behind her last customer. She pulled on her dress and smoothed a hand over her rumpled hair. She gathered up the money she had made that day, counted it, then dropped it into her pocket. She stepped outside, stood a moment on the small stoop, then took off down the street to where she hoped Hoss would be waiting. She smiled as she felt the weight of the money she had made that day slapping against her belly. Hoss would be pleased. Maybe he would forget the young whore if she brought in more money.

She and Hoss had had a hard time of it for a while after Deke sold her cattle on the sly and took off with the money. Aside from the cattlemen passing through, the town they were stuck in was sparsely settled, mainly with farmers. Farmers seldom had anything to do with whores. Hoss said it was because they worked so hard in the fields all day, they didn't have any energy left to do any humpin' at night.

But they had finally saved enough money to move on and had settled in a larger, more thriving town. Coldwater. Here they had done much better than they had hoped. She hadn't expected to have many customers considering the competition from the more attractive women who worked the saloons. They were young, wore pretty clothes and smelled nice. But they were also particular about the men they took to bed. They turned their noses up at men like Hoss.

When word spread about a new whore in

town who had her own shack, never turned a man away and would do most anything he wanted, they flocked to her.

The leather bag where she saved the silver dollars was growing heavier every day. Soon they would have enough saved to move on to San Francisco and open up the fancy Pleasure House they dreamed of. Hoss had promised she could service fewer men then. She certainly hoped so. She hadn't been feeling too well lately.

Bertha arrived at the shack and pushed open the door. Stepping inside, she paused. Who was rummaging around in their bedroom? Hoss was never home at this hour.

She slipped off her shoes and walked quietly to the small room off the kitchen. She stared in shock when she saw Hoss's carpet bag spread out on the bed, his clothes folded inside it. Then her surprise turned to outrage when she saw him lift the leather bag from the closet floor and tuck it into the bag.

"Just what in the hell do you think you're doin?" she roared.

Startled, Hoss jumped and spun around, growing angry himself. A man should never let a woman like Bertha Martin know she had unnerved him.

He gave her a look of contempt and sneered, "What do you think I'm doin'?"

"I think I caught you ready to sneak away and take my money with you."

"What if I tell you you're thinkin' right? What

are you gonna do about it?" he asked as he closed the drawstrings on the bag and tied them.

Bertha's face turned a mottled red, and she stared at Hoss in disbelief. He was doing the same thing to her that Deke had. Well, bygod, he wasn't going to take her money like Deke had.

"I'll show you what I'm going to do about it," she cried in a voice that didn't sound quite human, and her fingers curved into claws as she lunged at his face. Hoss tried to step back out of her reach but he stumbled over a chair, and she was upon him. Screaming like a wildcat, she brought her nails down his cheeks.

Swearing all kinds of threats at her as her nails furrowed skin and flesh, Hoss doubled up his ham-like fist and struck her full in the mouth. She went over backwards, hitting her head against the corner of the dresser. When she didn't get up to attach him again, he grabbed up the carpet bag and hurriedly left the shack. Outside, he ran to where he had left his horse, tied and waiting. He heaved his great weight into the saddle, and with a kick of his heels in the animal's sides took off down the street, headed for the Painted Lady Saloon.

A picture of the young, blond whore came to mind as he hurried the horse on. Wouldn't she be surprised when he showed up with a bag of money, prepared to take her to San Francisco. She had acted very cool toward him last night, said she didn't want to see him anymore. She probably doubted all the promises he had made her. But she would change her mind when she saw that he was going to keep his word about taking her away from Coldwater. How her eyes would shine when he emptied the pouch of silver dollars in her lap.

The proprietor of the saloon opened the door to his knock. She gave Hoss a dark frown. "You know the girls don't work in the daytime, Hoss. What do you want?"

"I just want to talk to Blondie for a minute. Just talk, that's all."

"After a slight hesitation, the woman nodded. "I'll go see if she wants to get up and talk to you." She closed the door in his face and he heard her climbing the stairs to the rooms upstairs.

It was several minutes before Blondie opened the door and scowled at him. She wore only a flimsy robe tied loosely together at the waist. Her large breasts were barely concealed. "What do you want, Hoss?" she grumbled. "We're not open for business for another couple hours."

"Can I come in for a minute? I want to show you something."

Blondie shook her head. "I'm not interested in anything you could show me, so you can go now." She started to close the door.

"But, honey, I've got the money now to take you away from here. We can go to San Francisco like I promised."

She stared at him a moment, then burst out

laughing. "I wouldn't go to the end of the street with you, you fat hog," she said contemptuously. "Take old diseased Bertha with you,"

"Diseased! She's not diseased!" Hoss protested, a tinge of alarm in his voice. What if the bitch did have a sickness and had passed it on to him?

"Are you so sure?" Blondie's lips curled in contempt. "That's the word that's going around town. Didn't you know that was bound to happen, the way she takes on every man who comes along? That's why I won't go to bed with you anymore. I don't want to catch anything."

He wanted to hit her, raised his hand to do so. But Blondie read the intent in his eyes and quickly closed the door and locked it. He could hear her mocking laughter as he climbed onto his horse and rode away. He guessed he'd best go back to Bertha, do a little crawling if neccessary. But he would never sleep with her again. He just hoped it wasn't too late.

When Hoss arrived back at the shack and walked into the bedroom, he stopped, a puzzled look on his face. Bertha hadn't stirred. She lay in the same position in which he had left her. When he felt for a pulse there was none. He jumped to his feet and ran from the house, cold sweat beaded on his forehead.

As he rode through the night he told himself that the sheriff wouldn't waste much time trying to find the killer of an old whore. They were done in every week.

He made dry camp in a stand of aspens around mid night. He was up early the next morning on his way to the border of Wyoming.

Hoss had been riding for about an hour when in the distance he saw a large cloud of brown dust rolling along. He drew in his horse and watched the dust ball draw nearer. He soon made out a dozen or so Indians racing toward him. He kicked his heels into the horse and raced it to a stand of cottonwood. When he was in the thickest part of it, he dismounted and ran to crouch behind a large mesquite. He peered through the brush, trying to identify the tribe galloping across the range.

He didn't think they had seen him until a bullet struck the dirt near him. He dropped flat on the ground when another shot scattered the leaves over his head. As he lay hidden he could hear them signal to each other.

What should he do? His face grew pale and sweat oozed out of his forehead. There were too many of them to try to shoot it out. Maybe if he surrendered, they wouldn't kill him, just keep him for a slave. Later he could escape. He took the kerchief from around his neck and tied it to the end of the rifle barrel. Taking a deep quavery breath, he stood up slowly, waving the flag back and forth. A full minute went by and he was breathing a sigh of relief when he was hit by a hammer blow in the chest. He gasped, his big body swayed drunkenly a moment, then wilted to the ground.

The Indians yipped and yelled and shook their tomahawks in the air. A minute later they rode off across the country.

Chapter Fourteen

There was a glimmer of light in the sky when Flame awoke. She lay in the comfort of the feather bed, trying not to think of Stone and Little Bird, how well they got along with each other.

She heard Stone's footsteps coming down the hall and swiftly rolled over on her side, facing the wall. If he should open the door, she would pretend to be asleep.

Several days had passed since they'd taken shelter from the storm in the abandoned house, and Stone had not suggested changing their sleeping arrangements again. To her surprise, Flame found she was disappointed.

She continued to lie in bed, making herself

plan her day. Ever since she'd seen that dilapidated old house, she'd been haunted by images of it. She couldn't seem to put it out of her mind. Should she go there again today?

She slid out of bed and walked over to the window. She shoved aside the heavy drapes and looked out at the usual sight. Every morning, fog lay over the river. It hung like a misty cloud a foot or so over the water, gradually disappearing as the sun rose higher.

Flame sighed. She loved this house, the area around it, the feeling of safety it gave her. She didn't understand the part about safety, but suspected that her previous life had been very different from the one she had been living the past month.

She turned from the window telling herself not to get too comfortable on the Falcon ranch. Stone showed no interest in making their sham marriage the real thing. The last few days, he'd acted like a friendly neighbor. Once she got her life together he would probably expect her to leave.

As Flame got dressed in clean pants and a cotton shirt, she heard the cowhands arriving at the cookhouse for breakfast. Yes, she would go to the old, abandoned house this morning. Somehow, she felt it held the key to unlocking her past. And she must straighten that out before she could think about her future.

Stone saw Flame coming across the yard and his heart, as usual, beat a little faster. With the sun striking flames from her hair, her body graceful as she came toward the cookhouse, he felt sure she must be the most beautiful woman God had ever created. As the doctor had suggested, he had not pressured her about deepening their relationship. It had cost him dearly to keep his distance from her the past few days. She stopped to have a word with Maria, the woman he had hired to do the housework. When the cowhands trooped into the cookhouse he followed them.

Everyone looked up when the screen door closed with a snap behind Flame. The men goggled at her as usual. He couldn't fault them for staring at her the same as he was. But it made him want to order the men to put their eyes back in their sockets.

Flame stood in the doorway a moment, a shy smile on her lips. That was another thing he liked about Flame. She wasn't forward; she never flaunted her beauty. He rose from the table.

"Good morning, Flame." He darted a look at her face as he pulled a chair out for her to sit down. It pleased him to see that she looked happy. "I hope you're hungry," he said. "Charlie has made flapjacks for breakfast."

"I love Charlie's flapjacks," she said, grinning at the cook as he placed a large platter of the thin pancakes in the center of the table. He blushed at her compliment as he poured coffee for everyone. The cowhands never said anything tasted good. They never opened their mouths unless it was to complain about something. But deep down he knew they liked what he put before them. They wouldn't stick around if they didn't like his cooking. Cowboys were particular about their grub.

"What are you gonna do today, Flame?" Stone asked as he forked several flapjacks onto his plate.

"I haven't made up my mind yet," she said, hesitant to reveal her plans to him. "What are you going to do?"

"There's some branding to be done before we start our spring drive to Abilene. I expect we'll be attending to that the better part of the day."

"That's a hot, miserable job. I was always glad when I had that job behind me."

A startled look came over her face. Why had she said that? she asked herself.

Stone's eyes wore a look of hope. Hope that Flame was beginning to remember a part of her past. The words she had just uttered cleared up the mystery as to why she preferred working with cows and horses, rather than working inside. She had probably worked the run-down ranch.

Silence settled over the table as Flame and Stone drank their coffee. Stone was trying to get up the nerve to ask Flame to attend the cattleman's annual spring dance with him this coming Saturday. Flame was trying to get up the nerve to tell her first lie.

Flame spoke first. "Stone, I want to ask a favor of you. But don't hesitate to say no if you don't agree."

Stone looked at her and answered softly, "I can't imagine saying no to anything you might ask me."

Damn him, Flame thought. Why does he have to pretend he has such tender feelings for me? He gets me all confused. She cleared her voice, then said hesitantly, "I thought I would pick some wildflowers today like you suggested. And since it's dangerous to be on foot around longhorns, may I use the wagon?" Somehow she was embarrassed to tell him that she wanted to go back to the old house again.

"Of course," Stone answered readily. I won't be needing it today.

"I guess I'd better get going. The men won't budge until I do." Stone grinned and reached across the table to squeeze Flame's hand. "I'll see you later." He left the kitchen and was half way to the barn when he realized he hadn't asked Flame about the dance.

Flame was mixed up at his show of affection. Was it sincere, or was it for the benefit of the ranch hands?

The man and the horse were weary but the Appaloosa plodded on even though its head was hanging low. It was as if he knew that the lean, middle-aged man with the tanned, lined face was anxious to get to his destination as soon as possible.

Rudy Martin had been on the road ever since Caleb had told him of Flame's disappearance. He had closed up his cabin, packed most of his belongings, and started down the mountain toward the ranch he'd left behind fifteen years before.

Rudy's first fearful thought was whether Flame was alright. On the heels of that question came another worry. Would he ever see her again? As long as she was at the old ranch, he'd felt satisfied that one day he would see his little girl again. Of course, when he found her, which he was determined he would, she wouldn't remember him, he thought, full of remorse that he had gone off and left her.

If she had been a little boy, he would have taken her along. But Flame was a delicate little thing, fair and fine of bone. She would have gotten sick, sleeping on the ground and eating game cooked over an open fire. But in the fifteen years that had gone by, a day hadn't passed that he didn't think of his daughter.

Now he had his life savings in his saddlebag and a forty-five strapped across one hip. On the other hip hung a canvas-covered canteen. A Winchester lay cocked across the saddle pommel. It had been years since he had been out of the mountains and he didn't know what to expect. Indians could be warring, cattle rustlers and bank robbers could be holed up in the valleys. Whatever he might run into, he was prepared.

So far, his journey had been uneventful.

As Rudy rode along his thoughts went back to his marriage to Bertha. Theirs had never been a love match. He'd married Bertha only because she'd told him she was pregnant with his baby. He'd known that she was man-crazy, so he had had his doubts that the child was his. But honor forced him to turn his back on the girl he had really loved, so that Bertha's child would have a father.

When the baby was born, one look at the tiny mite with the fuzzy, flame-colored hair told him that the little one was his. She was the image of Grandmother Martin. It was he who had named her Flame.

Bertha had wanted a son and had never paid any more attention to the child than she had to. She never cuddled her daughter, or talked baby-talk to her.

For the little one's sake, he had tried to make a go of his marriage. But Bertha became more and more flagrant with her infidelities. She slept with any man who came along, while he was working his butt off with the cattle.

When Flame was four years old, he came home one morning unexpectedly. He found Bertha in bed with the man he had hired two days before to help him with the branding. He hadn't said a word. He'd picked up little Flame, and his eyes wet, kissed her plump little cheek, hugged her close for a moment, then walked out the door.

He had ridden to the mountains, and like a lone wolf licking its wounds, he paced the animal trails there, mourning the loss of his child, the ranch where he had worked so hard.

Rudy hadn't noticed that the weather had

grown colder, the days shorter. Then one morning, hunched in his bedroll, he awakened in the clear, cold hour of dawn and knew what he must do. Like the geese flying south, he must move on, too. Until he could get his life back together again he must go back to the old uncle who had raised him since his parents had died of the flu when he was six years old.

His mother's brother was happy to have him back and asked him no embarrassing questions. He only asked about the welfare of little Flame. He had spent the winter up in the mountains with his relative, running a trapline. When winter broke and the passes opened up, he took his furs to the trading post down on the river. He was pleased with the good price he got for them. Having had cabin fever for the past month, he longed for some company other than his uncle's. He had lingered awhile at the post, drinking and talking with other trappers.

It was there he had met Caleb Greenwood. The two men had become fast friends. Over the years, as Rudy came down off the mountain less and less, he'd depended on Caleb for news of his daughter. Since his uncle had died the year before, she was the only family he had left in the world.

As he rode onto the land that he had last seen fifteen years before, Rudy's thoughts were interrupted by a rumbling and creaking behind him. He looked over his shoulder and caught his breath. A wagon was turning onto the ranch road. On the seat rested a huge basket of wildflowers. Handling the reins of the two draft horses was a beautiful redhead who could have been his grandmother Martin. He steered Sam across the dusty ranch road and reined him in.

Forced to stop also, Flame frowned at the stranger's action. Then he gave her such a friendly smile, she had to smile back.

"Is this your ranch, miss?" He took off his hat.

"No, it's not."

"Do you know who it belongs to?"

"I'm sorry, but I don't."

There is something very strange here, Rudy thought. He knew beyond a doubt that this was his daughter Flame, so why was it she seemed to know nothing about the place where she was born and grew up? And Caleb had told him that Flame had disappeared, yet here she was.

"I heard the place was for sale." He looked away from her as the lie slipped through his lips.

"I don't know. I haven't heard anything about it."

Rudy looked around at the grassy meadow, the river running through the property. How he had missed this place over the years. "It has everything a man could want in a ranch. Do you live on a ranch?"

"Oh yes. My husband and I have a big spread about ten miles from here." she answered proudly. "We run over two thousand head of cattle."

Husband? Rudy thought. Caleb hadn't mentioned any husband.

"The house on this land, what shape is it in?" he asked, hoping to prolong the conversation.

"It's kind of run down. It needs quite a lot of work done to it."

"Is it at all livable?" Rudy asked after getting an idea.

"Oh, yes," Flame answered, then added laughingly, "That is, if it doesn't rain. The roof has some leaks in it."

"The reason I asked is that I'm looking for a ranch to buy around here. I like this area."

Flame gave him an approving smile. "I like it, too. The ranch house is only about half a mile down the road. Why don't you come look at it?"

That was just what Rudy wanted to do, and he hurriedly accepted her invitation. "I think I'll do just that."

"Good." Flame gave him a warm smile. "Just follow the road. It will take you straight there."

Rudy rode along, the wagon rumbling along behind him. He couldn't believe his good luck. He wouldn't care if the old homeplace didn't have a roof at all. He'd live in it anyway. He was just happy that he had found Flame so quickly. By pretending to buy his own ranch, he would have an excuse to be around his daughter; he would have a chance to get to know her and she to know him. When the time was right, he'd tell her who he was.

It saddened him when he topped a ridge and looked down on the place he had built so long ago. He had felt so proud of it. Now the roofs of all the buildings looked about ready to cave in.

Even from this distance he could see that only half of the barn could be used.

He rode Sam up to the barn. As he dismounted and stretched his sore muscles, Flame pulled the team up and jumped down. "It's not much, is it?" She looked at him with a helpless shrug of her shoulders.

"It doesn't look so good right now," Rudy agreed, "but I see a lot of possibilities for the place." Remembering how everything had looked fifteen years ago, he itched to get busy and bring it back to its former condition.

Most of all, he itched to know what had happened to his daughter. Flame acted as though she didn't know anything about the place. But it wasn't an act. He could tell that the run-down house meant nothing to her. She had no memory of it. Why? Could he be mistaken about her identity?

Turning to the girl he believed was his daughter, he held out his hand. "I'm Jason Saunders," he said, deciding it would be best to use an alias until he knew the lay of the land.

"Flame," she replied, shaking his hand. She hesitated slightly before adding, "Flame Falcon."

"Pleased to meet you," Rudy said, even more pleased to know he hadn't been mistaken.

When he followed Flame into the house he couldn't believe the disorder, the jumbled mess that met his eyes. "Good Lord, Flame, it looks like someone came in here and wrecked the place. I wonder if anyone notified the law."

"I don't know," she replied.

"This room is in pretty good condition." Rudy stood in the doorway of the room he had once shared with Bertha. He wondered how many other men had shared it with her in the past fifteen years.

"I could sleep in here tonight if there's any clean bedding around," he thought out loud. "Then tomorrow I'll go into town and see about buying the place."

"There should be some sheets in here." Flame went past him to the linen closet at the end of the hall. "They may smell musty though."

How did I know there was a linen closet here? Flame asked herself as she reached for a set of sheets and pillow cases. Now that she was inside the house, she was getting little flashes of things she couldn't explain. When she returned to the bedroom where Rudy waited, she saw that he wore a curious look also.

"I was right, they do smell a little musty," Flame said as she stripped the bed and started remaking it.

"I don't mind as long as they're clean." Rudy didn't want to say that he didn't want to sleep between the sheets that Bertha and her lover had used. Flame would question him on how he knew about the woman and her lovers.

When they were finished with the bed, she went to the kitchen to get the broom that had always been kept behind the stove. It was there and as he wielded it on the floor, Flame began to haphazardly wipe the furniture down. She flung open the window and as the fresh air drifted into the room, he wanted to lie down and go to sleep. It had been a long day, full of surprises and bitter memories.

He walked over to the window and looked out at the familiar landscape. Flame watched him and, for some reason, she didn't know why, she was reminded of another man standing there when she was very young. He had looked as though he was sad, too.

"Well, Flame—" Rudy turned around—"I'd better go take care of my stallion and see about fixing my supper." He looked doubtfully at the rusty stove.

"You must have supper with me and . . . my husband tonight," Flame said. "I want you to meet him."

"I appreciate your invitation, Flame, and I'd like to meet your husband."

"Let's go then. Charlie will have supper ready by the time we get there."

Chapter Fifteen

Stone rose to his feet and leaned against the porch pillar, gazing toward the setting sun. When he saw no sign of a wagon approaching, he began to pace the floor. Flame should have been home hours ago. What was keeping her? Had the wagon lost a wheel, or perhaps broken an axel? Or maybe one of the horses had stepped in a gopher hole and broken a leg.

Enough of the maybes, he thought and sat back down. He would give her another fifteen minutes and if she wasn't back by then, he would go looking for her whether she liked it or not. She was trying very hard to be independent these days and that bothered him. What was wrong with her leaning on him a little?

Stone didn't like the answer that popped into his head. Maybe she was planning on striking out on her own.

It was near twilight when there emerged from the fringe of aspen along the river a wagon. Flame was sitting on the high seat. The glad smile on his face faded a bit when he saw a horseman riding alongside the big vehicle. Who was he? He and Flame were chatting away like old friends.

Stone walked down to the stables when Flame drove the wagon into the barn yard. "I was beginning to worry about you," he said as he lifted her down from the wagon.

"I would have been home much earlier, but I met a new neighbor." Flame grinned up at the tall, attractive, middle-aged man who was dismounting his horse. "Stone, meet Jason Saunders. He's going to buy that old house we were in the other day."

The two men gave each other a long steady look as they shook hands. Flame sensed a friction between the two men but told herself not to be silly. She asked herself how there could be animosity between them. They had just met. She looked at her guest and said, "I see the men going into the cookhouse. I guess we'd better get washed up and get in there before they eat everything in sight."

When the teenage wrangler unhitched the team and led the horses away, Stone followed Flame and Rudy to the wash bench alongside the cookhouse. When they had soaped away the sweat and trail dust, the three entered the building.

"Men," Flame said as she took her place at the table, "this is Jason Saunders. He's planning to buy that old ranch house in the foothills."

Rudy nodded to each man as she named him, then sat down beside Flame. Stone frowned. That was where he always sat. He stood uncertain a moment, debating what he should do. He decided that it would look petty if he made an issue of the stranger sitting beside his wife. He took a seat across from Flame. He longed to ask the man where he hailed from but knew better. It was nobody's business where he came from.

Stone knew two things for sure about the older man. That appaloosa of his was a fine looking horse, and the man who rode him was damn handsome. And he sure as hell didn't like the way Saunders kept looking at Flame; smiling at her, touching her hand. She didn't mind it, either. He jabbed at his steak. Saunders was old enough to be her father, for heaven's sake. Didn't it make any difference to him that she was married?

But she isn't married, Stone reminded himself. And the chances of her agreeing to marry him were beginning to look very slim. He wasn't sure he wanted her to get her memory back. Wouldn't it be better if things went on as they were? Perhaps in time she would fall in love with him without ever regaining her memory of the past.

Chairs were being pushed back from the table; supper was finished. As the men filed out of the cookhouse Stone had no idea what he had eaten. He followed Flame and her guest outside, and his eyes narrowed in anger when Flame said, "Come and sit with us for a while, Jason. We can go over what materials you'll need to fix up the house and I'll go into town with you tomorrow. I suppose you'll start on the roof first. It was leaking pretty bad when Stone and I took shelter in it the other day."

"That would be the logical thing to do, I guess, but first I must make sure I can buy the place," Rudy said as the three of them sat down on the porch. "How long do you think the house has been empty?"

"How long do you figure, Stone? A couple months?" Flame gave him an uncertain look.

"Something like that," Stone answered slowly. He had no idea how long the house had been vacant. Though it was not far from his own ranch, he had not known the owners. "We've been married for a month. It's been empty since then."

Where had Flame been the month before that, Rudy wondered, the darkness hiding his frown. He wouldn't ask her about that now though. He could sense her husband's thinly veiled hostility. He would get the chance to ask her a few questions tomorrow.

Far up in the mountains a wolf pointed his nose at the moon and howled a lonely sound.

Rudy gave a soft laugh. "That ole fellow doesn't sound very happy, does he? He probably doesn't like being all alone."

"I never liked being alone when I was little. I imagined all kinds of things lurking in the corners, or under my bed," Flame said, half laughing at her childish fears.

"Weren't your mother and father with you?" Rudy asked.

A startled look came over Flame's face. Why had she remembered being so young and afraid of the dark? And as for Rudy's question, she didn't know if her mother and father had been with her. Finally, she answered, "I suppose they were with me. I have a dim memory of a woman, but I don't think she was a very nurturing-type person. There was a man, too. A kind man. I have a vague memory of sitting on his lap, of his singing to me."

"What happened to him, Flame?" Stone held his breath, waiting for her to give him an insight into her past.

But Flame only shook her head. "I don't remember."

"My wife hit her head during a storm just after we were married," Stone explained. "She's had amnesia ever since."

A couple of owls called to each other from a patch of willows and the wolf howled again.

So that is why Flame has no memory of the ranch, Rudy thought. He pulled back his feet and stood up. "I guess I'd better be getting back to my new home," he said. "It's been a long day and me and Sam are both tired. I can't wait to stretch out and grab some sleep."

"Keep an eye out for that old lobo," Flame warned as she and Stone rose with him.

"I'm not afraid of wolves. They won't bother a person if they are left alone." Rudy smiled at Flame. "Thanks for supper. I'll see you tomorrow."

"I'll be over bright and early."

Stone didn't know if he was included in the invitation to the old house the next day, but he said anyway, "I don't know if I can make it. We're in the middle of rounding up cattle to drive to the market."

"Can I help you?" Rudy stood on the bottom step looking up at Stone.

"Thanks, but I have enough men to finish getting them together."

"Well, let me know if you need more help." Rudy stepped onto the ground and walked toward the barn.

"He's awfully nice, don't you think?" Flame opened the door and stepped inside the house.

"He appears to be," Stone answered reluctantly. "But there's a mystery about him. He looks very familar. I'm sure I've met him somewhere before. Did he mention to you where he comes from?"

"No, and I didn't ask. I figure he'll tell us someday."

"He's not a grub-liner. You can tell that by the clothes he wears and the horse he rides.

And that's an expensive Colt he has tied down on his leg. Another thing I can't understand is why a man his age should be riding around the country for no apparent reason. And why does he want to buy that old run-down place?"

"I don't know and I don't care," Flame retorted sharply. "Maybe he likes the area. He was impressed with the fact that the river runs through the property."

"Don't go getting so huffy about him, Flame," Stone said calmly, wondering at the sharp attitude she was taking because he raised a few questions about the man. "Tell the truth now, don't you think it a little odd that he would prefer an old place out in the country instead of one in town that would be more comfortable? It's kinda like he's hiding from someone, maybe the law. We don't know a thing about him."

"Think what you want. I have a feeling about him. I trust him."

"Flame, there's something you should know before you go back over there," Stone said, coming to a quick decision. "That old abandoned ranch house is where I found you. I think it may be where you used to live."

She stared at him for a moment. "Why didn't you tell me?" she whispered, then fled into the house.

A few minutes later Stone followed her. In his room he undressed to the skin and climbed into bed. There were so many things running through his mind it was a long time before he fell asleep.

* * *

Rudy lay in the silence, looking up at the star-studded sky through a large hole in the roof. He'd take care of that first thing in the morning, he promised himself. Otherwise the next rain would set the place awash. And a new mattress was in order to replace the lumpy one he was sleeping on tonight. It was not only uncomfortable, it smelled foul.

Rudy tossed and turned for several minutes, then gave up. Dragging the blanket off the bed he took up the pillow and walked to the barn. He would share it with Sam. The hay he piled into a mound was clean and comfortable. He stretched out on it, and being dead tired, he fell asleep right away. He didn't awaken until the first gray of day was appearing far off over the mountains. He yawned and stretched, then lay quietly, going over his plans for the day.

He wondered if there was a wagon on this disreputable ranch. He remembered the time when there was one. A fine, heavy vehicle that he had kept in good repair. He had been very proud of it. He had been proud of the whole place and worked hard to keep it up.

He sighed as he sat up and brushed the hay out of his hair. A lot had changed in the past fifteen years. His mark on the place was nowhere to be seen.

As Rudy pumped water into the leaking trough and washed his face and hands it came to him that he couldn't use a wagon if he had one. His stallion Sam would never allow himself to be hitched to one. He'd have to depend on Flame to take him to town to purchase the lumber he would need.

Flame. A soft smile curved his lips. It was hard to believe that whorish Bertha had given birth to such a sweet, beautiful girl. He had missed fifteen years of her life but he was going to make it up to her. He liked her husband well enough, he guessed, but he wished Flame wasn't married yet. He would like to have had her all to himself for a while.

He was drying his face on his bandana when he saw the wagon top the crest of a hill a quarter mile away. He recognized it, as well as the girl handling the reins of the two draft horses. His eyes sparkled at the prospect of seeing his daughter again.

"Good morning," Flame called, bringing the team to a halt a few feet away. "I'm happy to see you're up early. I was afraid you might still be sleeping."

"I've been up awhile." Rudy stretched out his arms to lift her to the ground. "As far as I'm concerned, there's no better time of the day while the dew is still on the grass."

"Me, too," Flame agreed. "I've always thought that way about it." She reached into the wagon and brought up a small cloth bag. "I brought some grub for our breakfast. I felt pretty sure there would be nothing here to eat."

"I hope you've got some coffee in there." Rudy grinned down at her. "I can't think straight until I get a cup of java inside me."

"We have something else in common, then," Flame said. "I've been told that I'm like a wild-cat until I drink a pint of coffee."

"Let's get some of that brew started then." Rudy took her by the elbow and steered her toward the house.

They went straight to the kitchen. Neither was anxious to see the rest of the place. Flame stood a moment, looking around the room, then took from the bag enough coffee beans to make a pot of coffee. She laid them on the grubby table then took a half slab of bacon from the bag. Next she emptied the bag by bringing out five eggs, a half loaf of sourdough and a salt shaker.

Rudy lifted a coffee pot off the stove. "What do you think, Flame?" He held it out for her inspection.

"Stone scrubbed it last time we were here," Flame said, "but the stove is a mess."

"I'll get some hot water ready." Rudy put the pot back on the stove and began to kindle a fire in the fire box. When a good-sized flame took hold, he filled a dishpan with water and started it to heating. Flame had been busy also. She had unearthed a coffee grinder from a cupboard. While she ground the beans, Rudy attacked the top of the stove.

"There's a bar of lye soap underneath the sink," Flame said, then snapped her mouth shut, puzzlement in her eyes. How did she know that?

By the time enough coffee had been ground

for their breakfast, the old stove was clean. When the brew began to perk, Rudy pulled out his pocket knife and started slicing the bacon.

Flame and Rudy worked in silence, but a compatible silence. In a short time the aroma of coffee and frying meat filled the dingy kitchen. Rudy had scrubbed the table top and Flame busied herself setting out plates and flatware. She added two cups, then sliced the bread she had brought along.

The meal was ready shortly and Rudy removed the meat and eggs from a dented, though clean, frying pan. Flame said that two eggs were enough for her and Rudy didn't hesitate to put the other three on his plate.

Very little was said as they ate. They were drinking coffee when Flame asked, "Have you ever been married, Jason?"

Rudy took a long swallow of coffee, then set the cup back down. "Yes, I have. My wife was a no-good hellcat."

"What happened to her?"

"I'm not sure what happened. I left her when I caught cheating. She's probably dead, killed by some man she was living with."

Flame reached across the table and covered Rudy's hand with her own small one. "Didn't you have any children?" she asked gently.

Rudy turned his hand over so that their palms met. "Yes, I had a daughter. She disappeared a while ago."

Rudy didn't speak for a minute or so. He wondered how he would ever tell her that she was his missing daughter. At last he spoke, but on a different subject. "I guess we should decide what we need in town."

"Quite a bit, I think," Flame said. "I can figure out what is needed inside, but you'll have to decide on lumber and such."

"I guess we both should make a list. I wonder if there's paper and pencil around here."

Flame walked over to a cupboard and pulled out a drawer. After rummaging around inside it a moment, she took out some paper and two pencil stubs. Her hand paused in mid-air as she started to lay the items on the table. How had she know that paper and pencil were in the drawer?

She was beginning to become quite nervous about these little happenings. Was Stone right? Had she really lived here before?

For some reason she felt a deep-rooted shame that she might have lived in this old house whose very walls cried out its misery, the dishonor done to it through the years. Was this the place where she had been born and grown up? If that was the case, she hoped her memory would never come back.

The only sound in the room for some time was the scratching of lead across rough paper.

Rudy finished first. His needs were mostly lumber, shingles and nails. For the time being at least, he thought. He felt sure that as he went along making repairs there would be many more things he would need. But right now the important thing was to get the roofs fixed over the house and barn.

It took Flame a bit longer to finish her list. There was so much needed in the house. The first thing she wrote down was stove-blacking for the rusty old range. Next was linseed oil to rub into the furniture. Once the pieces were cleaned up and the oil rubbed into the dry wood, they wouldn't look so bad. She wanted the place to look as nice as possible for Jason. She added bed linens, towels and dishcloths, plus soap, a mop and a couple brooms. The grimy kitchen window caught her eye then and she added curtains. She knew that the cupboards and storage room were empty so all she wrote at the bottom of the page was the word "food."

She laid the pencil down and folded the sheet of paper. As she slid it into her vest pocket she said, "I've written down everything I could think of. I must warn you, it's a long list."

"That's alright. I'm sure it's all needed." Rudy picked his hat off the floor beside his chair and slapped it on his head. "Let's get started then."

When they walked outside he asked, "Do you want to ride Sam. I'll drive the wagon. It's gonna be loaded down, coming back, what with the lumber and all."

"That's fine with me." Flame walked toward the stallion tied up at the sagging gate. After Rudy helped her onto the tall horse, he climbed into the wagon. He released the brakes, gathered up the reins, and snapped them over the team's backs.

The grass was wet with heavy dew as they took the wagon road through the old orchard. It was a short cut to Dogwood and Rudy remembered planting the apple, pear and cherry trees when he and Bertha first started ranching. He'd had such high hopes then, even though he hadn't wed the woman that he loved. The trees were old now, with mossy trunks and thin, twisted branches. Still, most were heavy with blossoms. Later there would be plenty of fruit to be picked.

The bunch grass stretched away to the mountains when they left the orchard and hit the main road. Rudy grinned and Flame laughed when a road runner darted across the track and ran along beside them for a short time.

Besides the half-dozen new business establishments that had sprung up in town since he'd been to Dogwood, there were now four narrow lanes branching off the main street. Alongside the short lanes were a few small, frame houses.

Rudy knew very well where the lumber yard was, but he remembered that he wasn't supposed to. When he stopped to ask its location, and was told it was down by the river, he said, "I'm going to go straight there. How long do you think it will take you to get what's on your list?"

"Close to an hour maybe." Flame jerked her

GET YOUR 4 FREE* BOOKS NOW—
A $21.96 VALUE!

Mail the Free* Book
Certificate
Today!

Get Four Books Totally
F R E E* —
A $21.96 Value!

PLEASE RUSH
MY FOUR FREE*
BOOKS TO ME
RIGHT AWAY!

Leisure Historical Romance Book Club
P.O. Box 6613
Edison, NJ 08818-6613

AFFIX
STAMP
HERE

thumb toward a small cafe across the street. "Shall we meet in the Sage Hen in a couple hours?"

As soon as the words left her mouth, Flame wondered where they had come from. How did she know the name of that little cafe? She had to have been to Dogwood before, and probably many times.

She didn't hear what Rudy answered. Her attention was on the small building on the other side of the street. If she stared at it long enough, hard enough, maybe some memory of it would come to her.

It was just a plain, little building with a large window. Flame could see people inside sitting in booths and at tables eating. Two cowboys came out, and stared at her minute. Though she smiled tentatively at them, it was clear they didn't know her. They would be unable to help her discover her identity.

With a tightening of nerves Flame rode up to the hitching post in front of Dogwood's largest mercantile. Several men lounged on its porch. A couple nodded at her pleasantly enough, but she felt their hot gazes traveling over her as she dismounted. Although their staring made her uncomfortable, she knew there would be no crude remarks made to her. As far as the town knew, she was Stone Falcon's wife. No one wanted to tangle with him. She had overheard some of the hands discussing him one day. It seemed it was a well-known fact that he was a mean one in a fight.

Flame walked the gauntlet of eyes and entered the general store. It held most anything a person would want in a frontier town.

As her gaze ranged over the well-stocked room she grew excited. If she'd ever been here before, she certainly didn't remember it. She was eager to look at everything. And best of all, she could buy things for herself. Just before she'd left the ranch this morning Stone had given her a roll of money that made her eyes widen in disbelief.

"I'll not waste it," she had said shyly.

"I intend that you spend every dime of it," he had said gruffly, but his eyes were soft as he looked at her. "Buy yourself some lady things . . . you know, dresses and bonnets and all the other things women like to wear."

Flame smiled wryly, remembering his words. She had a feeling that Stone knew more than she did what ladies wore.

However, the first thing she chose was a new white Stetson, then a pair of boots. She cautiously approached a long wooden rod hanging from the ceiling. Suspended from it were dresses, daytime and nighttime wear. There was such an array of colors, styles and materials, she could only stand and stare at the silks and satins, sheer muslins and velvets. There were also dresses like the ones Pearl wore. Plain and serviceable.

As she studied the lovely clothing, wondering what size would fit her, Flame became aware that an attractive middle-aged woman was standing at the counter watching her. Flame blushed in embarrassment. She felt sure that the woman could tell by her awkward handling of the garments that choosing clothing was something new to her.

She gave a start when a soft voice behind her said, "The colors are beautiful, aren't they?"

"Yes, they are." Flame smiled shyly.

"Which ones have taken your fancy?"

"I can't decide, they are all so pretty."

"Of course the first thing you must do is decide which ones are your size. I would say the smallest ones would be for you."

The woman started flipping through the dresses. "This blue muslin would look lovely on you." She held a pale blue, lace-trimmed gown up against Flame. "It goes perfectly with your eyes and glorious hair. What do you think?"

"Do you think so?" Flame smoothed her rough palms over the soft material.

"Yes, I do." The woman folded the dress over her arm. "And so would this black velvet for winter wear. It would show off your beautiful complexion." Folding the velvet creation over her arm also, she took from the rod a lavender satin that made Flame's mouth water. "This one you must have for the church social this fall," the woman said firmly. "You will look like a fairy princess in it."

"Oh, but I shouldn't. All these dresses will cost a fortune." Flame curled her fingers around the roll of bills in her vest pocket. "I need to buy everyday dresses . . . and other things."

The pretty woman smiled at her words. "You're Stone Falcon's wife, aren't you?"

"Yes, I am." Flame blushed. "But I don't see what . . ."

"You were going to ask, what difference that makes. I'll tell you you the difference, dear. You could buy this whole store if you wanted to."

Flame thought the woman was joking and she laughed lightly.

"I guess I was stretching the truth a little." The woman laughed, too. "I'm Rainee Devlow," she said as she added the lavender to the others on her arm. "But your husband isn't hurting from lack of money. I have a dress shop across the street. When you've finished shopping in here, come over to my place and I'll help you with other things." She winked at Flame.

Flame's eyes twinkled. Her new friend meant underclothing and such. She had been dreading purchasing such items from the pimply faced clerk who no doubt would be as embarrassed as she when she asked to look at some petticoats, camisoles and bloomers.

"Thank you so much, Rainee. I shouldn't be too long. I'll have to wait for my friend, Jason Saunders, first. He wouldn't know where to look for me otherwise. He's new here."

"I'll be there the rest of the day. Come on over when you're ready."

Flame watched Rainee walk across the street and enter a small shop. Flame began her shopping then by walking over to two shelves that held bed linens and towels. There were also a few mattresses. She told the young man who followed her around that she wanted two changes of sheets, pillowcases and blankets. She also purchased a dozen towels and washcloths.

Her next purchase was a can of stove-black for the rusty old stove. After Jason's scrubbing it was clean enough but it looked awful. A skillet and a coffee pot were added to the growing pile. Next came a set of plain white dishes and some cheap flatware.

Flame had been in the store close to two hours when she spotted some sweet-scented soap for the bath. She couldn't remember ever having such luxury before and she was quite a while choosing which frangrance she liked best. It didn't occur to her that she could buy more than one bar.

Her last stop was at the far end of the store, where shelves of supplies were stacked. She was another half hour selecting the many staples and supplies that the house needed. When she was finally finished, she looked at the young clerk and said, "When you have totaled up everything put it on Jason Saunder's bill. I will pay cash for the clothing." After the young man had taken her money, she turned and hurried out of the store. Jason would be waiting for her.

Flame saw him standing in front of the cafe and hurried along. He certainly is a handsome man, she thought and wondered why she was so proud of that fact. You'd think he was a relative.

"Have you been waiting long?" she asked, panting a little as she came up to him.

"Just a few minutes. I was at the lumber yard longer that I thought I would be. But I got everything I need. What about you? Did you get everything you wanted?"

"I think so, but there's one other thing I'm very happy about. I met a new friend."

"Oh, a female friend, I hope," Rudy said, half in jest, half seriously. "Stone isn't crazy about our friendship. If you show up with another male friend, he may throw a fit." He cast Flame an amused grin.

Flame smiled at the thought of Stone having a fit of temper. He was the sort who would take a man aside and warn him to stay away from his woman. But she seriously doubted that Stone would care how many men friends she might have.

"He's not going to object to my new dressmaker friend. I met her at the mercantile. She has a shop across the street. Her name is Rainee."

Continuing to talk about her new acquaintance, Flame didn't notice how still Rudy's body had gone. "I told her I'd meet her at her shop as soon as I met up with you. She's going to take my measurements for some winter dresses and such. She's so nice. I know you'll like her."

Rudy had no doubt that he would like Rainee. Years ago he had loved her. As he followed Flame across the street in a daze, he wondered if she would remember him? How would she react to him? It had been a long time since they had seen each other last. It was nineteen years ago the night he told her they couldn't marry, that another woman was carrying his child. He could still see the stunned look, the pain in her lovely eyes. How had life treated her? he wondered. Was she married? Did she have children?

He would soon know, he told himself with mixed emotions as he neared the dress shop.

Rainee saw Flame and Rudy coming across the street and sucked in her breath. Was the tall, handsome man walking beside Flame the one she called Jason Saunders? That wasn't the name she knew him by, and she knew him well. Had known him well, she corrected herself. After so long a time, she might not know him at all. If he had told the girl his name was Jason Saunders, he didn't want her to know who he really was.

Rainee decided she would play Rudy's game. She wiped her face of all the emotions that were running through her mind and waited behind the counter to face the man she still loved.

"Rainee, I want you to meet my friend, Jason Saunders," Flame said as they came in.

Rainee's gaze locked with Rudy's. The years melted away and they were young and in love again. Although no words were spoken, their eyes were speaking volumes. Flame would have been astonished at the looks they were

231

exchanging if she hadn't been exclaiming over some lovely bonnets that had caught her eye.

He has changed, Rainee thought, and yet he hasn't. His hair was gray at the temples, but it was still heavy and unruly. A few strands, as usual, lay against his forehead. There were fine lines fanning away from his eyes. From looking into the sun, she imagined. There were long grooves down his brown, tanned face, which only made him look more handsome.

But his eyes no longer twinkled with humor. Far back in their depths they said that he had suffered since she had last seen him.

Rudy was thankful that the counter was between them. He doubted that he would have the will power not to grab Rainee and kiss her until they were both dizzy. He finally broke the silence. "I'm pleased to meet you, Rainee."

"I'm pleased to meet you too . . . Jason." Rainee's eyes were soft as she looked at him. "Will you be staying in the area for a while?"

Rudy looked deep into her eyes and said quietly, "For the rest of my life if things go the way I want them to."

"Oh, I wish you would, Jason," Flame said, joining them at the counter. "That would be wonderful."

"Shall we look at some ladies' finery?" Rainee suggested, her heart pounding from the messages Rudy's eyes were sending her.

When Flame agreed, Rudy said, "While you two are doing that, I think I'll skip lunch at the cafe and get this lumber out to the house. I want to start patching some of the holes in the roof." He looked at Rainee. "Maybe I'll see you tomorrow. I'm sure I'll need more lumber."

Rainee started to say that it looked to her like he had enough lumber in the wagon to build a house, but something told her to hold her tongue. Maybe Rudy had some private plan. Wouldn't it be wonderful if he did make the old ranch house his permanent home? She didn't like to think of him moving on some day, that she would never see him again. She had lived through that pain once and she didn't want to do it again.

Rainee scolded herself for thinking that way. This man, now known as Jason Saunders, was a stranger whom she knew nothing about. For all she knew, he had a wife and children and friends tucked away somewhere, a life that he would return to later.

When the door closed behind Rudy, Rainee looked at Flame and asked, "How long have you known . . . Jason?"

"Not quite two days, but it seems like I've known him all my life. He is a really nice man."

"Yes," Rainee answered softly, "he seems to be."

"He's not married. Maybe the two of you could get together," Flame teased, her eyes sparkling.

Her pulse fluttering at Flame's information, Rainee said lightly, "I'm sure such a handsome man has a ladyfriend somewhere."

"I'll ask him."

"Don't you dare. Not on my account," Rainee exclaimed, appalled that her young friend might do just that. "Promise me that you won't."

"I promise, Rainee. I was just teasing you."

"Alright then. Let's look at some undergarments now. I want to take your measurements, too. I want to make you some clothes for when winter sets in."

A hot dry wind blew across the range as Rudy drove the horses toward his old ranch. It bent the grass, silverberry and wild roses before it. He looked up at the gray clouds that hung low in the sky. It was going to rain, maybe storm.

He fell to thinking about Rainee. When Flame had introduced her new friend, he couldn't believe that it was his first love who stood looking at him, wonder in her eyes.

With the reins loose in his hands, Rudy let his mind wander back to the time he courted Rainee Crawford, as she was known then. They had been so in love, planning on getting married the coming fall. Yet, Rainee would not give herself to him until they were married. He had gone around hurting until he had done what most young men in the area did. He began to call on Bertha Cronkin to get some relief.

He should have been warned when she stopped seeing other men and went to bed only with him. But he hadn't given it much thought. He had paid for that mistake for the rest of his life.

He stared unseeing at the road ahead. He would never forget that sunny October day when Bertha rode out to the small ranch house he was building for Rainee. The big raw-boned woman came right to the point of her visit. She informed him coolly that she was carrying his child. He remembered how he had wanted to smash her fat face as his dream of a life with Rainee crumbled to pieces.

He wondered now if it was possible that after all these years he and Rainee could have a life together. She didn't wear a wedding band. Did that mean she was divorced, a widow, or just that she didn't wear a gold band?

When Rudy reached his old homeplace, there was still enough daylight left for him to start mending the leaky roof. It took him about twenty minutes to unload the wagon. He laid aside three bundles of shingles, then covered the rest with a tarp.

Rudy went inside the barn to look for his old ladder. He found it leaning in a corner. If he wasn't mistaken, it was in the same place he had left it the day he said goodbye to his ranch. With a bundle of shingles slung over his back, he climbed to the roof and began to work. As he hammered away, his thoughts went back to Rainee. He couldn't believe that a woman as attractive as she wasn't attached to some man.

He remembered that Rainee had left town a week after he married Bertha. No one had heard of her since.

When had she returned? he wondered. Did she have children? He breathed a long sigh. He knew one thing for sure. If she wasn't tied to a man, he was going to move back into the house that he had built for her years ago, and he wouldn't stop courting her until she broke down and agreed to marry him.

Rudy had hammered a nail into the last shingle when Flame rode up. He climbed down as she slid out of the saddle. "You've been busy." Her eyes skimmed over the new shingles scattered about on the roof.

Rudy wiped his arm across his sweaty forehead. "Yeah, and I'll pay for it tomorrow. I've used muscles today that I haven't used in years.

"Will you stay and have supper with me?" he asked.

"No, I just stopped by on my way home to see how you were doing. It's getting near sundown and Stone will be worried about me."

"Well then, stop by again. See how my work is progressing."

"I will. I'll make a regular pest of myself."

"I doubt that, Flame. You ride over any time you want to."

She gave him a wide smile. "Thank you, neighbor."

Rudy stood in the weed-filled yard and watched Flame drive the team away with pride in his eyes. Handling a team was not new to her. This daughter of his was used to hard work, whether she knew it or not. Out of necessity, he felt sure.

Well, her father was back now and things were going to be different. But this memory loss of hers might make it a little difficult for him to help her as much as he would like to.

Chapter Sixteen

Shilo loped along the river trail, his long legs eating up the distance. He had held this steady pace for the last half hour. Thunder rolled in the distance and the air was hot and humid. Not a breath of wind stirred. He knew that a storm could break any minute and it would be a bad one.

He stepped up his pace, muttering angrily, "Where is that crazy girl?"

An hour ago it was discovered that Little Bird was missing. No one had seen her leave the village; no one had any idea where she had gone.

Had she gone to meet Stone? Shilo asked himself. The possibility was like like a stab in the heart. The blood in his veins began to boil. If he found her with Stone, he would marry her off to one of the braves who would beat her if she even looked at another man.

He shook his head. The thought of a stick being laid on her tender flesh made him flinch. But he would marry her off. Stone would never fool around with a married woman, whether she be white or Indian.

The Falcon ranch buildings appeared in the distance and Shilo slowed down to a fast walk as he approached the back of Stone's house. He could see the forms of the cowhands in the cookhouse. It was supper time. He hunkered down beside a large cottonwood and waited to see if Stone was among the men when they left later.

As he waited, he studied Stone's home. For a long time he had secretly yearned to own a house such as white men lived in. Not a fancy one like Stone's. He wouldn't want all those rooms, and he wouldn't go for all that furniture and fancy stuff, making a man nervous just being around them.

No, he only wanted a plain, well-built cabin. One that he would live in for the rest of his life. Maybe his long-time friendship with Stone was behind that wish.

How would Little Bird feel about living within wooden walls? Would she be content to gaze at the moon' through a window instead of a wigwam's peak where the smoke escaped from the fire-pit?

A dark scowl came over Shilo's face. What was he thinking? He and the Indian maid would never share any kind of home together. Little Bird didn't even like her chief, let alone care enough for him to wed. No matter what she'd said, she had her heart set on Stone, the little idiot.

Shilo stood up when he saw the cookhouse door open and the men began to file out. The last ones to step outside were Stone and Flame. They were laughing at something Stone was saying. He breathed a sigh of relief, but on its heels came another worry. This one worse than when he feared she was with Stone. Had one of the braves set upon her? Or maybe she'd been attacked by a bear or a cougar.

Where should he look? Which way should he go? Should he ask Stone to help him look for Little Bird? As he stood, undecided, some sixth sense turned him back toward his village.

It was early afternoon when Little Bird had decided to go into the forest to dig some roots and cut some greens for tonight's supper. She had overheard Shilo say to his mother that he was hungry for the special roots and greens. She would surprise him. Maybe he would smile at her when he learned what she had done for him.

She had decided to slip away from the children while they were taking their afternoon nap. When Little Bird had gone to tell Sholo's mother where she was going, she had found

Moonlight taking a nap also. She had decided not to awaken her. Chances were she would be back before anyone realized she was gone.

As Little Bird had struck off towards the woods, a reed basket on her arm, she'd noticed that a few storm clouds were gathering in the north. They did not worry her. She would be back home before it rained.

But she hadn't found the plant she was searching for. She'd been ready to give up and return home when she spotted a large growth of it beneath a stand of aspens. She hurried to kneel among them, her knife slashing and digging. In a very short time she had all the roots she needed. As she stood, brushing leaves and twigs off her skirt she became aware that the sun had lost its brightness and that a brownish haze hung in the air. When the wind picked up and a few raindrops struck her skin, she knew that she had run out of time. Jumping to her feet and uttering a white man's word that Shilo often used—a swear word, she suspected—she started sprinting toward the village. It was only a half mile away.

Suddenly a horse reared up in her path. She came to an abrupt halt and took a couple steps backward. As she stared up at the whisker-stubbled face of the rider, she began to tremble. He stared down at her and leered. "What have we here? Where are you goin' in such a hurry, little squaw? Are you afraid of a little ole storm?"

The man dismounted, and with a wolfish

smile walked toward her. "Don't be afraid. I'll take good care of you."

Little Bird let loose a scream as Deke Cobbs lunged at her. She dropped her basket, spun around on her heels, running as fast as she could. He was right behind her and grabbed one of her long braids. As he pulled her to the ground he growled, "Behave yourself, squaw, or I'll get rough with you. Do like I tell you and we'll get along fine."

All the time Deke was threatening her, his hands were busy. One hand tore the neckline of her shift while the other one was trying to get up under her skirt.

Little Bird only screamed that one time. She was saving her energy to fight him off. She had her legs crossed tightly as her small hands clawed at his face. When one of her nails brought blood streaming down his cheek, he freed his hand from her bodice and hit her hard on the chin with his fist. Lights flashed before her eyes. Now Deke was prying her thighs apart. As she felt them separating she let loose a scream that could be heard a mile away.

Deke had pulled her legs apart and pushed her shift up to her waist, when a heavy hand fell on his shoulder and jerked him to his feet.

Shilo's enraged face made Deke's blood run cold. As he moved backwards he snatched a gun from his waist and fired. When the shot spun Shilo around Deke jumped on his horse and put spurs to the animal. It tore away as the full fury of the storm struck.

With lightning flashing and thunder rolling, Little Bird rushed through the downpour to where Shilo lay. "Oh, Shilo," she cried as she knelt down beside him. "Are you badly shot? Where did the bullet hit you?" She ran gentle fingers over his chest and arms.

With the rain striking him in the face Shilo caught her hands and held them still. "He got me in my left shoulder, but it's only a flesh wound." He sat up. "Let's try to find some shelter. This rain is not going to stop soon."

"Where could we find shelter here?" Little Bird peered around.

Shilo took her arm and started running. "Over that knoll to your right is a cliff with an overhang of about four feet. We can stay dry there all night if need be."

"What about your wound? It should be dressed."

"It's fine. It has stopped bleeding already."

In a matter of minutes a huge cliff towered before them. There came a bright flash of lightning that revealed the overhang. "Crawl under, Little Bird." Shilo gave her a gentle push.

She dropped to her knees and crawled under the wide stone arch. She was surprised at how high its roof became after a few feet. Even Shilo could stand upright in the center. It was almost like a cave.

Shilo was right behind Little Bird. "Go all the

way to the back," he told her. "The wind is blowing the rain in a good foot."

Little Bird moved as far back as she could. She lay down and curled up on her side, to keep warm. Shilo lay down next to her and wordlessly pulled her shivering body into the curve formed by his chest and drawn-up knees. He began at once to rub and knead her small body.

The cave was warm and dry and soon Little Bird began to feel heat stealing through her body. Shilo didn't stop the stroking of his hands. They did move slower over her body, though, and were very gentle. This gentleness was so unlike him, felt so good, she grew still, not wanting to miss one rhythmic movement. His hands had now moved up to her breasts.

She held her breath when his slender fingers cupped her breasts in his palms. She gasped her pleasure when he stroked her breasts and gently tweaked the nipples. He was turning her over, then, his black head coming down to hover over the pebble-hard tips. She raised her arms and cupped his face in her hands. With a gentle tug she pulled him forward. A moan, low in her throat, sounded on the air as his lips parted and he sucked the tip of her breast into his mouth. She moaned again, a little louder, when he began to swirl his tongue around her nipple and nibbled a bit at the little nub.

Shilo's hand started a slow path down Little Bird's stomach, stopping when he came to the vee of her thighs. When she opened up to him, he inserted a finger inside her. He felt her feminine walls tighten around him and he knew that she was ready to accept him. He raised himself on his knees and climbed between her legs.

"You know that it will hurt a bit at first?" he said hoarsely.

Little Bird nodded. Taking his hard length into his hand, Shilo guided it slowly inside her.

She withheld a cry of pain as his largeness stretched the walls of her feminine core. He waited for her body to stop trembling, then ever so slowly moved a little deeper inside her.

Little Bird was sure she couldn't bear it. Each plunge of his manhood was like the stabbing of a knife.

She was at the point of begging him to stop when she became aware of something building inside her, a wave of something warm and wonderful. She raised her hips to meet his thrusting body, unable to get enough of him. He gave a deep moan, and gathering her hips in his hands, he lifted them as he slowly, but deeply thrust in and out of her.

Just as Little Bird reached her crest, she felt the warm spill of his seed flood inside her.

Shilo held his weight off Little Bird until his body stopped shuddering and his breathing calmed. "Are you alright?" he asked. He rolled off her, but kept her head pillowed on his shoulder.

He felt her head nod against his chest as she nestled closer to him. He turned his head and peered beneath the overhang. "It has stopped raining," he said. "Let's go home and get you into some dry clothing."

Little Bird was disappointed that Shilo didn't hold her hand as they walked through the meadow. She had hoped to hear tender words from him. After all, they had been as intimate as any man and woman could be.

But Shilo was his usual gruff self, saying very little, answering in grunts to anything she had to say. When they reached her wigwam, he lifted the flap for her to enter. He said only, "Get some dry clothes on."

Little Bird stumbled into her quarters, half blinded by the tears that welled up in her eyes. She stripped the wet shift off and pulled a dry one on. She sat down on her bed of furs and loosened her soaked braids. All the while the tears flowed. Even as she fell asleep.

Shilo kindled a small fire in his fire-pit, then stripped off his wet leggings. He sat cross-legged in front of the flames, his eyes staring into the fire. This coupling with Little Bird had been a wonderous thing, something he had never experienced before. She had opened herself up to him, giving him all of herself. No other woman had ever done that for him before, not even Opal. They had always held part of themselves back, something not to be shared.

He had been drawn to her from the first, but had fought the feeling. It was as if he somehow knew she would tame him, break him of his wild ways.

Was he ready for that? he asked himself. He knew one thing, he was ready to take her to bed again. Yes, now that he had had her, he would no longer be able to restrain himself. There was only one thing to do. He must wed the little orphan, whether his people approved of her or not.

Shilo stretched out on his furs with a smile. He would tell Little Bird his decision tomorrow.

Wet and hungry, Deke reined his weary horse in at the edge of Dogwood. The main street was six inches deep in mud from the storm that had passed through.

He fingered the two quarters in his vest pocket. Should he get a bowl of soup to fill his empty stomach, or a shot of red-eye to calm and warm his gut? He was still shook up from his encounter with the young squaw he had intended to rape.

A dark scowl came over his face. He had almost suceeded when that big buck seemed to appear out of nowhere. The Indian had meant to kill him. He'd seen it in his eyes. He knew his bullet had hit the brave, because he saw him go down. He did not know, however, if the bullet was a fatal one. He had better stay away from the Indian village, just in case he hadn't killed the brave.

Deke sighed. The faint light trying to penetrate the grimy window of the saloon beckoned him. Five minutes later he dismounted and looped the reins over the hitching post of the Red Lantern saloon. He stepped up on the mud-stained porch and, ever cautious, peered through the large window before entering the smoke-filled room.

This was a longtime habit of his. He had made too many enemies over the years to walk straight and tall like an honest man would.

When he didn't recognize any of the six men who lined the bar, he pushed open the bat-wing doors and stepped inside. He walked up to the bar and when the bartender came and stood opposite him he laid out his last pieces of money and said, "Whiskey."

He watched the amber liquid gurgle from the bottle neck into the glass. Even as he raised it to his lips, he knew he should have spent the money on something to eat.

"Do you think a man could get a job around here?"

"Doin' what?" the uninterested bartender asked.

"I'm a cowhand. I'd like to get hired on at some ranch or other. I used to work for the Bar FM. I guess you've heard of it."

"Yeah, I know it. I don't remember ever seein' you around here, though."

Deke ignored the remark and asked, "Does Bertha still run the place?"

"Naw. She disappeared some time back. Just up and left without a word to anybody. We heard that the man Bertha was with killed her, then the Indians got him."

"What about the ranch? Is it just sittin' there empty?" he asked, hoping that the man would say yes.

"It was empty for a while. Then this man by the name of Jason something or other showed up and kinda took it over. He's been fixin' the place up."

Deke hid his disappointment and said, "I wonder if he needs some help."

"Could be."

"I think I'll ride out there and ask."

And get some grub for your gut, the bartender sneered to himself.

Lamp light was still burning at the Martin ranch when Deke Cobbs rode his tired horse up to the yard gate. "Hallo the house!" he called and waited for a door to open.

Shortly he saw the silhouette of a man pass behind the window shade of the front room. A door opened and light spilled out onto the porch. "Who's there?" a rough voice demanded as the speaker stepped out of the light.

"The name is Deke Cobbs, sir. They said in town that you might need an extra hand around here. I can see the place is pretty run down."

There was a moment's silence, then, "I take it you know about ranch work."

"I sure do. I know all there is to know about cows."

Deke spotted the other man walking toward him. From the light shining through the kitchen window Deke saw that the fellows scrutinizing his face. Would he question him about the scratches the young squaw had put on his cheek?

Cobbs drew a breath of relief when the man said, "I could use an all-around cowhand. Like you said, the place is pretty run down. All I'm doing now is patching up the place, getting everything put in order. There's not even fifty head of cattle, so they don't need much tending. How are you with a hammer and nails?"

Dobbs couldn't speak for a moment. Was the fellow speaking of the cattle he and Hoss and Bertha had left behind? Finally he pulled his lips into a smile and said, "I'm fair. I know which end of the hammer to strike a nail with."

"That's good. There's going to be a lot of hammering going on around here for a while."

He stepped back from the horse and said, "My name is Saunders, Jason Saunders."

"Glad to know you, Mr. Saunders. My moniker is Deke Cobbs."

"Half the barn blew away in a storm, I'm told," Saunders said, "but there are a couple stalls that are in pretty good condition. Stable your horse, and if you're hungry, come on up to the house and have some venison stew. I don't know what shape the bunkhouse is in, but it's got to be better than the house."

"I'll take a look at it, then come up for some of that stew."

Deke couldn't believe his good luck as he stabled his worn-out horse next to the stallion. Old Bertha and Hoss were dead, and he had a job working on the Bar FM again. Maybe this time he'd rustle the rest of the cattle.

Chapter Seventeen

Flame spent the following day with Jason Saunders again, helping him to clean the ranch house. They had finished the kitchen by afternoon when it began to look as if they were in for another downpour. Flame beat the rain home. She unhitched the work-horses and led them into different stalls. As she gave each animal a measure of oats, she noticed that Stone's stallion wasn't in his usual spot.

"He'd better get home pretty soon or he's going to get caught in the rain," she said to herself as she wondered where he was.

On her way to the house she met the cook coming from behind the cookhouse. He carried an armload of wood for his big black stove.

"Is Stone out with the men?" she asked, smiling at tall, skinny Charlie. "If he and the men don't get home pretty soon they're going to get caught in the rain that's heading our way."

"The men came in about ten minutes ago. I don't know about Stone. He went down to the Indian village a couple hours ago. He and Shilo are probably hunting or fishing. Don't worry about Stone. That pair won't get caught in a storm. They'll hole up in a cave or something."

Along with Little Bird, Flame thought sourly. Everytime she saw Shilo it seemed the girl was with him. She still felt that friendship wasn't all Little Bird was interested in. Her adoration of Stone was easy to see when she looked at him with her soft brown eyes. But what did Stone feel for the pretty little maid? It was hard to tell just what his thoughts were when he looked at her or gently teased her. Flame only knew one thing: He never gave Little Bird the hot, smoldering looks that he sometimes gave his wife.

What did those looks from beneath lowered lids mean? Flame asked herself. What was Stone thinking? Was he remembering the hours spent with the girls at the Red Lantern? Was he picturing her doing the same things to him that they did? She knew he didn't respect those women, so maybe he didn't respect her, either.

But why wouldn't he? Did he know more about her past than he was letting on?

One thing I'm sure of, Flame thought as she

253

walked on to the house, Stone has strong feelings for Little Bird. She could only wait and see where they would lead.

Flame felt sorry for Shilo. There was no doubt how he felt about the maid. Even though he was gruff with her all the time, it was obvious that he loved her. Why didn't he marry her? Was it because he was a chief and she only a lowly orphan girl? Did he think she was beneath him?

Men! she thought as she stepped up on the porch. There was no use trying to figure them out. She reached for the door knob just as the first streak of lightning zig-zagged across the sky. She barely got inside when the rains came.

The rain and the wind beat against the house and Flame ran to the kitchen window and peered out through the yellow grayness toward the Indian village. In the occasional lightning flashes she could see the tossing trees. She hoped that Stone wasn't out in the storm, but at the same time she hoped that he wouldn't spend the night with Shilo . . . or with Little Bird.

As the thunder rolled and the wind whipped the top of the trees and half blinded Stone with rain he raced the stallion toward home. Ordinarily he would have spent the night in Shilo's village. That, however, was before Flame. Was she home, warm and dry, or was she out in this downpour, handling two large draft horses pulling a wagon?

Or—his lips firmed in a grim line as he neared the ranch—was she still with that man Jason Saunders? If so, would she spend the night there? He had the feeling it was going to rain all night.

Hard determination sparked in Stone's eyes. He was dammed if she would spend the night with that . . . that man. If she wasn't home when he got there he would go after her.

As Flame paced from one window to another, darkness descended. She gave up hope that Stone would be coming home tonight. Little Bird would get to enjoy his company. With a bitter look in her eyes she walked down the hall to the kitchen. She felt along the table top, searching for the jar of matches that always sat next to the lamp. Her fingers connected with the jar and she struck one on the floor and lit the lamp just as a heavy thud hit the porch.

Jubilation rushed through Stone when he saw the kitchen light up. She was home! He opened the door and stood dripping water on the floor as he stared at her, his eyes seeming to eat her. Flame looked no less joyful as their eyes met across the table.

"I see you didn't get caught in the rain." Stone gave her a wide smile.

"No, I got home just before it came down. You weren't so lucky, were you?" She gave him a teasing grin.

"We went fishing and forgot the time. Little Bird was the one who noticed that it was going to storm again. We picked up our fish and left the river in one big hurry.

"I thought at first I might beat the storm, but halfway here it caught me." He tugged his wet boots off.

When he began to unbutton his shirt, Flame remarked, "It seems that everytime you and Shilo go somewhere together, Little Bird is with you. Aren't there any young girls her age in the village that she could spend time with?"

"She's awfully shy. It's hard for her to make friends."

It set Flame's teeth on edge to hear Stone defend the Indian girl.

"I've noticed that the village maids are very friendly toward her. One day I heard them invite Little Bird to go swimming with them in the river. She turned them down. Her excuse was that she had already made plans to go fishing with you and Shilo. Stone, does she believe we are married, or does she think that it is all pretense?"

"Of course she thinks we're married." Stone looked surprised at her question. "I haven't told anyone anything different. Why do you ask me that?"

Flame shrugged her shoulders. "Just curious," she answered and went to her room. The door gave a loud snap as she closed it behind her.

Stone stared after her. He didn't quite know what to make of her attitude. He had the feeling that she was peeved at him, but he had no idea why. Of course he knew very little about decent women, what they liked and didn't like.

Stone went to his room and stripped off his drenched clothing. As he climbed into dry ones his stomach growled. He was starved. He hadn't eaten since morning. As he settled a dry Stetson on his head he tried to remember whether his slicker was hanging on the back porch, or whether he had left it in the barn the last time he used it. The lightning and thunder and thunder had ceased, But the rain still poured down. He would get soaked all over again if he didn't find the black slicker on the back porch.

He was surprised and pleased when he walked out of the kitchen and onto the porch. Flame was there ahead of him. He hadn't thought that she would show up to eat with him. He knew he was smiling like an idiot when she handed him his slicker. "Thank you, Flame," he managed to say and shrugged into the rain-repellent garment. "Ready to make a run for it?" He took hold of her arm.

"I guess so." Flame frowned at the rain coming straight down, then almost before she knew what was happening, Stone was rushing her toward the cookhouse. Just as they were ready to step up on the narrow porch, Flame slipped on a patch of mud. Stone lost his grip on her arm and she went down on her knees. Stone had her on her feet again in an instant. "Are you alright?" he asked anxiously, smoothing the hair off her forehead and face. He stared down at her then. What he hadn't meant to do was smear mud all over her face.

"I'm alright," she answered angrily. "If you hadn't made me run so fast, I wouldn't have tripped and fallen."

Stone started to apologize, then burst out laughing instead. His fingers had left streaks of mud all over her face. She looked like a tiger kitten, spitting and hissing.

"I didn't think my falling was that funny," Flame snapped. "I hurt my knees."

"Ah, I'm sorry about that, honey. Do they hurt a lot?"

"No," Flame admitted, somewhat embarrassed for even mentioning it. Her knees were barely scratched. "But I still don't think it was very nice of you to laugh at me."

"Oh, honey," Stone laughed and hugged her shoulders. "It's your face. It's covered with mud. Do you want to go back to the house and wash it?"

Flame stood a minute, then asked. "Do you have a clean kerchief on you?"

"Here." Stone dug a folded bandana from his back pocket and handed it to her. "What are you going to do with it? Cover your face?" he joked.

"No, you fool, I'm going to wash my face with it," she said and marched off toward the horse trough.

Stone caught up with her and took the kerchief from her. "Let me do it. I put it there."

Flame stood quietly with her lids lowered

while Stone gently cleaned her face. She is so beautiful, he thought as the rain pelted down on their heads.

A moment later his arms were around her, straining her body against his. She lifted a startled face to him and he bent his head and covered her partly opened mouth with his.

He had hungered for her lips for so long, he had to remind himself not to ravage them, not to scare her. He gentled the kiss and she began to relax and lean into him. He mentally cursed the heavy slickers between their bodies. He longed to hold her slender length against his body, feel her breasts crushed against his chest. When her arms wound themselves around his shoulders, he groaned his frustration. To hell with the rain, he thought and undid the fastenings of the heavy black garment that kept him from the body he ached for.

His hands were at her throat next, fumbling with the clasp of her slicker. It fell apart just as the loud voices of the men coming from the bunkhouse jarred him out of the fog of desire. Flame heard them also and she jerked herself out of his arms. Hurting as he never had before, Stone sighed, and taking her by the arm, ran with her toward the cookhouse.

They were laughing by the time they entered the long, warm room. Nothing had happened in their sprint from the trough to make them laugh; they laughed out of pure happiness.

When Stone helped Flame out of her slicker, Charlie handed her a clean, rough fustian towel. "Them curls of yours are dripping water on your shoulders. You'd better dry off before your dress is soaked."

Before Flame could attack her wet head with the towel, Stone took it from her. Beginning at the ends of her hair, he gently worked the cloth up to the top of her head. Each strand of hair seemed to have a life of its own as it wound itself around Stone's fingers and clung. "How's that?" he asked huskily when he could no longer bring himself to touch her hair without pulling her into his arms again.

"It's fine, Stone." Her voice was soft. "Thank you."

The cowhands were coming in then, sounding like a herd of buffalo. When they had all sat down, Stone and Flame took their usual seats at the end of the long table. Neither tasted what they put into their mouths. It they were questioned later what the cook had provided for supper, neither one would have been able to say what was put before them. They were only aware of each other and a feeling of excitement. Was something going to happen between them tonight? they were asking themselves.

Stone couldn't wait and Flame was uneasy. Was she a virgin, or had she known a man, or men, in the bibical sense? All she knew for sure was that Stone would make love to her tonight. She would know then whether or not she was pure.

When they found themselves sitting alone at

the table, they gave the cook a sheepish grin and stood up. Neither had noticed the men leaving. Wordlessly, Stone helped Flame into her slicker, then pulled on his own.

It was still raining as they made a rush to the house. They paused on the porch long enough to tug off their muddy boots before entering the house.

Inside the kitchen Stone felt along the table top until he found the jar of matches that was always kept beside the kerosene lamp. He scraped the sulphur end of the wooden stick across his thumb nail. When a small flame flared up, he lifted the lamp chimney and held the match to the wick.

Then, taking Flame by the hand, he led her down the hall to his room. He placed the lamp on his bedside table and turned Flame to face him. He slid her arms though the slicker's arms, and pulling it off her shoulders, he tossed it on the floor. His own wet garment soon followed and then she was in his arms.

Stone bent his head and planted small kisses all over her face. Flame tried to stop him when he began to unbutton her shirt. "Let me," he whispered.

When she released his wrist he slipped a hand down inside her camisole and curled his fingers around a firm breast. He gently massaged the silky mound until her nipple was like a hard little nub.

A smoldering heat enveloped Stone when

Flame moaned and whispered his name, and he soon had her shirt lying on the floor with only the camisole covering the richness he'd been dying to fill his mouth with, to taste, to savor.

He had to remind himself to go slow as he pulled the single garment over her head. She was not one of the Red Lantern's girls, who were used to having their clothes practically ripped off them.

He stood and stared at the perfection of Flame's breasts until she grew shy and brought up her hands to cover them.

"No," he whispered huskily, and taking her by the wrists, he held her hands down by her sides. As she stood helpless, he went down on his knees, and with a soft moan, he opened his mouth and sucked a hard nipple inside it.

"Oh dear," she whispered as he suckled her, his fingers working the nipple on the other breast. I'm going to faint, she thought, even as she shifted his head to the other breast.

Stone had loosened his hold on her wrists and she lifted her hands to hang onto his shoulders as sensations she had never known before rocked through her. When Stone left her breasts and stood up to remove his clothes, Flame grabbed his arm. "Where are you going?" she asked in a little girl's disappointed voice.

Stone chuckled softly and gave her a fast kiss. "I'm not going anywhere, honey. We're not finished yet. I still have to send you to heaven."

Flame wondered how he could possibly lift her to a higher bliss than he had already.

With his clothes now cluttered with Flames all over the floor, Stone knelt again in front of her. He placed a hand on either side of her waist, then holding her steady, he lowered his dark head to her breasts and resumed where he had left off.

Flame moaned low in her throat and whispered his name over and over as he swirled his tongue around her nipple, gently nibbling on it. The love noises she was making inflamed Stone. He slid his hands from her waist down to her hips. Holding them fast he began trailing kisses down her flat stomach. When he came to the vee of her thighs and the soft curls there, Flame stiffened.

Stone went no further. He reminded himself again to go slow with her. He rose and took her hand, bringing it down to his throbbing manhood. When she only rested her hand on his throbbing flesh, he curled her fingers around his hardness.

She gasped at its size. She gasped again when he guided her hand and his sex down to the patch of soft curls between her thighs. With his other hand he parted the thick mat until he found the core of her hidden there. He spread her legs, and drawing her close, urged her to stroke his maleness there.

A storm of need began to build inside Flame as the long, hard length rubbed against the little nub of her womanhood. She freed her hand from Stone so that she could hold on to him to keep from falling as he continued to massage her with his maleness.

When she began to whimper and dig her nails into his shoulder, he knew that she was ready for him. He picked her up and carried her to the bed.

When he laid her down she looked at him with eyes that were heavy with desire. Stone leaned over and kissed her forehead, then lay beside her. As she looked up at him, heavy-lidded, he gently spread her legs apart then climbed between them.

He hung over her a moment, then taking hold of her legs he drew them up around his waist. When he bent and drew a breast into his mouth, Flame sighed and bucked her hips at him. His pulse began to hammer. She was ready, ripe for him. At last he was going to get the wish that had haunted him day and night. He raised his upper body, and resting on his elbows, started a slow rhythmic bucking of his hips.

But that wasn't enough for Flame. She wanted to feel his entire length inside her, pushing and probing. She let him know this by grasping his narrow buttocks and pulling him closer to her.

In seconds she got her wish. Stone forgot

that she might be a virgin. He thrust as far as he could go inside her and made the bed springs squeak and the headboard slam against the wall as over and over he drove inside her.

Flame reached a climax twice and still Stone plunged in and out of her. He had wanted her for so long, he was going to make it last as long as he could.

His body shimmered with sweat as he worked over Flame. The time came then when he could no longer control his body's desire. He gave one last pump of his hips and his seed spilled inside Flame.

He groaned his elation as his wet head fell to rest between Flame's chin and shoulder. For a full minute his maleness quivered and jerked as he fought to get his breath. He told himself that he was half afraid to ever make love to Flame again. He had never given so much to any woman. His lips twisted wryly. She could very well be the death of him.

He knew he would take that chance any time he could.

Besides learning tonight that Flame was a virgin, he had also learned that a "good" woman could be as hot as any loose woman. His lips spread in a wide smile. He was really going to enjoy teaching her how good it could be between a man and a woman. As he rolled off Flame his lips twiched wryly. He had a feeling she might teach him a few things, also.

Stone turned over on his side and drew

Flame against him. He would rest awhile, then make love to her again. Right now he was like a wrung-out dishrag.

One minute later he had fallen into an exhausted sleep, his hand cupping one of Flame's breasts.

Chapter Eighteen

Rainee stretched and yawned as she jumped out of bed. Sometime during the night the storm had moved off and the rain had ceased to fall. Everything was washed clean and shone like a new copper penny.

A perfect day for an outing, she thought, pulling open the drapes in her small parlor. She had lived in the back of her shop ever since she'd returned to Dogwood where she had been born and grew up.

In her small kitchen she took out a loaf of bread, a crock of butter and one of strawberry jam. When she had wrapped and laid them in a reed basket, a jar she added of freshly brewed coffee and half an apple pie she had baked yesterday. Spreading a clean white towel over the food, she picked a hat from the supply in her shop and left the little store. As she saddled her mare she muttered, "Well, Jason Saunders, as you call yourself now, you and I have a lot of catching up to do." Nineteen years of it to be exact.

The day after Rudy Martin had married Bertha Conklin, Rainee had left Dogwood and crossed the Colorado border into Kansas. There was no way in the world she would live in the same area with Rudy and Bertha, see their baby, watch it grow into adulthood. Nor could she stand the looks of pity she would receive from her friends.

When Rainee rode into the small cow town where her older sister and brother-in-law owned a saloon, she was heartily welcomed by her sister Milly, and brother-in-law Johnny Thorton. Her sister was a matter-of-fact woman and wasted no words of pity. She gave Rainee a kiss and said, "We sure can use your help around here." When Johnny gave her a hug that made her grunt, she was more aware of their compassion than if a string of words had been said. She slid out of her slicker and walked over to the pot-bellied stove that warmed the saloon. In the winter it was necessary to have two such stoves. One at each end of the long room.

Milly motioned to a sturdy Mexican woman.

"Rainee," she said, "this is Rosa. The best cook in all of Kansas."

Rainee smiled and held out her hand to the cook. "If Milly says it, it must be true."

Rosa gave a jolly laugh. "People agree with Milly because they are afraid of her."

"Is she still bullying people? She made life miserable for me when we were growing up."

"Don't believe her, Rosa. I was the one who always got yelled at because Rainee was so little and would never do anything wrong." It was easy to see how fond the sisters were of each other by the way they laughed and hugged each other. Milly pushed Rainee away then, saying, "Rosa, would you please bring us a cup of coffee to hold us until supper-time?"

Milly motioned Rainee to a table in a corner of the room. "We'll have a little time to talk before the men come drifting in. Once they get here, carrying on like a braying herd of jack-asses, there will be no chance for a private word. I only got your letter yesterday, and it didn't tell me much. I can't believe that Rudy Martin preferred that whore to you."

"He didn't," Rainee sighed. "Bertha came up expecting and named him the father. I guess he thought there was a chance that he was."

"But the baby could belong to a dozen differ-ent men, couldn't it? She's laid with half the men in the area."

"The bitch was slick." Rainee gave a short,

bitter laugh. "I learned later that three months earlier she had stopped seeing other men. The slut was out to get Rudy."

Milly shook her head. "It isn't Rudy she's interested in. She likes all men. Just one man would never satisfy her. It's his ranch she has her beady little eyes on. And, of course, a husband to support her."

"It's all my fault," Rainee said, on the point of tears. "If I had just gone to bed with Rudy, he never would have gone near that whore."

"You just stop such talk." Milly gave her sister an angry look. "It seems to me that he could have kept his britches buttoned up for a while if he cared for you. Johnny did for me . . . six months."

"Don't you believe that." Johnny ambled over to their table and sat down. He picked up Milly's hand and kissed the knuckles. "Every time this one got me all worked up, I rode over to ole Bertha's, too."

Milly's eyes shot fire, and Johnny barely dodged the slap she aimed at him. "Aw, come on, honey," he laughed, holding his hands in front of his face. "You know damn well I was true to you."

The subject was dropped before Milly could give him a stinging retort. Three men had come through the bat-wing doors, loud laughter accompanying them. Johnny stood up, gave Rainee's shoulder a squeeze, then went to wait on his new customers.

Milly pushed away from the table. "Let's slip

into the kitchen and have our supper before you meet the men. There will be a bunch more coming in from other ranches. It will be best to meet them all at once. That way none of them will be able to pin you down to accept his marriage proposal."

"You're joking, of course." Rainee looked at her sister, not quite sure whether Milly was serious.

Milly gave her a cheeky grin. "Maybe yes, maybe no. Come on, let's go eat. Rosa made a beef roast."

"Look, Milly, I'm not interested in being romanced." Rainee gripped Milly's arm as they went through the kitchen door. "Promise me that you won't try to set me up with someone. The last thing I want to do is become involved with a man again."

"I figured as much. I just wanted to make sure. But be warned. You're a pretty woman, Sis, and since they won't know that you're getting over a broken heart, they will try to court you. Most of them are nice men, so go easy on them.

"I know you don't believe it, but some day you'll get over Rudy and change your mind about romance. If you've treated the men harshly in the past they might not forget it."

"I don't think that's apt to happen, Milly," Rainee said and took a seat at the table.

Rosa's beef roast was delicious and Rainee had two helpings of everything before her appetite was appeased.

It was time to go into the bar room then and Rainee dreaded it. She had dreaded it for the past half hour as the men began to come in. Their laughing and talking, joking and razzing each other brought back memories of the Red Lantern back home. She would never again see the place or the people who inhabited it.

With her lids lowered, she followed Milly into the big room. The raucous sounds there suddenly died away. She felt the hot stare of ten different men. She didn't feel insulted though. She knew that they didn't mean to insult her. They could spot a decent woman half a mile away and would treat her with respect.

"Rainee will be working here, starting tomorrow," Milly said. "I know you fellows won't give her a hard time." She narrowed threatening eyes at the men. "Will you?"

"Do you have to ask that, Milly?" a tall cowboy said, half insulted.

"I just wanted to make sure. Also, I wanted to ask you fellows to keep an eye out for any strangers that might come along and give her a hard time."

"Don't worry about it. We'll look out for her," a half dozen voices said.

Milly next introduced the saloon women, who served the drinks. Rainee learned later that they weren't above taking a favorite customer into their rooms, either.

Rainee also met the three prostitutes who

shared a house several yards behind the saloon. They eagerly responded to Rainee's friendly acceptance of them. In the weeks that followed they turned out to be better watch-dogs than the men when it came to looking after Rainee. She was the young daughter they had never had, or the sister they had left behind years ago.

Consequently, Rainee had many men friends but no lovers.

Then one night Aaron Devlow came through the bat-wing doors. She only glanced at him. He was average looking, not a man who would draw a second look from a woman.

When he walked toward the bar Milly whis-pered, "That is Aaron Devlow. I want you to meet him. He's about the only man around here I'd trust to court you."

Rainee lifted an amused eyebrow at her sis-ter. "Is he a preacher?"

"No, Miss Smarty, he's not a preacher. He's just a decent honorable man."

"He's not a youngster." Rainee watched the slim, tall man amble over to the bar. "How come he's not married? Don't the women around here like him?"

"I didn't say that the women don't like him. They like him fine. And before you ask, Aaron likes women. He takes them to dances, church socials." Milly grinned. "Of course, there's an occasional visit to the girls out back."

Rainee shrugged, not interested in Aaron Devlow's love life in the least.

Milly shoved away from the table. "I'm going to bring him over to meet you."

"I wish you wouldn't, Milly," Rainee protested, but her sister was already halfway across the room.

This time Rainee studied Aaron Devlow as Milly, her arm looped in his, led him across the room toward her. She saw a man in his early forties, of medium height and stocky build. Dust covered him from the crown of his hat to the toes of his boots. Even his eyebrows and beard stubble were gray with it. Weariness was in his red-rimmed eyes. It was plain he had been on a long cattle drive.

When they reached the table and Milly said, "Aaron, meet my sister, Rainee," a shy smile lit up his weather-beaten face. She returned his smile and offered her hand. His big, callused palm engulfed her slender fingers but held them ever so gently.

"I'm real pleased to meet you, Rainee," he said, his voice deep. "Will you be staying with us long?" he asked as he sat down across from her.

Rainee looked thoughtfully into her glass of sarsaparilla for a moment. Then, lifting her gaze to Aaron, she said, "I think I'll be living here for a long time. I like the country and I have a good job. I love my boss."

A hint of a frown flitted across Aaron's forehead. "You're lucky," he forced himself to say lightly. "Very few people like their jobs, much less love their bosses."

"I am lucky," Rainee agreed. "I work here in the saloon with people who really treat me well. And my bosses are Johnny and Milly."

There was relief in Aaron's laughter when he said, "You couldn't find two better bosses if you looked all over Kansas."

Aaron had a drink with Rainee and Milly, then announced that he must be getting back to the ranch.

"Rainee," he said as he rose to his feet, "I've enjoyed talking to you. I hope I can do it again."

"So do I, Aaron. Do you come here often?"

He looked at Milly and grinned. "Your sister can tell you that I'm a regular customer."

"Good, I'll see you then." Rainee gave him a warm smile.

When Aaron left them Rainee said, "I think he's one of the nicest men I've ever met."

"I told you that he's one-of-a-knid. Do you think you'd step out with him if he asked you?"

Rainee thought to herself that Aaron Devlow was not the sort of man who would break a woman's heart, so she answered, "I don't know. I might." There would be no racing of pulses, of course, no weakening of the loins when he kissed her, but she could be sure that he would be true to her, always be there for her.

By the time Rainee arrived at Rudy's ranch, her mind had traveled on to when she and Aaron had married. She'd had twelve years of contentment. She had always felt guilty that she couldn't love Aaron the way he loved her.

But she'd had a deep respect and fondness for him. When he'd had a sudden heart attack and died she'd mourned his loss for a very long time. She still missed him sometimes.

Aaron slipped from her mind when she topped the small knoll and looked down on Rudy's ranch buildings.

Chapter Nineteen

Rudy had been up since the break of dawn. He'd started work so early, he could hardly see to overlap the new shingles on the house roof. By the time the sun was creeping over the eastern horizon, the roof was finished. He sent the new hired man into town for additional supplies. Then he climbed down the ladder, and after washing his face and hands at the water trough, he entered the kitchen. In the semigloom he made a fire in the old cookstove and put on a pot of coffee. He wouldn't bother to fix breakfast for himself.

His mind was on Flame as he waited for the coffee to brew. His eyes grew grim as he thought of the years he had lost with her. He vowed silently to make them up to her. He didn't think it would be wise right now to blurt out that he was her father. She was trying to remember who she was and it might be disturbing to her to find out everything at once. After all, no one knew what had caused her amnesia. It might have been a terrible thing that had happened to her.

As Rudy drank his coffee, he decided that his first plan was the the best. Let them get to know each other, to like each other. He already loved Flame, but he wanted her to grow to love him all on her own, not just because he was her father.

Rudy had patched one large hole on the barn roof, then moved to another one. When he finished that one, he would undertake the big job. Rebuilding the whole eastern side of the barn. A wind storm must have blown it off, landing it a half-mile away.

He stood looking at the wreckage, wondering where to start, when he saw a rider top the rise beyond the ranch house. Squinting against the sun, he smiled broadly when he recognized Rainee.

He was so happy and surprised to see her, he could barely answer her cheery, "Good morning."

"Maybe I shouldn't have come." Rainee pulled the mare in. "You're very busy."

"Nonsense." He lifted his arms to help her out of the saddle. "Those holes have been there a long time. They'll wait."

"It must hurt you to see the place so run down."

"It does," Rudy answered after a long sigh. "But I'll bring it back to what it used to be."

They talked as they walked toward the house, Rudy carrying the basket. "I never forgot the place, the blood and sweat I put into it."

Rainee wondered if he had forgotten the girl whose heart he had broken. She kept the thought to herself. Neither did she ask whether he and Bertha had ever been divorced, whether he remarried.

"Shall we sit here?" Rudy asked when he and Rainee reached the porch. "It's still pretty bad inside. Flame was over yesterday helping me clean the place up, but there's a lot to do when she comes back today."

"She's an awfully nice girl, isn't she?"

"She's the nicest. It's a shame about her memory."

There was a short pause, then Rainee said quietly, "Is she your daughter, Rudy?"

"What?" Rudy gave her a startled look.

"You heard me. She is, isn't she?"

Rudy looked out over the weed-filled yard a moment, then looked at Rainee. "How did you know?"

"It's that tiny squint you both have in the corners of your eyes when you smile."

"I wonder if anyone else has noticed it. I don't want anyone to know until Flame regains her memory."

"I doubt if anyone has noticed it. Other people don't remember your past the way I do."

Neither spoke for a minute, then Rudy asked gently, "Has life been kind to you, Rainee? Did you ever marry?"

Rainee nodded. "I was married for twelve years. Aaron Devlow was a good man. I couldn't ask for a better husband. He died from a heart attack. Sadly, we weren't blessed with any children."

"How did you become a dressmaker? And a really good one, according to Flame."

Rainee gave him a crooked grin. "You're going to laugh at this, but it was truly the way I got started. With so much time on my hands, I started making dresses for the prostitutes in town. They wanted showy dresses with bright colors and lots of ruffles. The stores didn't have such creations." Rainee paused to give a short, little laugh. "When the 'ladies' in town saw the beautiful dresses I sewed for the red-light girls, they wanted me to make them the same. But they had a stipulation that I didn't like and wouldn't agree to. I wasn't to sew for the prostitutes anymore. They didn't like the idea of those lowly women being as well-dressed as they."

"So what did you do?"

"I stuck by my guns. I didn't need to work. Aaron was making a comfortable living for us. Then Christmas time rolled around and the banker's wife and her cronies wanted new outfits. I don't have to tell you how busy I was for a while." Rainee grinned.

"So when you returned here you were ready to set up shop?" When Rainee nodded, Rudy asked, "Where were you all time, Rainee? I asked around but nobody seemed to know. Or at least that's what they said."

"I was in Kansas with Millie and Johnny."

"How are those two? Does Milly still have her sharp tongue?"

"I'm afraid so. She and Johnny own a saloon, and every man who comes into the place is afraid of her." Rainee laughed.

"I guess she's not very fond of me?" Rudy asked with a raised eyebrow.

Rainee gave a shake of her head. "I would say that you are just about her least favorite person. She claims that since Johnny was faithful to her for six months before they married you could have done the same thing for me."

Rudy looked away from Rainee. "Do you think I haven't berated myself a hundred times for giving in to my bodily appetite? How much suffering it would have saved us if I had have used a little control. I paid dearly for my weakness, living with Bertha until I couldn't stand it any longer."

If Rudy expected forgiveness from Rainee, he didn't receive it. He had yet to earn that. Instead, she asked, "Did you remarry?"

"No, I'd lost the girl I loved. I never found another woman who could make me forget her, forget you. I would have gone looking for you if I'd had the first idea where to begin. Instead, I burred myself up on that mountain, living like a hermit.

"I'd be up there still if I hadn't heard that Flame and her mother had disappeared." He shook his head regretfully.

"But she's here now. Why do you look so sad?"

"She has no memory of me, Rainee. Of me, or anything else."

Rainee laid a sympathetic hand on Rudy's arm. "She'll remember. She just needs a little time. One of these days some little thing will trigger her mind and she'll remember everything."

"I certainly hope so. That's why I'm gonna work my butt off, getting the place in shape, so she'll have a decent home when does remember."

"But isn't she married to Stone Falcon? That's the talk, anyhow."

"I know, and she claims that she is." Rudy stared off at the distant river. "But somehow I don't believe she's married."

Rainee looked at Rudy in amusement. "That's because you don't want her to be. You want her to still be your little girl."

"You're probably right." Rudy laughed too. "I've been working since dawn. Do you have something good to eat in that basket?"

"I sure do. I thought we could have a breakfast picnic. And I brought half an apple pie."

"Apple pie, my favorite." Rudy smacked his lips. "My favorite."

"Yes, I remember," Rainee said quietly. "Should we go down to the river and eat?"

Rudy picked up the basket with one hand and assisted Rainee to her feet with the other. "That's a good idea. It will be cooler down there."

As they walked down the long incline to the water Rudy wondered if Rainee remembered the times they had spread a blanket beside the river and eaten whatever she had packed in this same basket.

As he took the folded blanket out of the basket and spread it on the river bank he thought to himself that nothing had changed much. The willows were quite large now, their branches hanging out over the water. While Rainee laid out the bread and jam and pie, he walked over to the largest tree there and stood looking at it.

He smiled when he saw, high up on the trunk, the shape of a heart carved in its bark. He stretched an arm up until he could run his finger tips over the initials inside the heart: R M & R C. The letters had widened over the years, almost smoothed away in some spots.

He looked over his shoulder and saw Rainee watching him. "Do you remember the day I carved these words?"

"Yes, I do. Do you?"

Rudy turned from the tree and walked toward her. "It was on the day that I kissed you for the first time." He sat down on the corner of the blanket. "I could never forget that." He grinned up at her. "It curled my toes."

Rainee chuckled softly and handed him a sandwich. "You did seem to enjoy it."

"Enjoy is hardly the word to describe it. I wanted you so badly it hurt like hell."

He bit into the sandwich, chewed a minute, then said as if to himself, "If I had stayed away from you some, not seen you every night, I'm sure I wouldn't have gone looking for Bertha. You always got me so heated up, I had to cool off somewhere."

Rainee made no response for a minute. When she did speak there was a slight sneer in her voice. "I expect she kept you cooled off all the time after you were married."

"Hah!" Rudy snorted. "You can believe this or not, but I never found much pleasure with her. You were the only girl for me."

In the silence that descended between them Rudy realized that he had better keep some distance between him and Rainee, not see her too often. A wild desire for her, like in the old times, was building inside him, as strong now as it had been then.

They finished their breakfast in silence, each with his own thoughts of days gone past. Then leaning back on their elbows, they talked aimlessly, prolonging their time together.

"Oh dear," Rainee exclaimed when she noticed how high the sun had climbed. "The ladies will be wondering why I'm late opening shop today," she said, gathering up the plates and cups and tossing them into the basket.

"They'll appreciate you more if they have to wait," Rudy said, folding up the blanket they had sat on.

They were halfway up the incline to the house when they met a man coming toward them.

"Hello, Deke," Rudy said when the three met. "Did you get everything in town?"

"Yeah. Now I'm going to clean out the bunkhouse. It needs a lot of work."

All the while Deke talked, his attention was on Rainee. Rudy noted it and didn't like it. He didn't say anything about it, though. All he said was "Rainee, meet Deke Cobbs. I've hired him to give me a hand getting the place back in shape."

Rainee nodded politely, but pretended not to see the hand Deke held out to her. He blushed a furious red at the slight.

"Deke, our neighbor Flame Falcon will be coming over today to help with the cleaning," Rudy went on. "She is a lovely person, but she recently had an accident that caused her to lose her memory, so watch your step around her." Turning back toward Rainee, he missed the look of astonishment on Deke's face.

When Rainee and Rudy reached the spot where her horse was staked out in a patch of grass, they heard catbirds calling in the willows. It was a soft sound and they smiled at each other, remembering the many times they had heard the calls when saying goodbye. Rudy saddled the mare and tied the basket on the cantle. Taking Rainee's arm to help her into the saddle, he asked softly, "When will I see you again?"

Rainee looked away from the eyes that were adoring her. "I don't know, I have a business to run. Maybe some Sunday I'll ride out."

"What if I ride into town and pick you up this coming Sunday? I'll hire a buggy from the livery and we'll go for a ride."

Rainee looked away from him. Did she want to pick up where they had left off so long ago? He had broken her heart once. Would he do it again? She didn't think that he would, but she hadn't thought that years ago, either.

She looked back at him. "Maybe after a while, Rudy. We're not youngsters anymore."

"I know what you're thinking, Rainee." Rudy boosted her into the saddle. "But like you say, we're not youngsters anymore. I'm no longer a hot-blooded twenty-year-old."

"Aren't you, Rudy?" Rainee grinned and gave a significant look at the bulge in his pants.

For the first time since he was a youngster, Rudy blushed. Rainee's laughter rang out as she nudged the mare into a gallop.

Chapter Twenty

Stone awakened late after a night of lovemaking such as he had never experienced before. He reached for Flame, wondering what time it was. The space beside him was empty. His body went rigid as he listened for her movements in the room. All was quiet. After a moment he sat up and looked for her clothes which had been strewn around the floor last night. They were gone.

Stone slid out of bed and hurried into his clothes, which were still lying in a pile on the floor. He was stuffing his wrinkled shirt tail into his pants when he stepped out onto the porch.

A shuddering sigh of relief rushed through

him when he saw Flame talking to his cook, Charlie. He hadn't realized it, but subconsciously he had feared that she had left him. He didn't know why he feared that. Maybe it was because he was ashamed of making love to her despite the doctor's warning to go slow with Flame.

Uncertainty was on his face when he walked up to her and touched her arm. When she looked up at him, he asked gently, "How are you this morning?"

From the concern in his voice Flame knew why he was inquiring about her health.

"Did I hurt you last night?" he asked in a low voice.

She smiled at him and shook her head.

"You didn't," she gave him a shy smile. "I feel fine," she added, wishing that Charlie would go away. She felt sure that after last night, Stone would ask her to make their sham marriage the real thing.

At last Charlie said that he'd better get into the cookhouse and start making lunch. It was already eleven o'clock. Flame was on tenterhooks as Stone took a towel and a bar of soap from the bench in front of the cookhouse and struck out for the river. He was going to bathe away the aftermath of their passion. She had done the same thing this morning before he got up.

She walked back to the house and sat down on the top step and waited for Stone's return. As she sat, planning her and Stone's life together, she saw him coming up from the river. His clothes clung to his damp body, outlining his broad shoulders and muscular arms. The sun shone on the beads of water in his black hair. Was there ever a man as handsome as Stone Falcon? she asked herself.

"Let's go eat," Stone lifted his hand to assist her down the steps.

Flame was disappointed that Stone didn't bring up their marriage right away as they walked to the cookhouse. She had imagined he would be as impatient as she to set their wedding date. However, although he was more attentive to her than ever, keeping a protective hand on her arm as they moved along, he didn't so much as hint about a wedding between them.

Flame and Stone were sitting at the table, making plans for a ride into town. Flame wanted to purchase new curtains for the kitchen and to order drapes for the dining room from the mercantile catalog when Shilo and Little Bird entered the cookhouse.

As usual, the Indian girl was all sunshine and smiles. Doesn't she ever have gloomy times like normal people? Flame groused to herself, then felt ashamed of her thought. She was only jealous of the way Stone was smiling at the girl. And as usual he and Little Bird began a teasing banter that excluded her and Shilo. Shilo's dark brow said that he didn't like it any more than she did.

Flame couldn't believe it when the girl

exclaimed joyfully, "I have a wonderful idea. What if we go hunting mushrooms? They always come up in the spring after a heavy rain."

Flame looked at Stone, then at Shilo. Shilo looked darker than ever, but Stone beamed like it was the best idea he'd ever heard. What had happened to the plans they were making only minutes ago? When she saw that he was about to agree to mushroom-hunting she wiped her mouth on her napkin, tossed it beside her plate, and stood up, the chair legs making a scraping sound from the force she used.

"I have already made other plans," she said coolly. "I promised Rudy I would help him at his ranch."

"But, Flame—" Stone stood up too—"I thought we were going to—"

"So did I," Flame snapped and slammed the screen door behind her.

"Flame sounds angry," Little Bird said. "Do you think she is, Stone?"

"I don't know, Little Bird."

"The hell you don't," Shilo growled. "Look, the reason we came by was to invite you and Flame to our wedding," he blurted out. "I want you to stand up with me."

"Wedding?" Stone repeated, dump founded.

"Little Bird and I are going to be married," Shilo said, not quite meeting his friend's eye. "My people have been urging me to take a wife for some time."

"Why, you son of a gun," Stone exclaimed. "Wait till I tell Flame."

With that he bolted out the door after his wife, leaving Shilo glaring at Little Bird.

"What did I do?" Little Bird demanded.

"What do you usually do whenever Stone is around? You make a damn fool of yourself."

The maid's eyes pooled with tears. He saw the tears slipping down her cheeks and put his arm around her waist. "I didn't mean to speak so harshly to you, but Flame gets her feelings hurt when you and Stone carry on so."

"What about you, Shilo? Do you care that we fun with each other?"

"No," Shilo grunted. "You are *my* woman now. Besides, I know that Stone loves Flame so much he has nothing left over for any other woman." He looked down at Little Bird's lovely face. "I hope you understand that."

Stone arrived at the stables slightly out of breath from his short sprint to catch up with Flame. He was seconds too late. She had already kicked her mare into a full gallop. Now what has set her off? he wondered, kicking out at a rock. One minute she was full of plans about what they would do today, then she was like a bitter wind blowing down from the mountains.

"Women," he snorted. There was no understanding them. Last night when they made love, she had freely given of herself, giving him a pleasure such as he had never had before. And now, a few hours later, she was treating him like a stranger, a man not worthy her attention.

When Stone saw Flame head the mare in the direction of the old ranch, he swore under his breath. She would spend the whole afternoon with that Jason fellow. He wondered what it was about the older man that drew her to him. He couldn't believe that she had romantic feelings for the man, despite his good looks.

But Flame was the type of young woman who would seek more than good looks in a man. The more he thought about it, the more he believed that the man was a father figure to Flame. Stone was whistling as he saddled his stallion. He would ride over to the old run-down ranch and help Saunders and Flame do some patching of the weathered buildings.

When Flame arrived at the ranch, Deke Cobbs was walking from the barn, a small keg of nails in his arms. Though he had known Flame was coming, he still stopped short when he saw her. He had almost forgotten just how beautiful she was, how strongly he had wanted her. He knew a moment of thanksgiving when he remembered Rudy Martin's words: she had no recollection of the past. He was being given another chance. This time he wouldn't mess it up. He would not force himself on her. He would treat her as a gentleman would do.

He took off his hat and smoothed down his hair and flashed his white teeth in a smile as she rode up to the barn. She gave him a curious smile, as if she was trying to place him. As she swung out of the saddle, she asked coolly, "Is Jason around?"

"Yes, he's working on the bunkhouse roof. It leaks like a sieve. I'll go call him down."

"Don't bother. I'll climb up to him. I rode over here to give him a hand."

"Yes, he told me you were coming. I'll turn your mare loose in the corral."

"Thank you," Flame said and began to climb.

"My name is Deke Cobbs." The information came hesitantly.

Flame fought the urge to ignore him. She'd felt an instant dislike of the man. But when she neared the top of the ladder she muttered, "My name is . . . Flame."

Some of the stiffness went out of Cobb's shoulders. Evidently she hadn't recognized him. However, he wished she didn't act so cool toward him. It was almost the same as when he was living with her and ole Bertha. He'd have to go slow and easy with her if he was to gain her confidence.

"Hello, Jason," Flame said as she stepped up on the roof. "How are you this fine sunny day?"

"I'm just fine, honey." Affection for her shone in his eyes. "How are you?" Rudy laid his hammer down.

"There's only one way a person could feel on such a perfect day."

Rudy didn't like Flame's answer. She hadn't really given him an answer, come to that. And he didn't like that look of pain far back in her eyes. All was not well with his daughter. Who was making her wear that look? He'd find out eventually, and when he did, God help the man. She didn't know it, but she had a caring man behind her now. A man who would not let her be harmed if he could help it.

"How can I help?" Flame hunkered down beside her father.

"You can hand me the shingles. Have you had lunch?"

"Yes. What about you?"

Rudy shook his head as he laid the piece of thin wood on the roof. "Deke and I will eat once I finish up here."

"Who is this Deke? Is he a friend of yours?"

"Naw. I just met him last night. He's helping me put the place in order." He looked up at Flame. "Says he knows all there is to know about cows."

A flash of reminiscence came into Flame's eyes. Although brief, it was so powerful it left her weak.

"What's wrong, honey?" Jason asked when he saw how white her face had become.

"I'm fine," she lied cheerfully. "It must be the way the sun is striking my face."

"Maybe," Rudy agreed half-heartedly. "Should I have Deke pour you a cup of coffee?"

Flame answered, "No!" so swiftly and loudly, Rudy gave her a curious look. Why didn't she like Deke? he wondered.

Was he a part of her past? A part she couldn't remember? He decided he would keep an eye on Cobbs. He didn't much like the man anyway. He didn't quite meet a man's eyes when he talked to him.

"Where's your husband today, honey?" he asked as Flame handed him another shingle. "I hope he doesn't mind that you're spending so much time over here."

"Oh no, he's off with his friend Shilo . . . and Little Bird."

"Little Bird?"

"A pretty little Indian maid who seems to have a crush on Stone." Flame tried to hide the bitterness in her voice but didn't suceed.

Rudy looked at her, a gentle humor in his eyes. His daughter was jealous of the Indian maid. "What is the relationship between them? Doesn't she realize that he already has a wife?"

"She doesn't care, as long as she can be around Stone. You see, he was the one who saved her from her white captors."

"She's probably very grateful to him. He saved her from a terrible life . . . a short one."

"I can understand that, but you should see the way she and Stone carry on when they're together. Stone never jokes or tease me the way he does her."

"He probably looks on her as a young sister. Believe me, honey, his real interest lies with you."

"He'd better start showing it then, or I'll move in here with you."

How very much he would like that, Rudy thought, but even if she did move in with him in a moment of anger, it would never last. She loved her husband and she should stay with him. He'd like to get hold of that Little Bird and tell her to stay away from Stone. Better yet, he'd like to have a strong talk with his son-in-law. But as far as Stone knew, Jason Saunders was nothing but a stranger to him.

His life was becoming awfully complicated, he thought as he hammered a nail into the last shingle that finished the roof. He shouldered the sweat from his face and looked down at the ground. His eyes hardened when he saw Deke sitting on the porch, lounging against a post.

"Hey, Cobbs," he called down, "make me a bite of lunch. We're about finished up here."

It was plain by the scowl that came over Cobbs' face that he wasn't pleased at the order. Flame, the female, should cook the noon meal. But one look at Rudy's stern face and cold eyes had him jumping to his feet. He must go along with everything for the time being, no matter how it griped him. This time he was going to play it different with Flame. He was going to be the gentleman all the way.

By the time Rudy washed up at the water trough, Deke had lunch ready. He had fried some potatoes, which were still half raw, and heated a can of beans. Flame and Rudy looked at each other with raised eyebrows, but neither said what they were thinking. Deke Cobbs wasn't much of a cook.

Flame was thinking of the much more appetizing lunch Charlie had prepared when she glanced through the window and saw Stone

"Thank you. I can use all the help I can get. The whole inside is in terrible shape. I hired Deke, over there, to give me a hand." He looked across the table to his new hired hand. "We were going to get started on one of the rooms as soon as we finished eating."

Deke, meet Flame's husband, Stone Falcon."

Neither man extended his hand. Instead, they measured each other with their eyes. What Stone saw was a man of medium height, not bad-looking in a rough sort of way. A womanizer if ever he'd seen one. Did Cobbs live at the ranch? he wondered, with a slight frown.

Deke looked at Flame's big husband and was quick to recognize a formidable and dangerous foe. He would make sure he didn't look at Flame in the man's presence.

"Well, shall we get to it?" Rudy rose from the table. "I think we'll tackle my bedroom first. It will take the rest of the day to shovel out the first layer of dirt."

Stone put his fingers around Flame's wrist, keeping her at the table. "We'll be along in just a minute. I want to tell Flame something."

What was he going to tell her? Flame's heart began to pump in her chest. Was he going to say he no longer wanted to pretend that they were married? That he wanted them to live apart? Had she disappointed him last night? Probably that was it. After all, it had been her first time, and she wasn't what he was used to.

All the fears that were racing through her

mind came to a stunned halt when Stone said, "Shilo and Little Bird are getting married."

Flame wanted to jump up and down and shout her thanksgiving, but somehow she managed to keep her seat and say quietly, "I'm surprised. They never seemed to be in love with each other."

A twinkle appeared in Stone's eyes and he said wryly, "Shilo said something about his people expecting him to take a wife."

"This seems to amuse you," Flame said sharply. "I wonder why."

"I can't keep from laughing at the idea of Shilo being tred to one woman because his people expect it of him. I wonder what Opal at the Red Lantern will have to say about that?"

"What about Little Bird? What is your idea of her? Do you think she is happy at having to marry a man she doesn't love?"

"Who says she doesn't love him? I believe she's quite happy about getting married."

Flame shrugged. "I have never seen Shilo act lover-like to her."

"It is not his style to act soft around a woman, but I can tell he cares for Little Bird." Stone gave a short, amused laugh. "The big lunk-head is even jealous of me."

"I wonder why?" Flame remarked cynically.

"What do you mean by that?" Stone gripped her wrist again when she started to rise from the table.

"Nothing. I don't mean anything." Flame jerked her hand loose and left the table. Stone lunged to grab her again but missed by an inch as she swept into the room they were going to work on. Stone's face wore a reddish tint as he walked in behind her. Rudy hid a smile behind his hand. Whatever Stone had told Flame hadn't smoothed her feathers. She looked more ruffled than when she'd arrived this morning. He wondered what Stone had said to her. It was none of his business, he thought, and turned to Deke.

"Deke, you can start in the small bedroom. It's a real mess. Haul the furniture out into the yard before you start scrubbing down the walls and the floor."

That was the last room Deke wanted to have anything to do with. It was in that room he had tried to rape Flame and Bertha had caught them together. Bertha had blamed Flame and had almost killed her that night. In fact, he and Bertha had fled, thinking that Flame was dead.

A thought that chilled him to the bone gripped him. What if Flame came into the room and her memory returned? If that happened, he'd better be ready to run, or make a grab for his gun. He didn't know how swiftly Stone or Rudy could draw leather. He hoped he'd never have to find out. He was only average with hardware.

Deke gritted his teeth and stepped into the small bedroom. He sucked in his breath. It was just the same as the morning he and Bertha had fled the ranch. In his mind's eye he could see Bertha dragging Flame off the bed, flinging her on the floor and beating her.

He was dragging the dresser toward the door when suddenly Flame stood framed there, her eyes huge and frozen on the bed that had been pulled to the middle of the room, the sheet and blanket disheveled, a pillow lying on the floor. Was she remembering? he asked himself fearfully.

"It sure is a mess, isn't it?" he ventured, his voice raspy.

When Flame didn't say anything, only kept staring, Deke realized she hadn't heard him. Should he call her name, bring her out of the trance she seemed to be in?

He decided that he should. If her thoughts were traveling backwards, he wanted them stopped before the past became clear to her.

He sighed a shuddering sound of relief when Rudy called Flame's name and she snapped back to the present. She looked confused though, as if she straddled two worlds and couldn't make sense of either one.

"What's wrong, honey?" Rudy came down the hall and stood beside her. "You look puzzled about something."

"It's the strangest thing," Flame answered quietly, her voice shaken, "but I felt like I had been in this room before, that I'd had a part in the way everything was torn up. I could vaguely see a big woman, hear her yelling at me. And there was a shadowy figure of a man in the background. Then you called my name and everything disappeared."

Stone had silently come down the hall and heard what Flame was saying. When he saw how shaken she was, he put his arm around her shoulders and drew her to his side. "Let it go, honey. Everything will be clear to you someday."

Flame leaned into the comfort of his arm. He was right. No matter how hard she tried, she hadn't been able to recall anything. Maybe if she just relaxed, her memory would return. "You're right." She smiled at Stone. "Should we get on with the house-cleaning now?."

Although the four worked diligently the rest of the afternoon, they could only finish cleaning the two bedrooms. "It's time we got started home," Stone said to Flame. "Charlie will have supper ready soon. I want to see his face when he hears that Shilo is getting married."

"When is the wedding going to take place?" Rudy asked.

"Probably in a couple weeks. Shilo asked me to stand up with him."

"It's to be like a white man's wedding then?" Rudy asked, a little surprised.

"Yes. A missionary spent a winter in the village four or five years ago. He converted a lot of the Indians, including Shilo and his mother and father."

"What about Little Bird?" Flame asked. "Is she a Christian, too?"

Stone shrugged his shoulders. "I don't know," he said, then added in a gentle voice, "I think she still believes in the old ways."

"You sound like you're fond of the girl," Rudy said and Flame tried to hide how intently she waited for Stone's answer.

"A person can't help being fond of her. She's a sweet girl. She's got no parents, had no home until Shilo took her under his wing. She's so appreciative of everything a person does for her, it makes a man feel protective."

"Will Shilo treat her well, do you think?" Rudy asked.

"Yes, he will. He'll provide for her and he'll never beat her. He probably doesn't realize it and wouldn't admit it if he did, but I think he has tender feelings and deep affection for Little Bird."

"Why would he want to hide his feelings from her?" Flame frowned.

Stone stood up and reached his hand down to Flame. "That's the way he is." He pulled her up beside him. "Always gruff and stand-offish. Even with me. And I know he'd give his life for me if necessary." Flame shook her head at such foolishness, then looked at Rudy. "I'll be over in a couple days to clean the bunkhouse. In the meantime you and Mr. Cobbs can get on with the outside work. Lord knows, there's a lot to be done."

Rudy looked at Stone, amusement in his eyes. "You'd better watch this one. She has the makings of being a hard boss."

"Don't I know it," Stone agreed. "You should hear how she lays the law down at the ranch. I have to get her permission to go to the privy."

"You big liar." Flame hit him on the arm with her small fist. He yelped and carried on as though his arm was broken.

Rudy watched Stone toss Flame onto her mare's back, then mount his stallion. He nodded his satisfaction. The big rancher loved his daughter. He looked at Deke, standing off to one side, planning to tell him that they would work at mending one of the corrals. The man was staring after Stone and Flame as they rode away. There was stark hatred in Deke's eyes, but Rudy couldn't tell which rider it was directed at. Why should the man hate either one of them? he asked himself.

He would let the man finish out the week, then he'd let him go.

It was a soft, warm evening and Stone and Flame urged their mounts into a ground-eating canter. Without saying it, they were eager to get home, eat supper, then go to bed. Stone would just as soon forgo the evening meal, but the men would ride him unmercifully if he hurried Flame straight into the house.

By silent agreement Stone and Flame joined in the easygoing conversation of the men after supper while everyone enjoyed coffee. As usual they waited to be the last to leave the cookhouse. But all pretense of being calm and composed deserted them when they walked into the house. Not pausing to light a lamp, Stone swept Flame into his arms, and by the light of the moon shining through the windows, made his way to his bedroom.

He stood her on the floor next to the bed and held her tight against his body for several seconds. Then slowly, he bent his head and settled his mouth over hers.

His lips were firm, yet soft, giving as he demanded. Flame sighed, and raising herself on her toes, lifted her arms and wrapped them around his neck. When she nudged her lower body at him he caught his breath. Spreading his legs, he drew her in between them. Cupping her small rear in his hands, he held her fast as he bucked back and forth against her.

Stone smiled a pleased smile when suddenly Flame shuddered, then went limp against him. He had given her a release, a foretaste of what was to come. It was time now for the real thing.

He began to slowly disrobe her. The shirt came off first then the camisole. The boots were next and when she bent over and grasped his shoulders to keep from falling, one bare breast was only inches from his mouth. The temptation was too great, and Flame moaned her pleasure when he sucked the nipple into his mouth. He nibbled it, pulled on it, suckled until Flame was sobbing.

Stone dropped the boot, then pulled off the other one. He next unbuttoned her pants, then gently nudged her on the bed and onto her back. When he had slid her pantaloons off her slender body, he hurried out of his own clothing. When he crawled into bed, Flame welcomed him with open arms and legs.

"Oh, Lord," he groaned as he slid his long length into the warm softness waiting for him. Flame immediately picked up his rhythm and they rocked slowly together, the bed springs squeaking and the headboard thumping softly against the wall.

An hour or so later they were both exhausted and wet with sweat. They curled up in each other's arms and fell into a deep sleep.

Chapter Twenty-two

Rainee was about half a mile from the old ranch house when she noticed a cloud of dust to her right down near the river. Were there wild horses churning up the dirt, or were cattle being driven along? Whose cattle? she wondered.

She reined the mare beneath a big cotton-wood when she heard the bawling of cattle. Rudy hadn't mentioned that he had any beeves, but he very well could. She would wait to see who was driving the cattle. They were headed toward the river and she would be able to see clearly who was driving them.

She hadn't long to wait before she recognized Deke Cobbs. They saw each other at the same time and uneasiness gripped Rainee when Deke broke away from the herd and raced toward her.

Her first instinct was to prod the mare into a fast gallop. She did not trust the man. The look he'd given her the previous day had made her skin crawl. Without saying a word he let'd her know what he was thinking, and it wasn't very nice.

"Good mornin', Rainee." He pulled his horse up in front of her mare, making it rear and dance around in fright.

"What's wrong with you?" Rainee demanded angrily, although she felt nervous. A fast glance around showed her that they were alone. There would be no help for her if Deke decided to do what his eyes were suggesting. "My horse could have thrown me and broken my neck!" she cried angrily.

"Oh, I wouldn't want that to happen to your beautiful neck . . . or any other part of your body." He leered at her.

Rainee lifted the reins of the restless mare, who was rolling her eyes in fear of the mean-looking stallion. When she attempted to go around the animal, Deke, with an unpleasant smile, kneed his gray in front of the mare again.

"You don't want to leave yet, Rainee. I thought maybe we could go down by the river and visit awhile. Like you and Saunders do. I've got a blanket we could sit on.

"Wouldn't you like that?" he coaxed. "You've been without a man for a while. You must be gettin' an itch down there. . . .

Deke stopped short, his eyes bulging. Rainee had slipped a Colt out of her waist band. It was aimed at his belt buckle. "Why don't we talk about some lead medicine instead," Rainee said coolly as she cocked the Colt. "Nothing is itchy about me except my trigger finger and it can hardly hold still."

"Now, Rainee, put that thing away! You know I was only foolin'."

"In a pig's eye you were. Now turn your horse around and ride the hell away from here before I put a bullet where it would stop you from ever wanting a woman again."

"You'd do that, wouldn't you?" Deke gave her a malignant look. "One of these days—" Deked grabbed for the reins as Rainee put a bullet between his mount's hoofs. The horse gave a frenzied squeal and reared up on its hind legs.

"Get going," she ordered as Deke fought the gray to the ground.

"Damn it!" he swored. "Give me time to get the cattle moving."

"Never mind the cattle. Leave them where they are until I tell Jason a few things. I think you were ready to rustle them."

Deke paled a little beneath his tan and sweat was suddenly beading his forehead. His manner defiant, he said in surly tones, "Jason told me to move them to a different part of the range."

"Why only fifteen? What about the rest of them?" She demanded, guessing that there was more to the herd.

Deke's face darkened with rage. "Well, I can see who the boss is at this ranch. You get him between your legs and he does whatever you tell him to do."

"That's right." Rainee smiled icily and placed another bullet between the stallion's front hooves. The horse screamed, reared up, then tore across the range like wildfire was at his heels.

"You damn saddle bum." Rainee stared after Deke. "I'd bet my dress shop that you meant to steal those cattle."

As she rode on, Rainee was glad she had strapped on the Colt before leaving her shop. She didn't trust that man an inch.

Where has Deke gotten off to? Rudy wondered as he cooked his breakfast of bacon and eggs. The sun was barely up and he knew that there was a lot to do today around the buildings. There were still roofs to be repeared, hinges on doors to be tightened, the barn door to be mended, as well as the stables. The man was lazy, he had soon learned, had to be prodded to finish a task he'd been told to do. And he liked women a little too much, Rudy thought as he poured himself a cup of coffee. Perhaps he'd spent the night in town and hadn't come home yet.

It didn't matter if he had or not, Rudy decided, finishing his coffee and standing up. He'd be leaving at the end of the week, he reminded himself as he stood on the porch, building a cigarette. He struck a match and held the flame to his smoke, then started to walk toward the barn. He took a couple steps, then stopped, staring. A rider was coming toward the ranch, a woman. A smile lit his face. It was Rainee.

"I knew it was going to be a special day," he said, gazing up at her smiling face as he lifted his arms to swing her out of the saddle. "I guess you couldn't wait till Sunday," he said with a grin. "Have you had breakfast? I can make you some bacon and eggs. And the coffee pot is still hot."

"A cup of coffee sounds good."

"Alright. Let's turn your mare loose in the corral and I'll have a cup with you."

"Do you have any cattle, Rudy?" Rainee asked as they sat on the porch drinking the coffee.

"I counted almost fifty head the day I rode in. I think that by rights they are mine. They're not my original animals, of course, but bred from them. Why do you ask?"

"As I was riding in I saw that man Deke driving a small herd toward town. I wondered about it since it was so early in the morning. I suppose you know about it."

"No, I don't. I didn't tell him to do anything about the cattle. He wasn't around when I got up. Would you mind keeping yourself company while I ride after that grub-liner and see what he's up to?"

"I don't think you'll find him." Rainee grinned at Rudy over the rim of her cup.

"Why do you say that?"

"He and I had a run-in. He tried to stop me by shoving that stallion into my mare. He said that by now I should be a little itchy for a man and that we could go down to the river and talk."

Rudy's face grew as dark as a thunder cloud racing out of the north. "I'll kill the bastard," he said, jumping to his feet.

Rainee grabbed his arm. "You won't find him, Rudy. I put a couple shots between his horse's hoofs and I wouldn't be surprised if the animal is still running. Deke wanted to take the cattle but I wouldn't let him. I expect they're still grazing down by the river. I came out here to help you today. Let's get started. What do you want to do first?"

"I was going to put some new shingles on the sheds. They leak like sieves. But we'll only work this morning. After lunch we'll take it easy."

"That sounds good." Rainee gave him a slow, lazy smile that made his loins begin to throb.

The morning air soon rang with the sound of a hammer hitting nails. A few hours later, Rudy squinted against the sun and the sweat that streamed down his face and said, "Let's call it a day, Rainee. What do you think about a dip in the river to cool off?"

"I think it's the best suggestion I've heard all day." Rainee took off her Stetson and drew her arm across her forehead.

Was he finally going to make love to her? Rudy wondered as he and Rainee rode toward the river. So much time had passed, he had given up hope of that ever happening.

Riding alongside him, Rainee was thinking along the same lines. She had long ago given up the hope of ever seeing Rudy again, let alone having him make love to her. Would she be disappointed now that it was finally going to happen? More important, would he be let down? She had only known one man, and he, good man that he was, wasn't very experienced in the love-making department, so she knew little about how to please a man. She felt sure Rudy was plenty experienced there.

For half the day they had been carefree, laughing and joking with each other like old times. But a shyness came over them when they drew rein beneath the willows that lined the river. They avoided looking at each other as they loosened the girths and lifted the saddles off the mare and stallion. They still didn't speak while staking the animals in a patch of grass.

And they were silent when they turned and went into each other's arms. Clasped tightly against each other, they sank down on their knees, their lips fused tightly together. The years of remembering and wanting were becoming almost overwhelming. Their breathing became ragged and their clothing hot and constricting. Their one thought was to get rid of them. Their fingers were busy with buttons from down river there came the laughter of young boys and the splash of paddles striking the water and hitting the sides of a boat. Barely breathing, they prayed the youngsters wouldn't see the horses and come to investigate.

It seemed a life time passed by while they waited for the happy laughter of children to fade as the boys paddled past them and floated out of sight round a bend in the river. Rudy and Rainee gave nervous laughs and Rudy said, "I'll spread the blanket, then we'll jump into the river and cool off . . . in more ways than one." He looked at Rainee, his eyes full of mischief.

It was mere minutes before they'd stripped down to their underwear and waded out into the river. When the water reached their waists, Rudy pulled Rainee into his arms. She clung to him, pressing her face into his shoulder. He took hold of her arms above the elbows and slid his hands up to pull down the straps of her camisole. He tugged the lacy garment up over her head and tossed it onto the bank.

Pleasure rose inside him as he stroked his hands down her sides and over her small rear. When she moaned, "Rudy," low in her throat a smoldering heat enveloped him.

"Rainee," he rasped her name, "don't send me away this time. I don't think I could bear it."

"I won't, love. I won't be that foolish again."

Rudy swooped her up in his arms and in seconds flat laid her down on the blanket he had spread on the ground. He came down beside her and she lifted her arms to welcome him.

"Oh, God," Rudy moaned as he slid inside Rainee's warmth. He had known that it would be wonderful, but this was beyond wonderful. It was beyond the power of description. He fully expected to die when he reached his release.

And because he didn't want to die, his pace was slow as he moved in and out of her, each stroke long, reaching her depths. But at last he could not hold back any longer. He prepared himself for death and gave one last plunge, hoping that he could take Rainee with him.

For a split-second as he rode the roller coaster of passion, he thought that he had. After one loud, passionate cry, Rainee lay as still as death. "Oh, Lord, I've killed her," he exclaimed, coming up on his elbows and stroking the hair off her forehead.

A shudder of relief slid over him when her eyes slowly opened. "Rainee!" he cried, "I thought you were dead, that I had been too rough with you."

She lifted limp arms to twine them around his neck. "Ah, no," she breathed, caressing her fingers up and down his back. "You were wonderful. I never knew it was possible to experience such passion. I am as weak as a kitten. What about you?"

"Aw, Rainee—" he dropped a kiss on her damp forehead—"I'm so weak a baby could beat the stuffins' out of me."

"That's too bad." Rainee pretended disappointment. "I was hoping that maybe we could. . . ."

"We can." Rudy dropped his head and pulled a hardened nipple into his mouth. Rainee waited for him to say more, but for several minutes he only busied himself with slow sucking and nibbling. He didn't stop his ministrations to the hard little nub until Rainee gave a small groan and bucked her hips at him. He hid a smile between her breasts.

As she looked at him in wonder he glanced westward at the mountains. The sky was growing pink there. The sun would set soon. "Will you spend the night with me, Rainee?" he asked softly. When she nodded immediately he said, "Let's do like old married folk then."

"And how do old married folk act?"

"Well, they do their chores, eat some supper, then go to bed."

"Go to bed before sunset?" Rainee teased. "Isn't that unusual, even for old married folk?"

"Not if the man has waited for nineteen years to get the woman in bed."

Rainee looked at Rudy, as though in deep thought. Then her eyes sparkling, she said, "In that case, I expect he's as eager as she is to get to his bed."

Chapter Twenty-three

It was a clear, cool twlight as Flame walked toward the Indian village. She was on her way to visit Shilo's mother Moonlight. She was unsure what kind of gift one gave to an Indian bride. The Ute women did not use the kinds of pots and pans that the whites used. They already had beautiful woven blankets. Of course there were quilts. They didn't seem to have those. In the winter when the cold winds blew, they stayed nice and warm in animal furs.

I think Little Bird would like a colorful quilt, Flame thought, thinking of the one she had begun a few weeks earlier under Rainee's direction. It was made from squares of bright silk. Stone had bought a bagful of the material from the dressmaker.

He had purchased the scraps, having no idea whether she even knew how to sew. When he had dumped the rainbow of colors on the bed and jokingly said, "Make me a quilt, woman," she had realized she had no idea where to begin.

The next day Rainee had shown her how to cut squares and triangles out of the silk. When she mentioned that she doubted there was a needle or spool of thread in the house, Stone purchased a packet of needles and several spools of colored floss.

In the many hours of constructing the bed cover, dim images would float like mist through her mind. The kind face of a handsome man would smile at her as he patted her on the head. She remembered fragments of a haunting song as though it had been sung to her as she drifted off to sleep.

She tried to hang on to those fuzzy moments but they were always chased away by the unattractive face of a large woman looming over her, a slender switch in her hand. For an instant she remembered the sting of that thin willow bough and cringed.

Were those passing images real? she asked herself.

Flame topped the small hill above the Indian village and stood beneath a tree for a moment, taking in the scenery. It was a serene sight she looked down on. Beneath the mist that hung over camp, a dozen small cookfires blazed. Children were playing in the last few minutes of daylight, and old men sat around the communal fire waiting to be called to the evening meal.

I'd best hurry along, Flame thought, if I want to get Moonlight's opinion about the quilt and get home to my own supper.

She was about to step from beneath the tree when she heard voices approaching. She recognized them as belonging to Shilo and Little Bird. They spoke in angry tones and she was about to let herself be known to them when she heard her name spoken. She stayed where she was and listened.

"I don't care to talk about it anymore," Shilo said, his voice hard, his words final.

"Well, I want to talk about it some more. I don't know why you couldn't have asked me to marry you, instead of ordering me to."

"If I had asked you, you'd have said no. Like a foolish child, you would have hung on to the hope that Stone would leave Flame and marry you."

"You think that, do you? Chief Shilo thinks he knows everything." Little Bird's voice was trembling as if she was near tears.

"I don't pretend to know everything, but along with half the village, I know that you sparkle and shine whenever Stone comes around. Now you tell me you carry a child, though I have lain with you only once. I am curious to see the color of your babe's skin when it arrives."

A gasp of rage exploded from Little Bird's throat. "And if it is a half breed, what then!" she demanded. "Will you turn us out?"

Flame felt that a hand had reached inside her chest and torn out her heart when Shilo answered, "I would never turn my back on Stone's child." When Little Bird flew at Shilo, furiously beating him on the breast with her small fists, Flame turned, and half blinded by tears, ran back down the hill toward the ranch house.

It was dark inside as Flame stumbled up the porch steps. Evidently Stone hadn't come in from the range yet. She was grateful for that, she told herself as she walked inside and moved down the hall to her room. A room she hadn't been using lately, but one she would be using from now on—for a time at least—until she could think through this last blow to her heart. She could not stay here much longer, she determined as she entered her bedroom and locked the door behind her. She could not bear to look at Stone tonight.

As Stone rode homeward the sky turned from twilight into darkness. He couldn't wait to get home, to see Flame. It hadn't been quite daylight when he made love to her, then left with his men to spend the day rounding up cattle. He wished there would be time for them to spend a short time in his bedroom before the supper bell rang. But that was out of the question. The little quarter horse he had used today was dead tired. He didn't have the heart to ask the little fellow to move faster than a walk.

After all, he and Flame had the entire night ahead of them.

As Stone unsaddled the horse and turned him into one of the corrals, he frowned when he looked at the ranch house and saw it was in darkness. That's strange, he thought. Why hadn't Flame lighted any of the lamps?

He took the porch steps two at a time, calling Flame's name as he walked into the parlor. He took the time to light two of the lamps in the large room, then walked down the hall to the bedrooms, calling her name again. Maybe she had lain down to wait for him and had fallen asleep.

He walked past her closed door, unbuttoning his shirt as he continued on to his room.

He needed no artificial light to show him that his bed was empty. He stood irresolute, wondering where she could be. Had something happened to her? A frostiness came into his eyes. Had she gone to Jason Saunders's place to help him? I wish she'd pay that much attention to her own home? he thought as he stamped back down the hall.

He didn't know what prompted him to look into Flame's room as he drew opposite it. He took hold of the glass knob and tried to turn it. It didn't budge. The door was locked.

"Flame?" He rattled the door knob. "Are you in there? Let me in." When only silence answered him, he rapped sharply on the door. "Are you awake, Flame? It's me, Stone. Let me in."

There was rusling inside, then Flame said, "I have a headache. You go on to supper without me."

"Is there anything I can do for you . . . get for you? Maybe a cup of coffee?"

"No, thank you. I just need to lie quietly in the darkness and let it run its course."

"If you're sure," Stone said after a short silence. "I'll have Charlie fix us a tray and we'll eat in your room."

"No!" Flame answered so sharply, so hastily, Stone gave a startled jerk. "I'm not hungry, and I don't feel like talking."

Stumped at her attitude, Stone didn't know what else to say. She couldn't make it plainer that she didn't want his company. Well, by God, he thought as he stamped away from the locked door, she was going to have it before he went to bed tonight. There was something damned strange going on here and he intended to clear it up as soon as he had his supper and calmed down. Flame was acting mighty peculiar.

A couple of the men inquired about Flame when Stone walked into the cookhouse alone. They accepted his explanation that she had a headache and no more was said about it. Most imagined it was her woman's time.

When the men finished eating and dug cigarette makings out of their shirt pockets, Stone took a tray out of a cupboard and began filling a couple plates for him and Flame. When the men cleared out, he said offhandedly to Charlie, "I hope Flame didn't go riding in this heat today."

"Naw, she didn't. She didn't go anywhere. She puttered around in the house all day, working on that quilt. She was still there when I started supper." When Charlie saw the concern in Stone's eyes, he said in his rough, though gentle way, "Don't worry about her, Stone. It's probably her woman's time. They sometimes get mighty strange at them times."

"I don't know much about that." Stone picked up the tray and headed for the door. "I hope she feels better tomorrow."

Stone entered the house, and balancing the tray on his hip, rapped on Flame's bedroom door. "I've got our supper, honey. Unlock the door."

When it remained quiet inside, Stone rapped again, a little louder.

"Stone!" Flame called impatiently, "I told you I wasn't hungry. Take it away."

Stone set the tray on the floor and leaned his palm against the door frame. "Shouldn't you get washed up and change into your night clothes? It's almost time we went to bed."

"I am in bed, Stone." Flame's tone was like that of a grownup explaining something to a child.

"Damn it!" Stone exploded, "I know you're in bed. Are you going to spend the night there?"

"I told you that I have a headache."

It slowly dawned on Stone that Flame didn't want any lovemaking tonight. "Flame," he said softly, "I only want to hold you while you sleep, that's all. Do you think I have animal lust that I can't control?"

There was sincerity in Stone's voice and Flame knew he meant what he said. The thing was, if she lay in his arms she would go up in flames, even though she had learned tonight that he might be the father of Little Bird's baby. She was afraid that where he was concerned, *she* had an animal lust she couldn't control.

"I'll see you tomorrow," she said finally. "I want to be alone tonight." Stone stood for a long, silent minute, his head hanging, his eyes on the floor. She was being unreasonable. If she loved him, she would want the comfort of his arms, she would not push him away. He had never felt sure that she cared for him . . . loved him the way he loved her. Her behavior tonight fueled his uncertainty. He remembered his grandfather saying once that in every marriage one partner loved more than the other. This relationship of theirs had been crazy from the begining.

He pushed away from the door and, with sagging shoulders, walked down the hall to his room, the tray of food sitting forgotten on the floor.

Flame heard his heavy retreating tread. When his door closed tears filled her eyes. He hadn't put up much of an argument against her sleeping alone in her bedroom.

But why should he? she asked herself. He had Little Bird tucked away, ready to fill in for his supposed wife . . . a woman who was moody most of the time, unsettled because she didn't know who she was, didn't know her worth.

Her lips twisted bitterly. Little Bird was always carefree, laughing and smiling about something. She was a young woman whose sunny nature drew people to her. Not only did she have Stone and Shilo running after her, she had half the young braves in the village giving her longing looks.

Flame sat up when she heard Stone's door open and close, then his footsteps going down the hall. Where was he going? To the Indian village to see Little Bird? She scooted off the bed and hurried to the window that looked out at the barn and corrals.

She stood there but a few minutes before she saw Stone lead his stallion out of the barn and climb onto his back. When he touched spurs to the horse and rode away, she pressed her forehead against the window pane and squeezed her eyes shut as though in pain. He was riding in the direction of the Indian village. Hot tears ran down her cheeks as she crawled back in bed. It wouldn't bother him at all that she wasn't sleeping beside him tonight.

What was she to do? she wondered as she knuckled her eyes dry. She could go on pretending to be Stone's wife, she supposed . . . until she could figure out what would be the wisest thing for her to do.

"But I will not sleep with him again," she declared in a whisper. But how could she stop sharing his bed? He would demand to know why. If she told him about overhearing the conversation between Shilo and Little Bird, Stone would only turn it off with a laugh, claiming that his friend was jealous.

Would Stone rendezvous with Little Bird after she and Shilo were married? Would Shilo allow it? He might if the baby turned out to be Stone's.

Another thing she didn't understand was why Stone didn't marry Little Bird himself if there was a chance the baby was his. Did he feel it was beneath him to marry an Indian maid? She hoped he wasn't the kind of man who would spread his seed indiscriminately with no intention of acknowledging his offspring.

It struck Flame suddenly that the same thing could happen to her. Stone could very well get her with child, then refuse to marry her. She hated herself for doing it, but she didn't let herself fall asleep until she heard Stone ride into the barnyard.

Chapter Twenty-four

A week had passed since Flame had moved back into her bedroom. The excuse she gave Stone was a half truth. She didn't like living in sin, she told him, and that was what they had been doing. She went on to say with carefully phrased words that if in the future she regained her memory, and they still wanted to, they would marry and share the same bed again.

Her explanation did not sit well with Stone and he went around like a lean wolf tracking a deer. Everyone gave him wide clearance, including Flame. There was no warmth in his eyes anymore when he looked at her, no curve of his lips. That had all stopped when time after time he asked her what was wrong and she answered that she didn't know what he was talking about. The last time she told him that, he yelled back, "Don't play me for a fool!" and slammed out of the house, leaving the door shuddering in its frame. Ever since then he had only talked to her when it was absolutely necessary to do so. This morning at breakfast they'd exchanged a few words, the first in two days.

He had asked as he poured himself a cup of coffee, "Are you still going to Shilo and Little Bird's wedding?"

She had answered shortly that yes she was going. She wouldn't want to disappoint Shilo.

"What about Little Bird? Don't you think she would be upset if you didn't show up?"

Flame shrugged her shoulders. "As long as you were there, she wouldn't even notice my absence."

"Now why do you say that?" Stone's voice had turned cold. "She would feel awful if you didn't come."

"Don't get yourself in an uproar for heaven's sake," Flame snapped. "I'm going with you."

A few seconds later, the timbre of his voice almost back to normal, Stone said, "Little Bird and Shilo are going to appreciate the quilt. The fact that you made it will mean a lot to them."

Flame thought to herself that it wouldn't matter a whit to the Indian girl that she had personally made the bed cover. "What are you bringing them?" she asked stiffly, wanting to end the conversation. His answer, however, put her deep in the doldrums.

A proud smile creased his handsome face. "I made the little fellow a cradle board."

Flame couldn't speak for a moment. A cradle board? Wasn't that a personal thing, something to come from the mother and father? She turned her head and looked away from him. She was sure tears were forming in her eyes. She managed to say stiffly, "What makes you so sure it will be a little fellow? What if it's a little girl?"

"It will be a little boy. His father wants a son in the worst kind of way."

It was too much. She could bear no more. She jumped to her feet and was out the door before Stone knew what she was about. He stared after her a moment, then with a shake of his head he rose and left the cookhouse.

The full moon was rising, the air soft and quiet when Stone knocked on Flame's door. "Are you about ready to leave?" he asked when she opened the door.

Stone's eyes narrowed and his smile disappeared. "Is that the dress you're going to wear?"

Flame's body stiffened at the hint of censure in Stone's words and voice. "Yes, I am. It's my nicest gown. What do you think is wrong with it? Did you want me to go dressed up in squaw doe-skin? I see that you are in full Indian regalia." There was a slight sneer in her voice.

"I dress in buckskin to honor Shilo's Indian blood," Stone said stiffly.

Flame grabbed up her comb and started dragging it through her curls. "Well, I have dressed to honor my white blood." She threw the comb on the dresser, picked her lightweight stole off the foot of the bed and left the room.

Stone stared after her, his temper rising. He was getting damned tired of her always going off without any warning. One of these days he would get enough and would not follow her.

He realized that would never really happen as he left the room and closed the door behind him. He would follow her to hell if need be.

Young Jamey, the horse wrangler, had the stallion and mare saddled and waiting for Flame and Stone. He helped Flame to mount just as Stone joined them. Flame dug in her heels and the mare was off and running before Stone climbed into the saddle. He swore a savage oath. He could see how this evening was going to go. For one thing, he would be ignored by his supposed wife.

But who would she talk with? She wouldn't know anyone there except Shilo and Little Bird, and for some reason she didn't like the friendly little Indian girl. His spirits lifted. Surely she would sit with him.

Flame soon slowed the mare down to an easy lope. The pace she had set in the beginning was tossing her curls about and whipping her long skirt around the horse's legs, making her increasingly nervous.

He didn't like the dress she had chosen to wear. Not that it wasn't beautiful, blue in color, but the bodice was cut low, showing quite a bit of cleavage. Indian women dressed modestly, although they wore beautiful necklaces and bracelets. But their fringed doe-skin shifts came past their knees and the sleeves past their elbows. He hoped the women didn't frown on Flame's way of dressing. He wanted them to like her.

When they crested the hill looking down on the village, lights from campfires twinkled like stars and the gray smoke from the fires hung over it all like a soft mist. Laughter and the soft beat of drums lifted in the air. The ceremony would start soon and the merrymaking would begin. There would be food and drink aplenty. He had sent a young beef over to the village a couple days ago. He could smell the delicious aroma of it roasting now. The drink would be of Indian make, not the raw spirits of the white man.

There was an eagerness in his voice that made Flame grind her teeth when he said, "Come on, let's go."

Some young lads had been stationed to take over the care of their guests' horses when they arrived. Stone noticed there were quite a few tied in the cottonwoods behind the wigwams. He recognized some of the animals and smiled. Shilo had invited some of his hands to the wedding and he was pleased that they had come. The nice part about it was that they had come on their own. He hoped they remembered the warnings he had always given his help. Don't play fast and loose with the Indian maids. The braves would slit their throats faster than they could unbutton their pants.

Shilo and Little Bird were standing in the midst of some young people, the smiles on their faces saying that they were very happy. What a handsome couple, Flame thought. Little Bird's shift of soft gray doe-skin was decorated with beautiful bead work and long fringe at the hem and along the sleeves.

And Shilo. Flame thought that with the exception of Stone, he was the handsomest man she had ever seen. He stood so erect, his head lifted proudly. The stance of a chief, she thought.

They were spotted then by the happy couple and Little Bird let loose a squeal that made some of the elderly woman frown. She ran toward Stone, her arms open. With a jolly laugh he caught her up and swung her around and around. Flame looked at Shilo and wasn't surprised at the dark scowl on his handsome face. She decided then that they should give the pair a taste of their own behavior, let them see how it felt.

She wrenched her attention away from Stone and Little Bird and fastened her eyes on Shilo. He sensed her gaze almost immediately and looked across the fire at her. He noted right away the mischief sparkling in her eyes. With a rouguish smile in his own eyes he circled the fire, and smiling down at her asked, "Can I fix you a plate of the wedding feast?"

"Yes, you can, Shilo. I'm starving."

"Come along then." He took her arm, aware that Stone and Little Bird were watching them and that Stone had a black look on his face. How do you like it, white brother? he thought.

Flame clung to Shilo's arm as they made their way to where the wedding feast was laid out. They warmed to their play-acting and made sure that every time Stone and Little Bird looked their way they smiled at each other.

With their plates piled high with beef and various Indian dishes, Shilo gave Flame a devilish grin and said, "Shall we give that pair something to worry about?"

"Yes!" Flame answered eagerly. "What do you have in mind?"

"That we take our food and go back in the trees to eat it. Far enough among the cottonwoods that no one can see us. What do you think?"

"I think it's the best idea I've heard in a long time. I don't mind telling you, Shilo, I've had about all I can stand of those two always falling all over each other."

"Don't take their carrying on too seriously, Flame. I believe that Little Bird is like a young sister to Stone and she worships him because he saved her from a life of hell. I don't believe that either one has a romantic feeling for the other." "Shilo," Flame said hesitantly. "I—I overheard you telling Little Bird that you thought Stone might be the father of her baby. Is it true?"

"No, that was only anger talking. She was untouched when she came to me, and I doubt she would have lain with my friend after. But like you said, I've had enough. My mother is growing concerned about the affection they show each other. She says that our people are beginning to talk behind their hands. She pointed out that I am their chief now and mustn't have any shame brought to me or my family."

"Why don't you come right out and tell her to behave herself?"

"I could say the same thing to you about Stone." Shilo looked at Flame with dry amusement.

Flame gave a nervous little laugh. "I don't have much control over Stone. As you very well know, he does as he pleases."

"We've been too soft with them, Flame, never reeling them in. I think it's time that we do . . . starting tonight. Is that alright with you?"

"That's fine with me. I'll enjoy every minute of setting Stone Falcon in place."

"Good. The first thing we'll do is take our time eating some of my wedding meal." Shilo gave Flame a crooked smile. "I've no doubt Little Bird and Stone are doing the same. After that, we'll walk around chatting with my people, with you clinging to my arm. My mother will think that I've gone loco, but I'll explain it to her later." The corners of his firm mouth lifted in amusement. "She suggested that I beat Little Bird."

"You would never do that, Shilo." Flame looked at him, alarm in her eyes. "Would you?"

Shilo burst out laughing. "I might if I could find a long feather."

Flame laughed also and took his offered hand to help her up. "I didn't think you would, but a lot of men, red and white, would have taken a stick to her a long time ago."

"She is young. She will learn. Let's go back to the festivities now. I think we've been gone long enough to cause some uneasy speculation between the pair."

"Or at least a lot of serious thinking to themselves." Glee spilled over in Flame's voice.

Shilo and Flame received a lot of strange looks as they walked into the village hand in hand. There was nothing strange about the look in Stone's eyes, however. Even the youngest child there could see that he was blazing mad.

Flame grew a little alarmed when she saw him striding toward her and Shilo, the wrath of hell in his eyes. She kept her trepidation well-hidden and was even attempting to smile when he grasped her by the wrist and jerked her away from Shilo. "It's time we were getting home." His voice was cold and raspy.

"But we've hardly arrived," Flame protested, digging in her heels.

"We've been here long enough for you two to

make everyone talk about you," he said, continuing to drag her along.

"We didn't do anything," Flame exclaimed angrily, keeping hidden the joy in her eyes as Stone tossed her onto the mare's back. Stone was jealous.

"You did enough by disappearing in the trees with a man not your husband."

"But Shilo is your best friend," Flame pointed out logically as she gathered up the reins. "Surely you can trust him."

"Well, I don't. I've seen the way he looks at you when he thinks no one is watching," Stone grated out and dug his heels into the stallion's sides. As it lunged away into a full gallop Flame wanted to shout with laughter. Shilo never paid any more attention to her than he would any other woman who belonged to a friend of his. Stone was so jealous he wasn't thinking straight.

Stone tried to calm himself as the stallion raced along, but one question kept creeping back into his mind: What were they doing so long, alone together in the dark? Any warm-blooded man wouldn't just sit and talk to Flame. And Shilo, he'd seen his friend with women before. He knew just how to make them surrender to him.

Stone ground his teeth in frustration. If he knew for sure Shilo had lured Flame into his arms, he'd ride back right now and shoot him in the heart.

Chapter Twenty-five

When Flame and Stone had gone, Shilo looked around at the wedding guests. Little Bird was not among them. He saw by the grim, forbidding looks on the elders' faces that he hadn't been wise to disappear into the woods with Flame. He slowly realized that their disapproval wasn't all because of his unseemly action. Little Bird was well-liked by everyone and the tribe was quite upset that he had insulted her.

He sighed and looked across the way at his mother's wigwam. She sat in front of it, her stong face telling him that he was in for a long tongue-lashing.

Shilo walked slowly toward the regal-looking

338

woman whom he adored and admired above all women. He sat cross-legged before her and said to her in English. "If you do not mind, mother, I will speak in the white man's tongue. There are too many waiting to hear what we will say to each other. I do not feel that my personal life is any business of theirs."

"In a sense, my son, you are right. However, as their chief you must hold yourself above reproach. What you did tonight was not the act of a chieftain."

"I know this is true, my honored mother, but tonight Flame and I decided that we'd had enough of our mates' unseemly actions. That is why we acted like we did.

"I know it will cause talk for a few days, but when my people see Little Bird settle down to being an obedient wife and observe that I pay no attention to Flame, everyone will understand."

He looked at Moonlight with a crooked grin. "I could not bring myself to beat Little Bird."

"It would have caused less talk if you had," Moonlight snorted. "You must have a serious talk with her tonight." After a moment she added, "And I will talk to her tomorrow."

"No, my mother, you will not. You may teach my wife how to cook, how to sew, how to tan leather, but when it comes to our personal life, you will have no say in it."

Moonlight looked as though she would give him an argument, then closed her mouth. Shilo's chin had come up and he looked very much the chieftain. She said only, "Your wife is waiting for you in your wigwam."

Shilo rose, and touching her shoulder affectionately, said, "Good night, my mother."

The flap to his wigwam was tied back and he could see Little Bird sitting on a pile of blankets staring into the small fire in the fire-pit. She looked so small, so sad. She sat, hugging her knees, her chin resting on them. In the light of the flames he saw a tear slip down her cheek. Foolish child, he thought. Did you really think I was going to put up with your craziness with Stone? You did not like the lesson you learned today, did you? You finally realized how Flame must have felt when you hung onto Stone's arms, told him jokes to make him laugh.

"I hope that tonight you and Stone learned a lesson, realized how Flame and I must have felt watching you two carry on," Shilo said, looking down at his wife.

"Oh, Shilo!" Little Bird cried, tears streaming down her cheeks. "I did not think how it must look to you and Flame when Stone and I joke around." She grabbed Shilo's arm and looked pleadingly into his face. "It is true that we are very fond of each other, but only in a brotherly and sisterly way. Stone loves Flame very much. It shows in his actions, in his eyes."

"And what about you, Little Bird? Have you ever loved a man?"

"Oh, yes, Shilo. I love a man. I love him very

much, but he doesn't care for me. He is always gruff with me."

Gentle words came hard to Shilo and he could only look at Little Bird, feeling tongue-tied and helpless. Finally, he cupped her smooth cheek in his hand and said gently, "Let us go to bed now. I plan that tomorrow we will take a wedding trip up into the mountains. We can get well-acquainted there, all by ourselves."

"I would like that, Shilo." Little Bird smiled up at him, then went and untied the strips of leather that held back the tent flap. Shilo opened his arms to her when she came back to the pallet of furs.

Dawn was just breaking when Shilo and Little Bird left their wigwam and walked toward the edge of the village. The grass was white with dew and the birds were fussing at each other as they scratched in the dirt for worms or flew about snapping up bugs and insects. They would break into song as soon as their little bellies were full and the sun had risen.

Shilo had slowed his pace to accommodate Little Bird's shorter stride. When they had left the village behind and the range was turning red as the sun rose slowly, Little Bird asked, "Where are we going, Shilo?"

He pointed northwest to the mountains. "We are going into the wild country. It is a place of dry gullies and rocky gorges, wild animals and the most beautiful wild horses man has ever seen."

"It doesn't sound very appealing, Shilo. Couldn't we go to a place that has some beauty?" Little Bird said as they reached the timberline and began to climb.

"There is beauty, as you will see. And the air gets cooler the higher we climb. We will need a fire tonight. Besides, I have relatives up there. Most of my youth was spent in these mountains. I want these relatives to meet my bride. Especially my grandfather."

He looked down at Little Bird, tender amusement coming into his dark eyes. "He will say that I will never be able to get such a scrawny little squaw with child."

"But he will learn better, won't he?" Little Bird wrapped her arm around her tall husband's lean waist.

A tingling started in Shilo's loins at his wife's touch. He wrapped his arm around her waist and said huskily, "There's a place of great beauty a short distance from here. We will stop there and rest awhile."

"Oh, but I'm not tired." Little Bird looked up at Shilo. She saw then the amorous gleam in his eyes and said with a wide smile, "Well, maybe a little bit."

Quiet mirth crinkled the corners of Shilo's mouth. His delicate-looking little wife liked love-making as much as he did and could out last him sometimes.

At first the faint trail angled gently up the

mountain. It became steeper then and just when Little Bird thought that her legs would give out, they came to a draw. With a sigh of relief they followed it down to a meadow of at least two acres of lush green grass. A narrow stream of spring water flowed through the middle of it, originating far back in the mountains. The water was so cold it hurt Little Bird and Shilo's teeth when they knelt and drank from the stream.

There was a stand of three large cottonwoods at the end of the draw. Shilo took Little Bird's arm and said with a light chuckle, "Let's go rest now."

He took the two blankets from where he had strapped them on his back and spread them under the tallest tree. He had barely smoothed out the corners when Little Bird flung herself down beside Shilo's kneeling figure. Laughing at her eagerness, he came down on top of her.

It took but a moment for him to shove her single garment up past her waist and for him to unlace his buckskins. It took less time for him to crawl between her legs and drive himself inside her.

Little Bird squealed her pleasure as he bucked against her, raising her hips to meet his every drive.

Once was never enough for them, so after a short rest to catch their breath, Shilo said, "Wife you can do the work this time. I'm tired."

"You're lazy," she laughed, straddling him.

He only laughed at her as he lifted her hips

and settled her over his throbbing maleness. As she sheathed him he sighed, crossed his arms behind his head and waited for Little Bird to start rocking against him. Several minutes passed and he had just achieved his release when he felt eyes upon him. He gave a start. A solitary white stallion, a ragged, shaggy, wild beast stood looking down at them.

As Shilo lay stiff, wondering what to do, the stallion's nostrils widened, he tossed his head, his ears pricked, and then he spun around on his hind legs and tore off down the draw.

Why hadn't he attacked them? Shilo asked himself in amazement. It had all happened so swiftly, Little Bird wasn't even aware that they'd had a visitor. It was an omen, Shilo felt sure of it. But of what?

Little Bird was climbing off him then. She walked over to the stream and cleansed herself with a piece of soft suede she took from a pouch at her waist. She rinsed the cloth out then and carried it back to Shilo, who still lay stretched out on his back. He let out a white man's curse when Little Bird began to wipe the icy cloth around his male parts.

Hungry from all the walking and excerise they'd had, they chewed on pemmican made from berries and buffalo meat. They sat in the warm air then, half dozing.

Little Bird slept. Shilo kept thinking of the stallion. Had the animal been trying to tell him something?

Two days later when he and Little Bird were

on their way home and passed the spot where they had napped by the spring, Shilo's eyes were drawn to the distant hill. The stallion stood there again, gazing down at them while his harem browsed contentedly around him.

It shook Shilo to his depths. What was the big white stallion trying to tell him?

Chapter Twenty-six

Stone sat on the porch, the chair creaking as he rocked back and forth. The slight wind had died, the trees were without movement and the birds were making the twittering sound they always made when getting ready to roost. The day was cooling off. There was a feel of autumn in the air.

Stone sighed a long, weary sigh. The close friendship between him and Shilo had changed. Now that they were both married, it was next to impossible to run into each other as often as before. And when they did talk for a while, nothing was the same. No plans were made to go fishing or hunting, nothing was ever said about the two men and their wives getting together for a Sunday dinner or to spend the day in town.

Flame continued to sleep alone, and things were cool between them. She visited Jason Saunders three or four times a week, and it was driving him crazy. What did they do all those hours they spent together?

When Flame suddenly emerged from the cookhouse, he was tempted to rise, go meet her and demand she tell him what went on between her and the handsome older man. But he would lose his pride if he did that. Impatient, he headed toward the barn. Maybe a long ride would work off some of his frustration.

As Stone walked toward the barn without a word for her, Flame stared after him, an ache in her chest. Where did he go on the many nights when he left the ranch without any explanation? It could be either to the Indian village or to the Red Lantern in Dogwood. She wished it was neither one. In the Indian village was Little Bird, and in town was the saloon where Opal and her girls carried on their business.

She hadn't seen Shilo and Little Bird since their wedding. The close friendship between Stone and Shilo had changed. The old camaraderie was gone. The light went out in the cookhouse and the quietness of night settled in as she took the chair Stone had vacated. A wolf's forlorn yowl floated down the valley.

Flame leaned her head on the chair back and half-closed her eyes. If only she could get her memory back. She felt so helpless, not knowing who she was, where she came from. Not knowing any of that made it hard to stand up for herself. She had been getting little snippets of memory that made no sense to her. There had also been some strange dreams.

There was one dream in particular that she partly welcomed. It always started out so nice, making her feel happy. Then suddenly everything was gray and she was a little child crying out to someone. Someone who had gone away and left her with a big, mean-faced woman who spanked her for crying. There was something else, however, that bothered her more than the dreams and the little snatches of memory that only served to confuse her.

Lately, every time she saw Jason Saunders, she was sure she had known him as someone else, someone she was very fond of. She wanted to see him all the time, made thin excuses to ride over to his ranch, even though the old run-down place made her very uneasy every time she stepped inside it.

And that was another thing that bothered her. Why did she have that feeling, almost of fear, every time she stepped inside the old place? She had once suggested to him, half jokingly, that he should tear the house down instead of spending so much sweat and money on it. His answer kept her from ever bringing the subject up again.

"I have a very special reason, Flame, and I won't rest until I've rescued the old woman. I have a feeling that she started out with much love; then fate stepped in and the young woman was doomed to live in shame and despair." Rudy paused and gave a small, embarrassed laugh. "I guess I'm waxing quite poetic, but that's how I feel about this old place. It has waited a long time to renew her pride, to hear her rooms ring out with laughter instead of tears."

She had half wondered if he was really talking about the house. It halfway sounded like he was talking about a woman; a woman he had loved once. She smiled sadly into the gathering darkness. Jason Saunders also had a dark past. The only difference between them was that he could remember his.

Flame dragged a foot, stopping the rocking motion of the chair. It was getting late and she didn't want Stone coming home and finding her still sitting out here. She didn't want him thinking that she was waiting for him to come home.

But she would wait for the sound of his step on the porch as she lay in the darkness of her room. She did that every night when he had gone off somewhere.

Geese were flying overhead and the wild howl of a timber wolf echoed through the hills as the stallion carried Stone toward Dogwood. Stone had no desire to go there. He would much prefer staying home, spend the evening with Flame. They couldn't do much about planning their future. How could they when she didn't know who she was, wouldn't marry him until she did? She had slept with him awhile, then got it into her head that she was living in sin by doing that. He didn't know what had put that bee in her bonnet.

Stone was thankful when the lights from town showed through the darkness. The wind was picking up. They were in for a storm, he knew. As he tied the stallion to the hitching post he told himself that he must get home before it struck. Maybe a couple hours from now.

There were a couple ranchers and half a dozen cowhands at the bar when Stone entered the smoke-filled room. He knew them all. The bartender had placed his drink before him when suddenly the hair on the nape of his neck prickled. Someone was staring at him, and not in a friendly way. When he had taken a long swallow of his beer, a whiskey-roughened voice asked, "Are you too proud to speak to an out-of-work cowhand, Falcon?"

Stone turned his head and looked at the speaker. His dark brows knit together in a scowl. "Howdy, Cobbs," he said coolly, then turned back to his drink.

"That man who calls himself Saunders is an arrogant bastard. I'd watch him if I was you. That purty little wife of yours visits him an awful lot. He's a handsome devil. He'd—"

"Look, mister—" Stone swung around to glower at Cobbs—"I don't want my wife discussed in a bar room." His words were so cold, they froze the blood of those who stood within hearing distance.

"Now ain't that too bad," the drunken Cobbs sneered and jerked a wicked-looking hunting knife from his waistband.

The men at the bar stepped back and chairs scraped on the bare plank floor as a few customers scampered for cover. They had seen Stone Falcon fight before and it wasn't pretty.

As an ominous quiet hung over the room, Cobbs sprang at Stone, the knife aimed at his stomach. Stone side stepped quickly and smashed Cobbs in the mouth. Blood splashed from a badly cut lip.

As Cobbs sat down, stunned, he spat four teeth onto the floor. Stone stalked after him and pulled him to his feet. "Come on you blustering bastard," he ground out. "Say some more about my wife so that I can beat the life out of you."

Cobbs shook his head, holding up supplicating hands. "I'm not going to fight you. I apologize for what I said. I'm sorry," he muttered through the blood that ran from his mouth.

"You'd better be." Stone put some money on the bar and walked out into the night.

Stone was still seething when he mounted Rebel and sent him galloping toward the end of town. How dare that saddle bum mention Flame in a saloon? He had to fight the desire to return to the Red Lantern and beat Cobbs again. He hoped the man would leave the area.

Stone was more than half way home when suddenly there was a loud roll of thunder and almost immediately a sprinkle of rain. He swore under his breath. He had hoped to beat the storm home.

But within a minute the rain broke with a thundering roar. He gave Rebel a jab of his heels and raced for home.

The stallion was galloping toward the closed barn door when a ragged streak of lightning tore through the sky. The crack of thunder that followed it hurt Stone's ears. He was able, however, to hear Flame's terrified scream. In one movement he left the saddle and flung open the barn door. He didn't wait to see if the animal would go inside. He knew that the stallion would take shelter as soon as possible.

Stone sprinted toward the house. Flame had sounded scared out of her mind. Maybe the storm had brought back her memory, something terrifying.

He reached the porch, then dashed into the house and sprinted down the hall to Flame's room. Her slender body was curled under the covers, only the red of her hair showing on the pillow. He hurried to kneel at her side and gently called her name as he peeled the sheet off her.

She almost knocked him off the bed as she sat up and flung her arms around him. "Don't be afraid, Flame," he soothed, folding her shaking body into his arms. "This house is strong.

Lighting, thunder and rain will never get inside it." He gently stroked her back.

She made no answer, but snuggled into him as though saying, "I believe you."

When her body stopped quivering, he said in joking tones, "The rain can come in, though, if a window has been left open. Will you be alright while I go close the kitchen window?" She nodded against his shoulder and Stone lowered her back under the sheet. "I'll be right back."

He hurried down the hall to the kitchen. As he had feared, his feet squashed in water when he neared the window. He pushed aside the dripping wet curtains and hurriedly closed the window. He was turning away, to go back to Flame when a brilliant streak of lightning zig-zagged across the sky. In its flash he saw a man running from the barn. Why would a man run from dry shelter on a rainy night like this? he asked himself and wasn't long in guessing why. Whoever the man was, he was up to no good.

He wanted to go after the intruder, but Flame was waiting for him. When he heard the sound of running hooves over the sound of the rain, he hurried back to Flame's room. He found her in the same position he had left her. "I'll be right with you," he said, sitting down on the edge of the bed. "I've got to get out of my wet clothing."

Stone didn't know whether Flame would accept his lying in bed with her in only his underwear, but he was damn uncomfortable in his soaked denims.

When she made no answer he shucked off his boots and socks, then his shirt and pants. He waited a moment, then pulled back the sheet far enough for him to slide in beside Flame. He was pulling the white cover up to his chest when lightning hit a nearby tree with an ear-splitting crack. Flame gave a terrified scream and threw herself at him. His arms automatically closed around her. She snuggled her head into his shoulder, and moved against him as if she was trying to crawl inside him.

Stone held her as the storm raged on, determined that he would not give in to his wild desire for her. He told himself it would be almost an act of rape. If Flame wasn't scared out of her wits, she wouldn't be lying in his arms now.

The storm finally abated, the thunder faded away and the lightning only occasionally flashed a yellow glow. Stone felt Flames body go limp and he knew she was sleeping. He started to ease out of bed, then sucked in his breath and went statue still. Flame had flung an arm across his waist and a long leg across his hips.

As he lay there, hardly breathing, he asked himself what a man was supposed to do when the woman he loved pressed the length of her body against his.

I'm not made of stone, he thought in answer to the question, and with one hand he dared to pull her close against his chest. Whe she made no demur he slid his other hand slowly up her thigh. Never before had he felt anything so satiny smooth. He breathed softly, thinking that any minute she would become aware of his stroking hand and order him out of bed.

But minutes passed as he continued to smooth his hand up and down her leg and thigh, even daring to slide his palm over her hip, and still she made no move to reject him.

Stone, on the other hand was hurting badly. If his male member became any harder, it would surely snap in half. And he didn't know how much longer he could bear the pressure of her breasts against his chest. He had swollen so, he was afraid his sex would escape the bounds of his underwear any minute and would be nudging the patch of curls between Flame's thighs.

He groaned deep in his throat when that very thing happened. He lay perfectly still. Had he awakened her? He didn't know if he had or not. He did know she had sighed and whispered his name as she curled her fingers in his long hair. He sat up and it took him only seconds to be rid of his underwear.

Flame lay on her back now, her arms lifted. She was definitely awake, welcoming him. He positioned himself between her legs, and as he slid into her warmth, he whispered huskily, "I love you, Flame."

Flame wrapped her long legs around his waist and said softly, "I love you, Stone Falcon."

Half an hour later Stone and Flame, both sweating and exhausted, lay side by side waiting for their breathing to calm down. When Stone thought he had breath enough to speak, he turned his head and looked at Flame. She returned his look steadily and he propped himself up on his elbow and smoothed the damp hair off her forehead. "I can't go on this way, Flame. You must marry me or I'll go out of my mind."

Flame turned to face him. "I can't marry you, Stone until I know who I am. There might be shameful things in my past. There could be things that you wouldn't want in a wife. I might even have a husband."

Amusement twisted Stone's lips. "One thing I'm sure of—you don't have a husband."

"How can you be so sure, Stone?"

"Because—" he leaned over and planted a kiss on her nose—"I was the first man you had ever been with."

Flame blushed at her ignorance. "I guess you would know."

Stone sat up and reached for his underwear. As he pulled his clothes on, he said half jokingly and half seriously, "Be advised, little miss, the next time I make love to you, I'm going to make you pregnant."

Before Flame could respond to that remark, Stone had left the room. Would he really do that? she asked herself.

Chapter Twenty-seven

The morning sun was pleasantly warm on Shilo's face as he stood on top a rocky ledge and gazed down into the valley. In the distance came the shrill cry of an eagle. He tilted his head, his gaze eagerly searching the sky for the proud bird. How he envied its freedom to soar through the air. Every once in a while the lure of the high lonesome came over him and he felt it today.

A dullness came into his black eyes. He couldn't strike off and climb the mountains like he used to. He had a wife now, a wife who was expecting his child. A gloominess settled over his face. Stone wouldn't be going with him, anyhow. Half the excitement would be gone if his friend wasn't with him.

Shilo wished, as he had a dozen times before, that he and Flame hadn't gone off together on his wedding day. They had wanted to make Stone jealous, but the thoughtless act hadn't worked that way. It had only broken up a friendship of years.

He wondered how Stone and Flame were getting along. Had Stone finally realized that his behavior with Little Bird in front of Flame hurt his wife? He somehow doubted it. His friend was as smart as a whip about most things, but sometimes he was as dumb as an ox.

He, himself, had learned one thing from that dumb trick he and Flame had pulled—Little Bird loved him and not Stone. Further more, she had convinced him that Stone thought of her as a sister, and that she only cared for him like a brother.

Shilo decided that the day would be a fine one to go hunting. He would slip away from Little Bird, though. She must learn that her place was in the village with the other woman. Now that they were expecting a child, they each had responsibilities to attend to.

He hoped his first born would be a son. There was so much a man could teach a son. He would love a daughter, but there wasn't much he could teach her. That duty would belong to her mother.

When Shilo saw his wife enter his mother's wigwam, he hurried to his own. There he lifted the lid from a clay pot and took out a handful of pemmican. When he had tucked the strips into his vest, he took up his rifle from its place beside the door. As his long strides took him up the slight knoll to the timberline, he heard Little Bird calling out to him. He pretended not to hear her as he increased his pace. He felt no guilt. This wife of his must learn that she could go places with him only if she was invited.

Little Bird stamped her foot in frustration. What was she to do with herself all day? Shilo would be gone all day, hunting. His mother had just said that she was going to visit a friend. "She and I haven't had a good private chat in a long time." Those words had told her that she wasn't welcome to come along.

"I'll go fishing," she decided as she walked toward her own wigman. It was always pleasant down by the river.

She, too, visited the olla and took out a handful of pemmican. Stepping outside, she picked out one of the birch fishing poles that leaned against the wigwam wall.

Little Bird noticed geese flying south as she reached the river. Summer was over, but its warmth lingered today. She would enjoy the coolness that would come off the river. It was no more than two feet deep, and it moved slowly. Almost always a fisherman could land enough fish for his dinner or supper.

Little Bird knelt on the bank and cupped the cool water to her flushed face. She picked a spot beneath the willows, and baiting her fishing pole with a piece of pemmican, she tossed the line out into the middle of the stream.

She sat, half dozing, thinking of her aunt, wondering if she was dead or alive. She smiled when she thought of her baby, hoping it would be a son. She was thinking how proud Shilo would be when suddenly the fishing line was jerked so hard, the pole was in danger of being pulled into the river.

She gave an excited cry, and jumping to her feet, reached for the pole. She did not know what kind of fish it was, but she knew it was a large one as she freed it from the hook caught in its mouth. She and Shilo would have it for supper.

Little Bird tossed the fish onto the river bank, where it flopped around in the gravel. She was asking herself if she should catch a couple more or be satisfied with this big one. When without warning she was tackled around the knees and brought to the ground. The breath was knocked out of her and she lay on her back staring up at a man who held a knife at her throat.

"Make one move, little squaw, and I'll slit your throat from ear to ear. Do you understand me?"

Little Bird was trembling so hard she couldn't answer. She recognized this man—he was the one who had attacked her before. "Now here are all the things I'm gonna do to you, and all the things you're gonna do to me."

She listened aghast, shaking her head and whispering, "No, no. You will kill my baby."

"Good," Deke Cobbs grunted. "The world will be better off with one less squalling red brat." He stood up, unfastened his trousers and pushed them down to his boot tops. "Now, little squaw, get ready for the ride of your life."

Stone sat under a tree, idly stripping leaves off a willow twig. His stallion, Rebel, cropped grass a few yards away. If ole Caleb was here he'd say I had a bad case of the dismals he thought.

And he'd be right. Despite their incredible lovemaking the night before, he was no closer to making their marriage real than he'd been before. It didn't look like she would ever regain her memory. And on top of everything else, he missed Shilo. Without his old friend along, all the excitement of fishing and hunting was gone. He had tried to hunt a couple times and both times had come home empty-handed. One time he almost walked right into a young deer.

This split of theirs was crazy. He dropped the now leafless twig and picked up a stone. He came to a decision as he skipped it across the river. Before he could change his mind he was going to the Indian village to straighten out things between him and Shilo.

Stone had been riding about ten minutes when he heard a woman scream. He jabbed the stallion with his heels and raced down the river road. A profane oath ripped out of his throat when the stallion rounded a bend in the river and he saw the slight figure of Little Bird struggling to fight off a large man who was straddling her.

He pulled Rebel's reins and was off his back before the stallion had come to a complete stop. In half a dozen running steps he had the man's shoulders in his hands and was tossing him onto the ground. When the man staggered to his feet, Stone stared at him, cold fury growing in his eyes.

His lips curled in contempt. "Deke Cobbs! I should have known it was you!"

Deke's face grew pale. He licked his lips nervously before whining, "It ain't my fault. The little squaw begged me to lay with her."

Stone didn't say a word. suddenly, his right fist shot out, catching Deke on the jaw. His boots flew out from under him and he fell onto his back. Stone straddled him immediately. His lean body was agile as his fists rained shattering blows on Deke's face.

"Enough! Enough!" Deke begged, his face a bloody mess.

Stone climbed off the groaning man and walked toward Little Bird. He was almost beside her when she cried out, "Behind you, Stone. Deke has a gun!"

Stone spun around and found that Deke had gotten to his feet and had a gun in his hand.

Before the cowhand could fire, Stone's right shoulder dipped down and his Colt seemed to leap into his hand.

Faster than the eye could see, he aimed and squeezed the trigger. Deke screamed and grabbed his crotch. His body swayed drunkenly a moment, then he crumpled to the ground. "You've ruined me, you bastard," he blubbered when Stone stood over him.

"Be glad I didn't kill you, you no-good back shooter. I've done you a favor, actually. You won't have the desire to rape women anymore, so there won't be a danger of any husband looking to kill you."

When Stone walked back to Little Bird, Deke cried after him, "Are you going to go off and leave me to bleed to death?"

"You won't bleed to death. I only nicked you," Stone laughed scornfully. He raised Little Bird to her feet and said gently, "Let's get you home to your husband." He turned back and looked at Deke. "And speaking of her husband, if I was you, I'd head for different country before Shilo comes looking for you."

When Stone and Little Bird reached the village, they found it in an uproar. Shilo had returned from hunting to find his wife missing and ordered his people to search for her.

In the midst of this commotion, Shilo caught sight of Little Bird, her face dirty, her dress torn and bedraggled as Stone helped her up to the wigwam. He froze for a moment. Then in three long strides he had enfolded his wife in a crushing embrace.

"I prayed to God I would find you safe," he whispered. "Now I understand the omen of the white stallion. Like, him, I wanted only my freedom. But you have tamed me, my love." Shilo tenderly wiped a tear from Little Bird's face, then looked up at her friend with a smile. "This is the second time you have saved her for me. I thank you."

Stone hadn't understood Shilo's reference to the white Stallion, but he understood that this would mark a turning point in his friend's marriage. And he knew that the break between him and Shilo was mended at last.

Chapter Twenty-eight

Rainee pulled the sheet up around her shoulders and scooted her bottom nearer to the warm body holding her close. She smiled and snuggled deeper into the welcoming hollow of bare legs and slim hips.

She'd been spending as much time with Rudy as she could. They had already lost so much time together. She wanted to be able to go to bed with him every night, get up with him in the mornings. She wanted to close her shop in town and do nothing but be a wife to Rudy, keep his house and make his meals.

But he hadn't mentioned their ever getting married. And yet she knew that he cared for her. His every action, every look said so. Did his silence about marriage have anything to do with Flame? She couldn't imagine what Flame could have to do with their relationship. If he was holding back because of Flame's memory loss, they might never have a life together.

Rainee was debating whether to come right out and ask if he had any plans for their future when she felt his long fingers stir on her breasts. Everything else left her mind and she rolled over on her back, giving him free access to her breasts. When his warm mouth closed over one swollen nipple, she moved her hand down his body and curled her fingers around the hard flesh that was prodding her thigh. With a low moan he pulled her beneath him and eagerly entered her.

They had learned what each wanted from the other, and the sun was well up by the time all the rituals of pleasing each other had been performed.

"Ah, Rainee," Rudy laughed weakly as he rolled off her, "you've drained me. I don't think I can do a lick of work today."

Rainee gave him a lazy, satisfied smile. "I'm not sure I've got the strength to ride into town."

Rudy gave her a wicked smile. They both knew that all they needed was a few minutes rest and they'd be at each other again. Rudy heaved himself out of bed before it could happen. Ready or not, he had a lot of work to do today. He took his clothes from the foot of the bed and pulled them on. He took Rainee's clothes which had been folded beside his, and tossed them to her. "Are you going to make me some breakfast before you leave, woman?" he asked, grinning at her.

"I guess so, if I've got the strength." Rainee reached for her dress as he walked into the kitchen to fire up the stove.

She was just buttoning up the dress when Rudy came rushing back into the room. "Flame is coming! What are we going to do?"

"The first thing you're going to do is settle down and stop acting like you've shot her dog. We'll go into the kitchen, and while you set the table I'll put on a pot of coffee and slice some bacon. If she asks, we'll say that I just arrived and am making you some breakfast."

When Flame stepped into the kitchen a fire was burning briskly in the range and Rainee, a towel tied around her waist, was grinding coffee.

"Good morning," Rainee said. "As soon as I got here Jason talked me into making him breakfast. Have you eaten yet this morning?"

In a few minutes they were sitting down to breakfast, while Flame told them of Deke Cobbs attack on Little Bird and how Stone had rescued her.

"I always thought there was something low down about that fellow," Rudy said. "I'm just sorry he didn't leave the area altogether when I let him go."

"I hope he's gone for good now," Rainee said as she poured coffee and Rudy built a cigarette.

Wanting to change the subject, Flame asked, "What are we going to do today?"

"I thought maybe we'd finish up inside," Rudy said, striking a match and holding the flame to the white cylinder. "We've got paint for the walls. Linseed oil for the furniture, curtains for the windows."

"And don't forget the bedspreads and small rugs for the floors," Flame chimed in.

Rudy looked at the two women in his life and felt warm and happy that they liked each other. He could hardly wait until the day he could ask Rainee to be his wife and to tell Flame that he was her father. What a day of thanksgiving that would be.

While Rainee and Flame washed and dried the dishes, Rudy exchanged his boots for a pair of old worn moccasins he'd found in the barn. He had worn them fifteen years ago. Today he would wear them while he took care of the horse, brought in some wood for the range and filled the barrel on the porch with water.

It wasn't long before the smell of linseed oil wafted through the house. Rainee paused in her task of rubbing oil into the dry furniture. She dragged her arm across her sweating forehead. The place sure was shaping up, she thought, looking around the room. From where she was standing she could see parts of the kitchen and one bedroom.

Flame had spread a colorful cloth on the kitchen table, and hung bright yellow curtains at the window. In the bedroom she could see the corner of a dresser and half of the bed. It wore a flowered bedspread. That room wasn't meant to be Rudy's, she guessed with a grin. She couldn't imagine his very maculine body sleeping under a patch of daisies.

With a long sigh Rainee returned to rubbing a shine into the old furniture. The house was pretty enough for any woman now. But did Rudy want a woman in it? A wife? He seemed more concerned with getting the out-buildings mended before winter set in and the snows came.

She wondered again if Flame had anything to do with his silence on the subject of marriage. She knew it bothered him to see his daughter so unhappy. Whenever he asked her if everything was alright her cheery answer was, "I'm fine, Jason. The heat gets to me sometimes."

But Flame couldn't blame the heat these days. The early fall days were pleasant now. The evenings were cool, a blanket needed in the late night. Geese were flying south and a couple mornings ago she had found a thin film of ice on the water in the horse trough. The weather was going to change soon, she knew. She could feel it in the air.

And when the snows came, with snow up past a persons waist, how was she to see Rudy then? She wondered if he had thought about that.

Flame had just departed when the doorway darkened and Rainee looked up, a wide smile forming on her lips. "Rudy, I was just thinking about you." She capped the oil bottle and tossed the rubbing rag into the woodbox.

"That's strange." Rudy caught her around the waist and pulled her up tight against his chest. "I was just now thinking about you. What were you thinking?"

"I was thinking that after the first blizzard hits, we won't get to see each other very often."

"I've given that some thought, too. Do you have any ideas?" He planted a quick kiss on her throat.

"I thought I'd leave that up to you." She gave him a slow, flirty look. "This winter will show me just how much you like to see me."

His arm still locked around her waist, Rudy backed up against the table. "You know how much I like to see you," he growled and spread his legs apart wide enough to pull Rainee in against his suddenly hard maleness.

"Is that the only reason you care about seeing me?" Rainee teased, bucking her hips against his. "I miss you every day I don't see you." She deftly unbuttoned his denims and slid her hand inside them.

"Oh, Lord, Rainee," he groaned as she freed him. "You shouldn't do that to a man in broad daylight, in his kitchen. I'll have to do something about it." His hands gripped her waist and lifted her to straddle his hips.

Fifteen minutes later old man Caleb stopped by to get a drink of whiskey before climbing back up the mountain. But when he stepped up on the porch and saw through the window what was going on, he grinned and turned around, leaving without his drink of spirits.

Another fifteen minutes passed and Rudy withdrew from Rainee and let her slide to the floor. With a wicked light in his eyes, he asked, "Will that hold you until tonight?"

Rainee laughed softly. "The way I feel now I can manage for a week. But all joking aside, what are we going to do when winter sets in and a person can hardly leave her house, let alone try to get through snow taller than she is."

"I've been thinking about that." Rudy was serious as he tucked his shirt tail into his pants. "I've never asked you, Rainee, but you're bound to know that I love you and want to marry you. I've been holding off, hoping that Flame can become healthy in her mind again. But I'm beginning to realize she may never regain her memory. Maybe I should just tell her I'm her father instead of waiting for her to recognize me."

"You know, Flame is not really your responsibility anymore. She has a husband. Isn't it up to him to look after her? He might not show it, but Stone Falcon is crazy about his wife."

After a few silent minutes, Rainee said gently, "Don't you think it's time you and I had a little happiness together? We've waited a long time."

"I know we have, honey, and I'm sorry about that." Rudy pulled Rainee into his arms and rested his chin on top of her head. "What do you say we tie the knot two weeks from Saturday?"

"I say that's wonderful." Rainee put her arms around Rudy's waist and squeezed. "I'll ask Flame to stand up with me. Who will you ask?"

"I don't know anyone around here. I guess I'll ask Stone."

"I've got to get home." Rainee was all business now. "I've got to decide on a dress to wear." She paused in the doorway.

"When will you tell Flame?"

"Probably tonight at the church social. She told me she and Stone will be there."

Rudy walked Rainee to the door. She turned to him, and with shining eyes said, "I can't wait to start bringing some of my things over here. With my own little nick-nacks around me it will truly seem like my home."

As Rainee rode back to town her mind was full of the things she would bring to the ranch. She hardly noticed the way the temperature had dropped or the dark clouds sweeping down from the mountain.

Chapter Twenty-nine

Deke Cobbs stood in the shadows of some pines, his gaze steady on Stone Falcon's barn and ranch house. Only when he had to remove a coat from his saddlebag to stop his shivering did his eyes stray from the buildings.

He had been watching the ranch for days now, waiting for the right moment to strike. If only he'd never strayed down to the river, never tried to rape that Indian squaw. His groin ached from the wound Falcon had dealt him.

Stone Falcon. His eyes burned with hatred. He knew just how to get back at the man. And he would have his fun with the girl he'd been hankering after at the same time. Tonight.

Deke had waited for just such a time when

he would find Flame alone. Of the dozen times he had hidden in the pines and watched the Falcon ranch, Flame was never alone. There was always the cook and a couple stable hands close by.

But this Saturday night there was a big to-do going on in town and most everyone in a twenty-mile radius would be there. Falcon was nowhere about, and Deke had just caught sight of Flame galloping toward the ranch. She'd been gone most of the day and he'd almost given up waiting for her to return.

Now if only Falcon stayed away long enough for him to finally get his hands on Miss Snooty. She wouldn't have that nose of hers so high in the air when he finished with her. He would take her up the mountain where there would be nobody to help her.

A deafening crack of thunder startled him so, he almost dropped the reins. And on the heels of that threatening blast freezing rain was suddenly coming down in sheets. He peered through the wet, gray curtain as Flame hurriedly dismounted and led her mare into the barn.

The look of the devil came into his eyes. Things couldn't have turned out better. It would be easy to grab her there, in the dark.

Flame had tied up her mare when suddenly she was gripped so hard around the waist the breath whooshed out of her lungs. She was being pulled to the ground then, her hands held over her head.

"Oh, dear Lord," she prayed, "help me." As the last word left her mouth a streak of lightning lit up the barn, and her attacker's face. A humming began in her head as she looked at the man who had her pinned to the floor. That same face had loomed over her before. As if a door had been thrown open to let in light, everything that she had lost came rushing back to her.

She was released from her paralysis and scream after scream tore through her throat. This crazy man was finally going to rape her.

But instead of tearing off her clothes, Deke was tying up her arms with a piece of rope around her waist.

"What are you doing?" she exclaimed.

"I'm making sure you don't run away," he said and tossed her into his saddle, mounting behind her.

"Where are you taking me?" she pleaded.

His answer was a snarl of bared teeth.

Deke sat in the saddle like a drunken man, weaving from side to side. His groin was a steady beat of agony and he feared he was gripped with fever. His head throbbed and his wound felt like it was on fire. To make matters worse, as they ascended the mountain trail, the freezing rain changed to snow. He knew he must find shelter soon. He was going to fall out of the saddle any minute. His grip tightened around Flame's waist. If he went down she would go with him. He had waited a long time to get his hands on her.

There was a hammering in his head and he had almost given up hope of finding any kind of shelter, when he spotted a cabin in a stand of aspens that had lost most of their leaves. No smoke lifted from its chimney, for which he was thankful. The place was vacant.

Deke rode his horse right up to the front door and pratically fell out of the saddle. He reached up and jerked Flame with such force that she fell to her knees. He forced open the cabin door and staggered into the room, dragging her with him and tying her to a heavy table. She felt like the rope was cutting her in half and her knees had been rubbed raw from the way he pulled her along.

Even frightened as she was, there still sang in her mind the words, I know who I am and that I must get free of this mad man and get back to Stone.

Deke's staggering progress across the floor finally brought him to his knees. He swayed back and forth there a moment, then toppled over on his side. Flame watched as a large pool of blood formed between his legs. Is he going to die? she wondered, praying that he would. The wind howled outside, drowning out the sound of Deke's heavy breathing. It was hoarse and erratic, sometimes stopping altogether for a moment or two before continuing on.

Flame's gaze scanned the room, looking for anything near enough at hand for her to use to get rid her of her bonds. There was nothing within reach except a candle stub of about two inches and three or four matches lying beside it. She sighed in frustration. Unless . ... hope sprang in her chest. Maybe she could manage to strike one of the sulpher sticks and light the candle stub. She could then hold its flame under the knot where it had been tied around her waist. The knot was not so close to her body that she would be burned, and she knew Deke had pulled it so tight that she would never be able to undo it.

She watched Deke a minute, the slow rise and fall of his chest. When he only continued to moan and curse at Stone, she began to ease away from him. Inch by inch she worked her way to where the candle stood. Deke's breathing was getting raspy by the time her fingers closed over one of the matches. Just as she raked it across the floor and a flame shot up, Deke gave a long shuddering breath, then his body arched upward, his heels digging into the floor. His body went limp then, and he lay so still she knew that he was dead.

All the more now Flame wanted to get distance between her and Deke. With her left hand she pulled the knot as far away as she could from her clothing, then carefully, with her right hand, held *the little* light under the knot.

As the flame ate into the rope she could smell it burning, also feel its heat. Would her clothes be set on fire? Would she burn to death? With that last awful thought, the rope fell apart. She sobbed her relief as she flung it into the cold fireplace.

Flame's first thought was to bring in the poor horse standing outside in the snow. She dashed out the door, and grabbing the horse's trailing reins, she led it inside the cabin. She unrolled the bedroll wrapped in a tarp and spread it out. She used one of the thin blankets to wiped down the shivering horse. "Just don't mess up the place, alright?" She patted the spot between the animal's ears.

Not expecting to find much, Flame opened a narrow, inside door, and gingerly holding the flickering little flame shoulder high, she peered into the bedroom. There were a bedstead, a small table and a chest. On the table was an old family Bible. Curious, she opened the cover and held the candle so she could read the name scrawled on the fly leaf: Rudy Martin.

She remembered her full name now—Flame Martin—knew that Rudy was her father. She could connect that name with the image of the kind-faced man in her dream. Had her father been living up here on the mountain all the years since he'd left Bertha? But where was he now?

Shivering violently, she opened the chest, found some warm, dry clothes, and put them on, though they were far too big. Then she went back into the other room.

There were several large pieces of wood lying among the ashes in the fireplace. Flame was raking them together, wondering if by some miracle she could set them afire, when the horse wuffled and stamped its foot.

Jumping to her feet she unsaddled the horse on saying, "I'm sorry, fellow. I've got nothing to give you." The horse nudged her shoulder as if he understood. She patted his rump. Now for a fire, she thought.

After several attempts, and with one match left, Flame managed to coax a fire from the charred ends of the wood. It flickered and hissed when some of the snow fell down the chimney. The sound of the crackling fire was soothing, but Flame kept her face turned away from where the dead Deke lay.

She wearily lay down on the floor, her feet stretched out to the fire. She wouldn't sleep, she knew. She had too much on her mind, she thought with a yawn.

That was her last conscious thought for several hours.

His heart heavy, Stone paced the floor until the stars grew pale, signaling that day wasn't far off. He had returned from an errand in Dogwood the previous evening to find Flame's little mare tied still saddled in the barn. There was no sign of her owner, but marks of a scuffle in the straw made his blood run cold. He was only waiting for daylight to set off after her.

He stuffed his grub bag with pemmican and hard tack, coffee beans and a blackened coffee pot. When he had pulled on his jacket, he stood a minute, then took Flame's mackinaw from the rack beside the door. She might not have a coat on.

Stone braced himself against the freezing rain that still pounded the earth as he made his way to the barn. A pain struck him in the chest when he saw again the signs of the desperate struggle that poor little Flame had put up.

He led the stallion outside, halted him a minute while he swept his gaze inch by inch along the line of the horizon. He had no trouble spotting hoof prints in the frozen mud outside the barn. They led straight toward the trail up the mountain. Stone smiled grimly. He and Shilo knew every path up that mountain. Flame's abductor didn't stand a chance.

As Stone rode higher up the mountain, the rain changed to snow covering the tracks he'd been following. The pines were heavy with the white flakes. And to worsen matters, the wind had risen, and it was getting colder.

Rebel snorted and shook his head, jets of steam coming out of his nostrils. The stallion would be glad to get back home and get warm. But Stone would not turn back until he'd found Flame.

Suddenly Stone thought he heard angry voices, like those of people arguing. He strained to hear through the wind and the muffling snow and decided that it was definitely a couple men going at it. He hesitated, wondering if he should ride on. It was none of his business why they were at odds.

Then he heard the faint squeal of a woman. He reined Rebel in and slid out of the saddle. A few steps and he was hunkered down in the brush, peering through the dry, brittle branches.

He recognized the two men who were squared off at each other immediately. It was the Jackson brothers, the two from whom he had rescued Little Bird.

"You had her for an hour after supper," one of the men declared angrily, "It's my turn with the squaw."

"I say no, because when I got drunk and passed out last night, you had her until the next morning."

"It ain't my fault you got drunk," the first brother said. As the two argued back and forth, Stone looked around for the squaw. He almost exclaimed out loud when he found her crouched beside a campfire. It was Little Bird's aunt who fearfully watched the two men. How could he get her attention? he wondered.

The snow had melted from the heat of his knees where he knelt and he became aware of something sharp biting into his flesh. He reached down and discovered a small, sharp pebble digging into him. He picked it up and carefully tossed it toward the woman. It landed at her feet. Startled, she looked up, then scanned the area. Stone cautiously raised his head just inches above the brush.

It was enough. The woman's black eyes saw him immediately. He saw her choke back a cry of surprise. He lifted his right hand and motioned to his right. Would she get his meaning? he wondered. He wanted her to get out of the way of a bullet if they should start flying.

He saw that she had understood when she began inching her way in that direction. He felt pretty sure that she had recognized him.

When Stone thought she was sufficiently safe from bullets, he stood, his six feet two inches plainly visible. With a Colt in each hand, he called out, "I'm going to settle the argument between you two men. I'm taking the woman."

"The hell you are!" the elder of the two yelled, and went for his gun. Stone squeezed the trigger of the Colt in his right hand and the man reeled back, blood soaking the front of his shirt.

The other brother's gun bellowed. Stone opened fire again, the bullet smacking the younger brother in the chest. He wavered, then slowly his knees buckled and he fell flat on his face, dead.

The woman stood, looking uncertainly at Stone. He gave her a warm smile and said, "Come on, woman. I'm taking you to your niece, Little Bird."

When Flame awoke, her body was cold and her teeth chattering. She unwound herself from the fetal position she had lain in all night and with grunts and groans managed to get to her feet. She was cold and miserable and when she put her clothes back no they were still damp, but she had much to be thankful for. Deke Cobbs was dead. She was free of him. All she had to do now was find her way home, back to Stone. She had so much to tell him now. What would he think when she told him she was Flame Martin, daughter of Rudy and Bertha, that she was born in that old ranch house and had lived there all her life?

She came back to the present when the horse stamped his feet. She found him rested and in good shape. "I wonder if by some miracle there's food in this," she said as she picked up Cobb's saddlebag.

Her rummaging fingers found only some beef jerky mixed with tobacco flakes. She cleaned the dried meat as best she could and bit into it. As she chewed hungrily, she saddled the horse and led him outside. She paused to let him paw away the snow and crop some grass before mounting him.

While she waited for the horse she looked around, peering through the rain. She recognized no landscape, no trees, no trails. She had no idea where she was. She looked up at the sky and vaguely made out the pale, almost white, sun behind the snow clouds. Something told her to ride east.

It was near noon and the snow had finally stopped when two teenage Indian boys stepped out in front of her. It was hard to say which of the three was more startled.

Flame gathered her wits first. She smiled at

them and said, "Young braves, I am lost. I wonder if you could show me in what direction I should go to get home."

The oldest boy, around fourteen, she judged, asked "Do you know what village you come from?"

"Yes. I come from Dogwood. Do you know of it?"

"Yes, I have heard of it. It is about twenty miles distant." He jerked his thumb over his bare shoulder. "Ride to the Platte just over the hill. You can follow it all the way to your village."

"Thank you, young braves." Flame smiled at them again and turned the stallion's head in the direction of the river. The boys eyes followed her, bright with curiosity. "She is very pretty," one said. The other boy agreed and wondered what she was doing out alone.

Flame felt she had been riding at least an hour and still she hadn't seen anything she ever remembered seeing before. Once a herd of wild horses surged forward, moving through the low-lying river fog. She almost jumped out of her skin as they thundered by and it took several minutes to calm the stallion down.

She noted as she rode along that the willows along the river had lost all their leaves to the onslaught of slashing rain. She thought of Jason Saunders. He had barely finished getting all his roofs mended before the rain came.

She would have to tell him about her memory returning. He would be happy for her. He was the kindest, sweetest man she had ever known.

It was nearing sunset, and Flame was weary and tired to the bone when she saw light shining a mile or so down the river. "It has to be Dogwood," she cried out joyfully and turned the stallion's head away from the river and towards the old ranch. She hoped Jason had something to eat. His house was nearer than Stone's place and she was half starved.

Rudy sat on his newly mended porch, his long legs stretched out to the railing, his feet crossed at the ankles. He had just finished a supper of fried steak and potatoes and his stomach was pleasantly full.

He had planned on sharing supper with Flame but she hadn't shown up today. She hadn't been at the church social the night before either. He hoped that she was alright. He would ride over to the Falcon ranch tomorrow and check on her.

It was hard, not telling her who he was and he didn't know how much longer he could go without telling her that he was her father. Especially now that he and Rainee were going to be married. He had waited so long to be reunited with his little girl. All these years he had paid the taxes on the old place so that she would have a home. Evidently he had returned just before the buildings fell to ruins.

He yawned. It had been a long day. He had been up at the break of day, checking on his cattle. He found them huddled in a gully with water up to their knees, in danger of drowning as the rain pounded down. As he drove them out of the water he decided that it was true what was said about cattle. They were the dumbest animals on earth. You would never catch a horse standing in water, meekly waiting to drown.

Rudy yawned again, then rose to his feet. It was early, but he was going to bed. He took a last drag on his smoke, and as he flipped it into a puddle of water he saw a horse and rider coming toward the house. He walked to the edge of the porch and peered through the early evening.

"Flame, is that you?" He stepped down into the yard and waited to help her dismount.

"What brings you here at this hour, girl?" he demanded as she slid into his raised arms. "And how come your clothes are wet? Have you been out in the rain?"

"Yes, I have. And up on the mountain it was snowing."

"Up on the mountain? Come on in the house and explain to me what you've been doing up there."

"It's a very long story and before I start it, do you have anything I can eat? I haven't had anything but an old piece of beef jerky."

"Yes, I have something you can eat, but first you've got to get out of those wet clothes. Go into the small bedroom and take the blanket off the bed and wrap it around you after you've undressed. While you're doing that, I'll find you something to eat."

It didn't take Flame long to get out of the uncomfortable wet clothes and to wrap the blanket around herself. She brought the garments with her to the kitchen. She pushed chairs around the stove and spread them out to dry.

Meanwhile Rudy had heated a pot of soup Rainee had made the day before. He placed a steaming bowl of it on the table and handed Flame a spoon. "Eat up, honey. Get some color in your face."

The wood crackled and the fire blazed in the cookstove. The warmth it produced crept into Flame's chilled flesh. When the soup was almost gone, Rudy poured her a cup of coffee. She took a long swallow of it, sat back and announced, "Now I will tell you all the things that have happened to me the last two days."

She told it as it had happened. How Deke had caught her in the barn, his attempt to rape her. She told of the long ride in the rain and snow, how they came to the cabin, how Deke died there. She ended part of her story by telling how two Indian boys had directed her toward Dogwood.

"Honey, you must have been scared to death." Rudy knelt down beside her. "You must try to put it all behind you."

"I'll admit I was plenty scared, but, Jason, when Cobbs was trying to rape me, everything came flooding back. One night when a terrible storm was raging, he tried to rape me then, too. My mother came into the room and saw what he was doing. She was drunk and blamed me. She beat me badly and threw me out into the storm. That was when Stone found me and I had no memory of who I was. He's going to be surprised to learn that my full name is Flame Martin."

Rudy got to his feet and sat down beside her. "I have a surprise for you, honey," he said, reaching for her hand. "My real name is Rudy Martin."

Flame gave him an uncertain look. "Then I think it was your cabin I stayed in last night." When Rudy gave her a warm smile certainty began to grow in her eyes. "Are you my dad?" she asked hopefully, coming to her feet.

"I am, honey." Rudy folded her into his arms. "Your long lost dad."

"Oh, Dad," Flame sobbed, "I never expected to see you again. I can't believe it's you."

"It's me, Flame baby, and I'm here to stay."

Rudy held her close and rocked back and forth as she sobbed quietly on his shoulder. When only hiccups were left, he held her away from him, and drying her tears with a dish towel, he said, "I imagine your clothes are pretty dry by now. Why don't you get dressed while I go saddle a couple horses. We've got to get you home. Your husband will be worried sick about you."

"Stone will be worried about me, but he's not my husband."

"He's not?" Rudy's hand froze on the door knob. "Why not? Everybody thinks he is."

"With my memory loss and all, we thought posing as a married couple was a good idea so he could look after me." She gave him a gamine grin. "We'll get married for real now that I know who I am."

Chapter Thirty

Stone dismounted in front of Caleb Greenwood's cabin, leaving Little Bird's aunt mounted on Rebel. The sun was behind the mountain and the wind was rising. It was going to be a cold night.

Old Caleb hurried out of the cabin, curious to see who his visitors might be.

"What the heck are you doing here?" was Caleb's greeting to Stone when he recognized his friend. After Stone had explained his desperate search for Flame, the old man said, "It's gonna be a long hunt, Stone, and you're not prepared for it. Let me help you. We need to go to your ranch and pack some grub, get dry bedrolls and clothes. If it's alright with you I'll borrow one of your horses . . . a mountain-bred one. My old mule doesn't have much speed left in her. Besides, we've got to take the Indian woman to Shilo. Having her along will only slow us down."

Stone immediately shook his head. "I could never rest, not knowing what is happening to Flame, wondering if she is hungry and cold. I have to keep looking for her. I know every trail on this mountain. She's got to be here somewhere."

"And I agree, but you're so tired now you can hardly stand up and you say you've been the saddle since the first streak of dawn. The state you're in now, you could ride right past Flame and never see her. The right thing to do is get a good night's rest and sleep, and start out fresh tomorrow."

"You're right," Stone agreed reluctantly. "I'm dead on my feet. We'll go back to the ranch."

Stone thought he had never seen anything so beautiful when he and Caleb topped a hill and looked down on his ranch buildings. He could make out each one, the full moon was so bright. But no lights came from inside the house, the cookhouse or the bunkhouse. It was past midnight and everyone was asleep. They had made a brief stop at the Indian village to reunite a tearful Little Bird with her aunt.

"We'll not wake Charlie up to fix us something to eat," Stone said. "I'm sure we can find something to put in our bellies. I just hope there's some coffee in the pot," he added as he started the tired horse down the hill.

It did not take them long to strip the rigs off the animals and to stable them. Each one got a scoop of oats before they left them.

When they entered the cookhouse, Stone and Caleb moved about as quietly as possible, so as not to wake Charlie. In the warming oven they found the bony parts of fried chicken on a platter. No doubt Charlie planned on feeding them to the old ranch hound in the morning.

Stone felt the coffee pot and found it still warm. He filled a couple of cups and he and Caleb sat down to the best meal they had ever eaten. They slipped out of the cookhouse and parted there. Stone knew there was no use inviting Caleb to sleep in the house. The old man would bed down in the barn.

"In the morning at daybreak we'll have a good breakfast and start out again," Stone said as he climbed the porch steps.

He had no trouble finding his way through the house. In the moonlight streaming through the windows each piece of furniture stood out clearly. He paused at Flame's room and stood there, letting his gaze roam over everything inside it. There was her robe lying on the foot of her bed, her little house slippers sitting on the floor.

Would he ever see her again? he wondered, his eyes damp. He must. He couldn't imagine a life without her in it.

His shoulders slumped, Stone walked down

the hall to his room. He was thinking of the lonely nights he had spent there, longing to have Flame sleeping beside him.

He tugged his damp boots off, then peeled off his denims and shirt. With a weary sigh he crawled into bed and pulled the blanket up over his shoulders. He turned on his side, preparing to go to sleep, then went dead still. His bare legs had encountered warm flesh, smooth as silk.

He slowly raised himself up on an elbow. It couldn't be what he was thinking. He had to be hallucinating. He was so tired. Maybe he was dreaming. He slowly pulled the cover off the warm body. He gasped a sound of pure joy and thanksgiving as he gazed on Flame's sleeping face.

As he continued to gaze at her, a hundred questions ran through his mind. How had she escaped her abducter, then found her way here? And why was she sleeping in his bed? Had she changed her mind about marrying him? He lifted his hand and gently stroked her cheek. She gave him a sleepy smile as she turned on her side to face him. A shock went through him. Flame didn't have any clothes on either.

His arms went out to gather her close. With a happy little murmur she laid her head on his shoulder and continued to sleep. Stone kissed the top of her had, then fell into a deep sleep.

* * *

It was high noon when Flame and Stone were awakened by the raised voices of Caleb and Charlie.

"I say let them sleep," Charlie was saying.

"But they'll be wanting some grub. Stone will have your hide if you let him sleep through lunch."

The door to the cookhouse slammed, reducing their loud argument to a muted murmur.

Stone and Flame looked at each other, the love they felt shinning in their eyes. Stone bent his head, his lips taking hers.

It was a long, lingering kiss that built and built.

At last Stone raised his head so that they both could breathe. "We'll talk later," he said as he pulled Flame's eager body beneath him. "Right now I want to show you just how glad I am that you're back."

Two hours later Caleb had departed, and Flame and Stone were finishing their first full meal in two days.

While Charlie had fried two large steaks and a skillet full of fries, Flame filled Stone in on all that had happened to her, the good and the bad. He hadn't interrupted her, but his face showed anger and shock many times. He looked stunned when she told him that Jason Saunders was actually Rudy Martin, who was her father.

Flame looked at Stone over the rim of her

coffee cup, and with a teasing gleam in her eyes, said, "Dad expects us to get married. He does not want his daughter living in sin."

"Nor do I," Stone agreed. "As old Caleb would put it, 'By the bear that bit me, I love yah, girl.'"

Raven
Norah Hess

When Raven's two-bit gambler husband orders her to entertain a handsome cowboy at dinner, she has no idea of the double dealings involved. How is she to know that he has promised the good-looking stranger a night in her bed for $1,000, or that he has no intention of keeping his word? Cheated of his night of passion, Chance McGruder can't get the dark-haired little beauty out of his mind. So he is both tantalized and tormented when she shows up at the neighboring ranch, newly widowed but no less desirable. What kind of a wife will agree to sell herself to another man? What kind of a woman will run off with $1,000 that isn't hers? What kind of a widow can make him burn to possess her? And what kind of man is he to ignore his doubts and gamble his heart that when she gives her body, it will be for love.

___4611-3 $5.99 US/$6.99 CAN

Wild Fire

NORAH HESS

The Yankees killed her sweetheart, imprisoned her brother, and drove her from her home, but beautiful golden-haired Serena Bain faces the future boldly as the wagon trains roll out. But all the peril in the world won't change her bitter resentment of the darkly handsome Yankee wagon master Josh Quade. Soon, however, her heart betrays her will. His strong, rippling, buckskin-clad body sets her senses on fire. But pride and fate continue to tear them apart as the wagon trains roll west—until one night, in the soft, secret darkness of a bordello, Serena and Josh unleash their wildest passion and open their souls to the sweetest raptures of love.

___52331-0 $5.50 US/$6.50 CAN

Lark — Norah Hess

Trapped in a loveless marriage, Lark Elliot longs to lead a normal life like the pretty women she sees in town, to wear new clothes and be courted by young suitors. But she has married Cletus Gibb, a man twice her age, so her elderly aunt and uncle can stay through the long Colorado winter in the mountain cabin he owns. Resigned to backbreaking labor on Gibb's ranch, Lark finds one person who makes the days bearable: Ace Brandon. But when her husband pays the rugged cowhand to father him an heir, at first Lark thinks she has been wrong about Ace's kindness. It isn't long, however, before she is looking forward to the warmth of his tender kiss, to the feel of his strong body. And as the heat of their desire melts away the cold winter nights, Lark knows she's found the haven she's always dreamed of in the circle of his loving arms.

___4522-2 $5.99 US/$6.99 CAN

KENTUCKY BRIDE

NORAH HESS

Fleeing her abusive uncle, young D'lise Alexander trusts no man...until she is rescued by virile trapper Kane Devlin. His rugged strength and tender concern convinces D'lise she'll find a safe haven in his backwoods homestead. There, amid the simple pleasures of cornhuskings and barn raisings, she discovers that Kane kindles a blaze of desire that burns even hotter than the flames in his rugged stone hearth. Beneath his soul-stirring kisses she forgets her fears, forgets everything except her longing to become his sweet Kentucky bride.

___52270-5 $5.50 US/$6.50 CAN